· PICUS THE THIEF ·

*knowe us by poppies in golden fields
of wheat splashd red lyke blood*

Picus the Thief

TRANSLATED BY ROBIN BENNETT

monster books

Small Vampires. Picus the Thief
(Aktuel Translations Ltd. 7043141. Monster Books)
Originally published in Great Britain by Monster Books, 2011
The Old Smithy, Henley-on-Thames, OXON RG9 2AR

All rights reserved. No part of this publication may be reproduced or transmitted in any form or by any means, electronic or mechanical, including photocopying, recording or any information storage retrieval system, without prior permission in writing from the publishers.

The right of Robin Bennett to be identified as author of this work has been asserted by him in accordance with the Copyright, Designs and Patents Act 1988.
Text copyright ©2011 Robin Bennett
Illustrations copyright ©2011 Rob Rayevsky

This book is sold subject to the condition that it shall not, by way of trade or otherwise, be lent, resold, hired out or otherwise circulated without the publisher's prior consent in any form of binding or cover other than that in which it is published and without a similar condition including this condition being imposed on the subsequent purchaser.

ISBN 978-0-9568684-0-4 hard cover
A catalogue record of this book is available from the British Library

Printed in China by CTPS.
Book design by Medievalbookshop (www.medievalbookshop.co.uk)
Cover illustration: the talented Rob Rayevsky©
Small Vampires device: the inspired Adam Curtis

🐟 Humble gratitude to all those who gave up their time to help get this book into some semblance of shape – so, in no particular order: Josie Kember, Charlie Norfolk, David Mossop, Patrick Walsh at Conville & Walsh, Barry Cunningham and Imogen Cooper at Chicken House, Sara Hornby and finally Serena Jones – without whose careful editing this manuscript would have been buck-shot with the sort of spelling and basic grammatical errors that sent regiments of my English teachers into towering rages.

🐟 Thanks also go to the staff at Royal Holloway, (London Uni not women's prison) who work in the Founders library and the superb and utterly original Miller's Hotels (London, Devon and Somerset) where most of this book was conceived on gin and written on builder's tea.

🐟 Lastly, and not leastly, thanks to my patient wife and noisy children who serve to keep all things in perspective.

🐟 Grovelling apologies go to anyone I have forgotten.

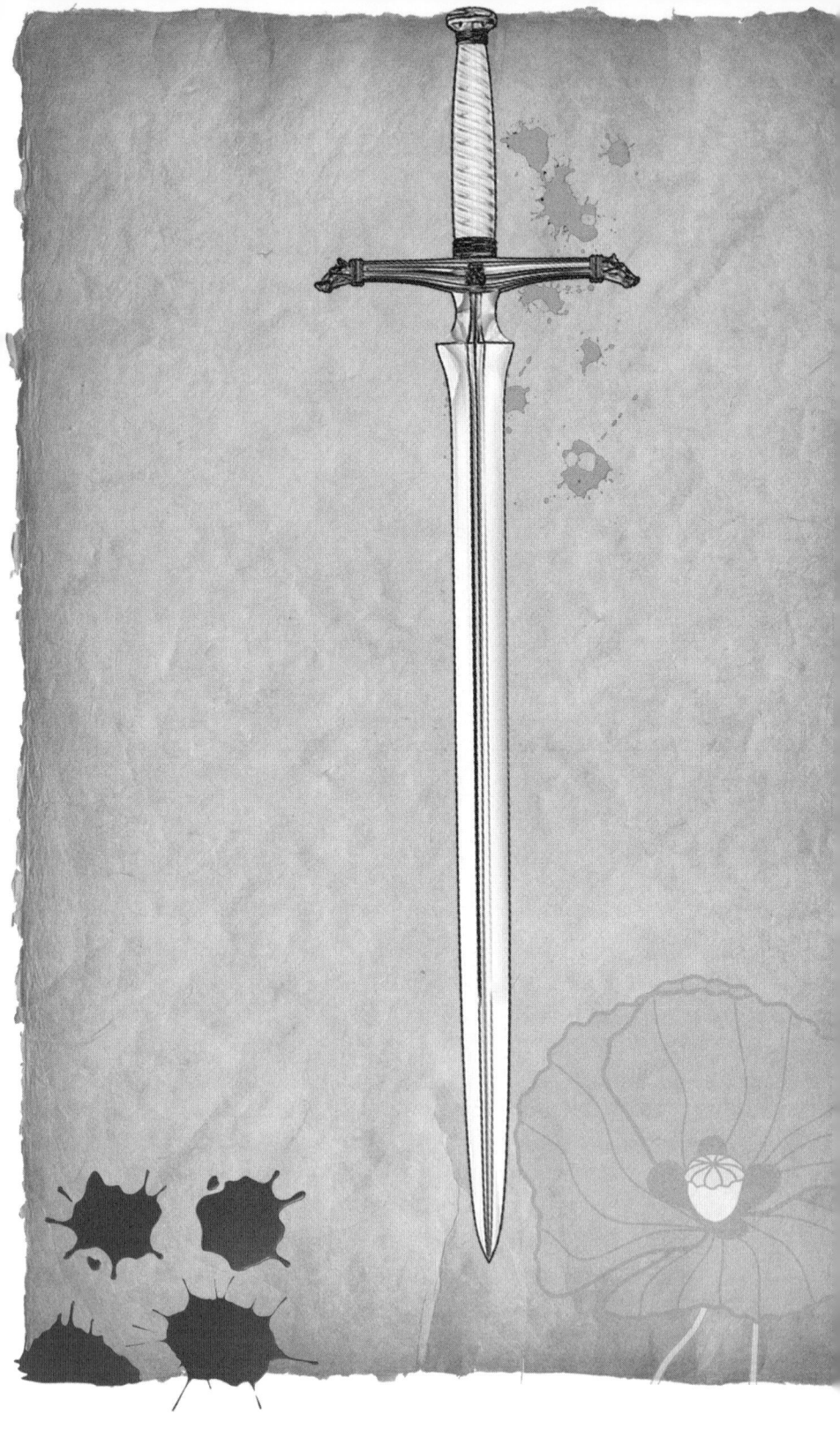

'Excellent ... there's so much to LOVE here ... a thoughtful and great beginning.'
Barry Cunningham, OBE - pioneer of Harry Potter books.

'Fantastic story-telling.'
Faber

'It is really well put together and strong.'
Hachette Childrens Books

'... a great sense of glee ... THIS IS SUCH A GREAT BOOK.'
Conville and Walsh

'Goodness - how fascinating ... he's a talented writer.'
Egmont

'Can't wait to read it!'
Chicken House

'I think there's so much that good, fun and funny here. It's so imaginative and filled with great details.'
Greenhouse Literary

'...this book has huge charm.'
Short Books

'I did enjoy Small Vampires ... a lot of potential in the story.'
Random House

'... accomplished writing.'
HarperCollins

'The biggest mistake we Vampires and others in the Hidden Kingdom ever made was to hide away – for what you Humans cannot see, you fear and what you fear, you would make monsters of.'

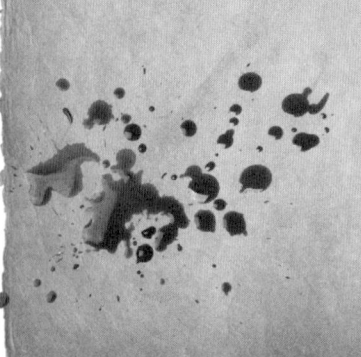

dear sirs

quarto translations

One very cold day, just over ten years ago, I found myself standing alone at a wind-swept train station in Newcastle. My being there was thanks to a letter from a complete stranger. I did not know it at the time, but this letter and the short walk I was about to take would change my life forever.

My name is Robin Bennett, and I am the founder of a small language translation bureau called Quarto Translations in Henley-on-Thames. The letter I had received a week previously invited me to come to Newcastle in order to view three large volumes that appeared to be in an *unknown* tongue. A pretty generous fee for my time was offered, plus a lot more money if I was able to identify (and translate) the strange writing.

The letterhead itself bore the name *Tyne Antiquarian & Rare Books*, gave a residential address but no phone number and ended with the initials, A.G.F-P.

The lack of a proper name at the end of the letter and the general air of mystery about the whole business meant that, when I arrived at the right street, I was very much looking forward to the interview with 'A.G.F-P' and to seeing the volumes themselves.

After a few wrong turns, I finally tracked the address down to a nondescript house in a nondescript street. The entrance was half-hidden in an alcove whose door seemed to have been shut several years previously and not opened since for any reason. I pushed through the poppies that seemed to be thriving in the otherwise bare front garden and looked for a buzzer in vain. I then gave the door a tentative knock, followed, on reflection, by a good kick.

Inside I heard an odd noise as something scuffled across bare wooden boards. I leaned closer to the door, to locate the source of the noise but as I peered into the grubby, stained-glass window panel, some primitive instinct suddenly told me to be fearful. Nothing, at first, stirred within and all I saw was the blurry outline of shelves and boxes and books; however, some indefinable sense of danger made the hairs on the back of my neck rise and I gave an involuntary shudder.

Then, just as I was about to pull away from the murky view I had of this old room with its lurking presence, something moved – *right* in front of my eyes. The figure was small – no larger than a few centimetres from head to toe – and it seemed to hover in front of my face. Just then, whatever it was moved closer and, for the briefest of instants, I had a very clear view of a pair of small but exceptionally piercing dark blue eyes that bored into mine. Almost as soon as the connection between me and *It* was made, it was severed as the creature flicked away from my view and was gone.

Since I had turned into the street there had been no sign of life anywhere, so I was startled when I heard a loud sniff that appeared to come from my left leg. I turned this way and that and eventually identified the source of the sniff as being a small boy standing just behind me. 'Hello,' I said and had turned to resume my assault on the door when I was interrupted.

''Ee's not 'ere.'

'Who's not here?' I asked mid-thwack.

'Mr Fancy-Pants.'

'Mr *Who*?' I asked instinctively. 'Go away,' I added.

The boy didn't seem at all put out. 'Arnold G. Fancy-Pants. That's what me mam calls 'im anyway. I think 'is name's Fal-something-Palmer. But anyway, likeisaid, 'ees not 'ere.'

Right initials, I thought. 'So where is he then?'

''Ees *ded*... they carried 'im out in a box on Sunday... 'e was that *owld*...'

'Oh,' I said, 'I see.' I ran my hand through my hair. 'Does anyone else live here?'

The boy chewed his lip. "'E used to 'ave a cat,' he said eventually. 'But I ain't seen it for ages.'

'Thank you,' I said, feeling irrationally cross with Mr Arnold G. F-P. for dying and not telling me about it. However, there was nothing for it but to walk back to the station and catch the next train to London. I looked with mixed feelings at the closed door, noticing for the first time that it had the outline of a cup carved intricately into the wood. Then I gave the small boy fifty pence, a short lecture on personal hygiene, and went home.

Three weeks later there was a further turn to these mysterious events when a bulky package arrived from a firm of solicitors in Sunderland.

Their client, Mr Arnold Falaise-Palmer, had left recent instructions that in the event of his death (which, given the weather in the North of England, was most likely imminent), the three volumes enclosed be sent to me for language identification. The books were in poor condition and unlikely to be worth much but any proceeds from the sale should be given to his niece and sole heir, Ms Natalie Falaise, of Lille, Northern France.

The books, when I unwrapped them, were certainly antiquarian *looking*, as far as I could tell. Nevertheless, as the solicitors pointed out, they seemed to have been ill-treated over the years and they may well have been fairly new, just beaten up. The binding looked like it had been done in someone's kitchen using cheap glue and a blunt knife and the pages were dog-eared and contained an array of stains: some of which, on closer scrutiny, looked suspiciously like dried blood.

As for the language, it looked familiar but at first glance I hadn't a clue as to its origin, except to say it was probably Indo-European in root. This didn't help me much – nearly everything is Indo-European *in root*. However, nothing I looked up and none of the translators I asked could make out any meaning in the sentences, even if some of the words looked strangely familiar. I eventually concluded that it was most probably written in some sort of private code.

I sat down to write Ms Natalie Falaise a letter explaining the background to the books, her uncle's stipulation in his will and my opinion as to the origin and (most probably) limited value of the books. I suggested that, as a blood relation[1], it would be better if she took it upon herself to sell the books. If she made some money out of it, then I would be grateful for a small fee for an hour or two's work; if not, then no matter. I added that I had not known her uncle but was very sorry, all the same, for her loss.

A few weeks later I received a reply from Ms Falaise in perfect English. She started by thanking me for my letter and suggested we meet at the Eurostar exit in Waterloo station that weekend where she was getting a connecting train to visit old university friends in Exeter. As to the value of the books, she begged to differ with me – her uncle, whom she had only met a few times in as many years, had spoken of them on a number of occasions and had strongly hinted that their value was greater than anything he had acquired in his long career as a rare book dealer.

This time at least, there was a phone number on the letter and I rang to confirm with her. That job done, I went to put the books back in the packaging. I was reflecting on what a sweet vivacious girl she sounded on the phone, when a sheet of paper that half fell out of the first volume caught my eye. I instantly recognised the handwriting as that of my late correspondent, Mr Arnold *Fancy-Pants*.

On it he had written simply, *GK/Ltn/AROM…?*

Given the context, I presumed the first two were his shorthand for Greek and Latin and whilst I wasn't sure what 'AROM' actually was, I was pretty confident that it was simply his abbreviation for another language. Looking it up in *Dalby's Dictionary of Languages*, 1990 edit., confirmed that it was most probably Aromanian: a dialect of Greek spoken in the North of the country and a root and relative neighbour of modern Transylvanian.

---

[1] If only I had known the real importance of that phrase then!

I met Natalie at the station. She was blond, very pretty and unreasonably cheerful, considering she'd been stuck on a train for nearly four hours, and before long we were getting along very well. In a nearby pub by the river, I fished out the books and showed them to her, and I also handed over Uncle Arnold's short handwritten note. She tucked her hair back behind her ear, stared at the paper for a few moments and then thumbed the volumes. Meanwhile I was quite happy to drink my beer and enjoy studying her in profile. When she looked up, she smiled almost apologetically and said, 'I'm sure you've thought of this already but could the writing not simply be a mixture of all three?'

And there you have it.

I knew immediately that firstly she was almost certainly right and that secondly, if I wasn't already, that I would very soon fall in love with Ms Natalie Falaise of Lille, Northern France.

In fact, we were married in the spring of 1997. Since then, on and off, the business and children allowing, I have worked on the translation. At first it was hard going but initial successes and a growing fascination in the actual contents kept me going. The writing was indeed an odd mixture of all three of the above languages, and after some time I realised that the writer was just lazy and had simply used whichever word in whatever language came to mind first.

The volumes told the explosive and moving story of an intelligent species – no larger than the forefinger you are using to hold down this page – that has lived amongst us, largely in secret, for thousands of years. These creatures are very close to the best of us in so many ways – in their language, good humour, courage and sense of fairness – but utterly different in others, such as their inhuman turn of speed, the grace of angels, their obsession with blood and, most importantly, their gift for magic. They go by many names: Nosferatu, Vykolakas, Strigoi...

However, these days, we simply know them as *Vampire*.

Small Vampire is a name all of my own – they never refer to themselves in this way. They do not actually see themselves as small, rather that we Humans are lumbering, ungainly and ridiculously B I G . Another title for these stories might also have been, *Vampires – the truth*, or, *The Secret History of the Hidden Kingdom*. But I am calling it simply *Small Vampires* simply because it is catchier and because it describes them in a way that at least partly explains why so few Humans have met one. It also explains why most of us stoutly believe Vampires only exist in books, films and in the imaginations of people who find the idea of knowing someone who wants to bite them on the neck romantic.

A Small Vampire is actually about the size of a dragonfly. They travel widely, and you've almost certainly *seen* several and indeed been bitten by one or two right in your own back garden. You most probably thought that it was a mosquito, or a horsefly, and then forgot about the bite because it didn't itch or go red. But if you looked very carefully, you would have seen not one tiny pinprick bite mark, but T W O . I put this in capitals because it is important. The T W O holes represent one for each of the sharp little teeth of the Small Vampire.

If you happened to catch one, which is very unlikely given their skill at magic and how fast they can move, and you looked at him (or her) under a magnifying glass, you would see that he had dragonfly-like wings that fold neatly away behind his back and (if he is not wearing his usual light armour) you would see very soft, mole-like down or fur covering his body. This velvet fur is mostly black, but with a flash of white around the neck and where his tummy starts. The effect is as if they are wearing a perfectly tailored evening suit. Even more striking are their faces, which are basically human, in a way that's hard to explain. Under a very strong magnifying glass, female or *Duchess* Vampires are nearly all very beautiful, and the males elegant and charming, with just the hint of something proud and rather dangerous about them.

Apart from their size, it is important to know that Vampires are most certainly *not* the wicked creatures of the night with foreign accents that Hollywood has had us believe. However, they *are* steeped in magic and, like any other creature from the Hidden Kingdom, they are unquestionably cleverer than any of us.

How they came into being is lost to us but what is almost certain is that they have been here from the start. The first volume you have here begins nearly two thousand years ago, when civilised Humans were only just starting out – mostly unaware, even then, of the existence of these small but immensely powerful creatures.

However, my part in their story doesn't end there and this leads me to my reason for writing to you.

For some months now, I have had a growing feeling of unease – usually at night. We live in the country on the edge of a very ancient wood. This does not normally worry me but lately I have heard an unusual noise – something like a low chuckle – coming from the line of trees outside the barn, and, once or twice, I have caught the flash of a pair of cold, insane eyes, reflected in the moonlight, staring out at me from the shadows: Very different from those I saw through the grubby door pane all those years ago, but no less intense. Recently I awoke in the early hours with the distinct impression that someone had been stroking my hair as I slept.

Then, about a week ago, I received a parcel postmarked from Newcastle. I immediately checked the sender's address and was surprised to see it came from the same part of England as Mr Arnold Falaise-Palmer's letter all those years ago.

The package contained three items, each carefully wrapped in cotton wool:

1. A small but surprisingly heavy sword – no more than three centimetres long but beautifully made and *very* sharp;
2. A tiny crystal phial containing a dark red liquid;

3. And a pair of dried wings – like that of a dragonfly – though longer, tapered and beautifully iridescent.

When I picked up the envelope, a note dropped out. Initially all I saw was what looked like a reddish smudge on the yellowing paper but, on instinct, I grabbed a magnifying glass and peered at the ink. Now the writing was clear – a beautiful but minute copperplate hand.

> 'I hope you enjoyed our histories, Mr Bennett! I saw you once (and I believe you spotted me too), many years ago, when you came to the home belonging to the late Mr Arnold Falaise-Palmer, my last Human friend. At that moment I formed the impression that you would be an excellent custodian of these precious volumes.
> However there are those of your race (and ours) who would seek to destroy them and quite possibly harm you, should you misuse their secrets! And so I bitterly regret the danger I have put you in. One day the contents of this package may be of great use to you. Humbly yours, Clan Karl of Brasov – Picus.'

My first reaction was to dismiss the letter writer as a lunatic, but then I remembered the strange things that had been happening and got to thinking about the actual contents of the books and what it would mean were they actually true.

My next instinct was to light a fire in the garden and burn the books and then to go into hiding – preferably somewhere really warm and sunny.

In fact that was what I resolved to do until a couple of days ago when I had a rare brainwave – I told my wife all about it. However instead of running up and down the stairs screaming, as I supposed she might do, she just shrugged.

'Um,' I prompted, 'you did hear what I said – bad guys and possibly their friends with big teeth are out to get us…etcetera?'

She shrugged again. 'Yes,' she said, 'for I am not deaf. I was thinking of a solution and now I have one – voila!'

'Oh yeah, what's that?' I asked, a little cross, I have to admit, that she didn't seem to be taking all of this very seriously.

'C'est evident! Simple! And I am quite sure you would have thought of it too, my darling – sooner or later.' She patted my arm at this point, which was also quite annoying. 'In brief, I would make the contents public – as public as possible! In this way, the books *we* have will no longer hold their value, as nearly everyone will have a copy. What would be the point of destroying them and – let us be honest here, the two of us – if thousands of copies were printed that people all over the world will read? No use shutting the door of the barn when the cat has already escaped.'

I thought about it. 'Surely if what is in these books is true and we told the whole world all about it, then that would make the bad guys even more angry?'

'Angry – certainly! But if these secretive, extremely powerful and possibly dangerous Vampires or People know you have the books, then it is much more likely that sooner or later they are going to come around the idea that they better get rid of us *before* we do anything. Just in case. If everyone knows about the Hidden Kingdom, then what would be the point of attacking just us?'

I didn't reply right away.

Instead, I went over to the window and looked out at the wood that borders the house. A spray of poppies I had never seen before caught my eye – scarlet, nodding in the breeze and out-of-season. I peered into the shadows and the hollows as I thought about what else lay hidden in there, beyond our gaze. The books I had translated told of other secretive creatures, some just as magical, and some even more dangerous than Vampires: Faies with their Leaf Castles that lay all over Britain, Weres, Wights...and we had proof it existed, all written in her uncle's books!

At that moment I had to admit, despite all the danger, it was exciting. Publishing the books would change everything, and not just for us.

Finally I came to the conclusion that – as usual – my wife was right. Making the entire contents of the book wasn't a perfect solution but it was better than sitting around doing nothing, hoping that they (whoever they were) would be nice enough to decide to leave us alone.

So here it is then, the secret history of Small Vampires. It is a story that started when the Empire of Man was still new and Vampires, the most powerful but also the best of all creatures, ruled with fairness, grace and good humour…

Yours faithfully

robin bennett

Turn your gaze to a half-remembered world of childhood that exists below the tall grass and flowering hedgerows. Look very carefully and you may be able to trace faint pathways through the undergrowth, leading to small mounds of dry foliage in curious, deliberate shapes – Leaf Castles! These are perhaps the last visible remains of the Hidden Kingdom.

Chapter 1

Picus the thief

This story starts on a night nearly two thousand years ago, in the dense forests that surround an area known today as Transylvania. The countryside all around is pitch black and freezing rain tumbles from bruised clouds.

Now, pick a solitary droplet of rain and follow it through the swirling clouds as it is buffeted by winds: past the rocky outcrops and down into the canopy of trees, right to the forest floor. Imagine it land with a small pat – like a bead of blood falling on wet leaves – amongst the tangled roots and briars; where dramas, unseen by Human eyes, play out.

Through the storm someone is running for their life. It is the Vampire, Picus. Picus the Thief.

Needless to say, almost as soon as he had stepped outside, the rain had found a way to gush down the back of his neck. His wings were sodden and refused to work. Swerving to avoid an arrow that zipped silently through the trees, narrowly missing his exposed neck, he stumbled into a miniature, evil-smelling swamp at the towering base of a tree and lost a boot.

Picus, who liked the finer things in life, such as good footwear and not smelling like a blocked drain, cursed the day he was born. It was one thing to be pursued through a dark wood during a thunderstorm, battered by raindrops the size of his head, shot at with arrows and called terrible names but it was quite another thing to lose one half of his second favourite pair of magic boots.

The immensely powerful, fat and furious Vampire who was catching up with Picus despite his best efforts to escape was currently wearing his favourite pair.

'When I get my talons into you, I'll rip your fangs out with white-hot pliers!' Picus heard the thunder of large feet behind him. And they were getting closer. 'I'll chop your miserable, thieving head off and boil it. I'll shred your tongue and use it to string my harp. I'll ... I'll make you eat your own feet!'

That's just weird, thought Picus.

Without warning, a Were burst out from behind an acorn husk just ahead of the fleeing Vampire. The monster shook its greasy pelt and pounced at Picus, who suddenly found himself staring into a mouth full of pitted, yellowing teeth – the beast's jaw working like an industrial meat grinder.

Picus laughed. The Were was just one of Raben's defence mechanisms. Nothing more than a Summoned Ghost. Without slowing, he turned his wrist in a complicated series of pentagons and the spectre vaporised into a thick, black fog that briefly obscured Raben's path, making him run headlong into a tree root.

Despite missing footwear, Picus accelerated and, to take his mind off the rain, had a think about how he came to be in this mess: Gambling!

In a word.

More like licensed thieving, he thought bitterly. You sit down for a relaxing game of Blood Tarot with some apparently honest Vampires and before sunrise you've lost your shirt. And all your money.

And your best boots.

Going to Raben's castle in the dead of night and stealing Raben's property was sweet revenge and had seemed like good fun until he'd been caught slipping out of a ground floor window by the old crook's disturbing son, Corbeau. The latter had raised the alarm by yelling so loud that half the Vampires in their family crypt probably woke up for the first time in centuries. Very shortly after this, Corbeau threw a priceless goblet from Atlantis at Picus' head at which point what had seemed like a bit of a prank suddenly became a desperate fight for survival: Raben, wearing boots that made him move as if running on air, despite his size, and Picus zigzagging past Raben's sentinels through the forest surrounding his lonely eyrie that perched high on a mountain at the far edge of Vampire country.

Picus grinned.

It would still be quite something, though, if he did get away. Raben was not just a card cheat but also one of the most vicious, dishonest and generally cowardly Vampires Picus had ever had the pleasure to nick from. At least I'm honest about pinching stuff, he had time to think, before three Wood Sprites darted down from the canopy of foliage above his head and started firing their nasty little arrows at his face. 'Stop that!' he said, batting the first two away. One got through and stuck in his cheek. 'Ow!' Another embedded itself in the back of his hand. 'I *said*, "Ow". What's wrong with you guys?' The arrows were tiny but they hurt like hell and he knew, from past experience, that the little holes they made itched for days. 'Look, seriously, you little squirts, I'm warning you …' Clicking his fingers, and making a curiously metallic sound in the back of his throat, he conjured up a large hammer out of thin air.

But then he had second thoughts. Sprites were usually OK; these had probably been put under some kind of off-the-shelf Loyalty Charm by Raben, who seemed to have a magical menagerie working for him in the forest.

Picus blinked and traced an outline in the air with the tips of his fingers. A bottle replaced the hammer, hovering just below his attackers who were chattering away, enthusiastically re-loading their pig bristle bows. Picus blinked again and the bottle flexed, gave a sort of inhalation and sucked all three very surprised Sprites in. A large cork appeared from nowhere and stuck itself firmly in the neck of the bottle with a *bung* sound, whereupon Sprites, bottle and cork disappeared into thin air.

By now Raben had untangled himself from the thick roots under the tree he'd run into and was back on track, thundering towards Picus. 'You think you can steal my possessions and get away with it!'

'You started it, fatso!' Picus had broken into a sprint again and was shouting over his shoulder. 'Card cheat!' A flash of lightning lit up the forest like a negative. Picus risked a backward glance: Raben was drenched, his fur covered in mud and matted; all in all, he looked menacing, murderous and ever-so-slightly mad. He had thrown away his bow and arrow but had now drawn the largest, sharpest-looking meat cleaver Picus had ever clapped eyes on.

'I won fair and square, these boots are mine and so is that dagger – a family heirloom you just stole from our sacred Crypt.' Raben rushed towards him.

'Rubbish, I happen to know you stole it from Count Oradea three hundred years ago, and *he* actually lifted it from the Great Tomb in the Keep. I'm just following tradition. Anyway, if the Eltern[2] knew you had it, they'd make you into black pudding.'

'Well they'll never find out, will they? By this time tomorrow, all that'll be left of you will be a pile of dry bones and a nasty memory.'

Picus heard a thrumming sound that he didn't recognise at first. Then he felt his eyes widen in sudden realisation. He ducked just in time as the meat cleaver tumbled over his head, missing him by less than the thickness of an eyelash, and took the top off some wild garlic. The burst of fumes made both Vampires lurch, as if suddenly very drunk.

Picus, being young and extremely fit, recovered quickest. However, he was tiring fast and knew he had to get away from Raben very soon before he collapsed. Over the last two years of using magic to steal things and get away fast, Picus had learnt, first-hand, that it consumed huge amounts of energy very quickly.

So, whilst Raben was still staggering about, knees buckling, Picus whispered something in a strange sing-song voice and

---

[2] [Translator's note]: Vampire elders who supposedly run things at the Keep and almost everywhere else, if you believe them. The Keep is the spiritual home of Small Vampires the world over. It is situated in the Carpathian Mountains, somewhere between modern day Hungary and Romania.

a jagged edge, like a half-open door, appeared in the rain.
He slipped sideways into the Shadow World.

※

OK, now, this was definitely the riskier side of magic. Shadow Worlds occupied the unseen space between the real world and that of the dead – a sort of cavity wall between Earth life and Eternal life. Like all cavity walls, they contained any number of things that scrabbled about in alarming directions. Some Vampires and Faies referred to it as the Chaos. And with good reason. Picus had used this escape route before and each time he visited he felt an increasing sense of despair in that place – everything seemed forlorn and somehow hopeless. You never knew what to expect with Shadow Worlds either. The last he had been in was an exact replica of the real world but made entirely of grey glass; another he visited when trying to avoid a particularly nasty Demon prince, a few weeks before, was covered in a velvety green moss that burned and blistered the skin when you touched it. This time – to the untrained eye, at least – it looked no different from the place he had come from. Picus was in the same wood, surrounded by the same trees and still getting soaking wet under the same rain. But even in the dark there was a strange transparency to everything – nothing really looked solid. The Moon that appeared briefly through a break in the tumbling clouds was duller, somehow. Picus stretched his hand out tentatively and touched the nearest plant that towered above him. Instantly it crumbled into dust, making him spring back in alarm. He touched another trunk and felt something like sponge give beneath his fingers. It took him a few moments to work out that everything in this world seemed to be made of charcoal and ash, as if, at some stage in history, it had been scorched to cinders by an immense heat source.

Picus glanced to his left, though a gap he had left between the Shadow World and the real world, like a narrowly parted curtain. Amongst the trees he could make out the blurry form of

Raben stumbling around, still shaking off the effects of the raw garlic fumes, whilst looking about for Picus, who seemed to have vanished into thin air.

Which, technically, he had.

Picus felt a small upswing of pride: there were few, if any, Vampires who could carry off the stunt he'd just pulled without hours or even days of careful preparation. Magic was something that came naturally to him. Rather like pinching things.

Although this was not the sort of place where you wanted to loiter about, Picus knew he probably wouldn't have to wait long until Raben moved off, to continue the search further down the valley. So long as Picus kept quite still he wouldn't attract any attention. The half-formed creatures that stalked the Shadow World would fall upon any live prey, biting and gouging with misshapen claws and broken teeth in an effort to enter a warm body and so leapfrog into the real world. Dozens of gruesome fireside stories told of creatures from the Chaos suddenly appearing in the real world literally wearing the bloodied carcasses of their victims, like a still-warm coat.

So, to take his mind off his immediate surroundings, Picus looked down at the bundle of sodden rags he was holding. One corner of the grubby material had fallen open and something bright glinted through the darkness. Ah, gold *always* cheered him up. It was his now – he could take a peek if he wanted, remind himself what all his hard work that evening was for and dispel the gloomy thoughts that crowded in on him in this desolate, dead place.

He was staring at the bundle so hard that he didn't notice something large and shapeless stir behind his left shoulder.

Reverently, Picus slipped the dagger from its bundle and marvelled silently at how it shone through the forest, almost of its own accord, as if lit within, like a symbol of hope. Jewels encrusted the hilt and the blade rippled like liquid mercury. Picus had read about this in the library at the Keep. Apparently the blade was made of a metal from a meteorite that had fallen to Earth in pre-history: the Lost Dagger of Eden, said to be the sister of the much larger Human blade that cut the apple from the Tree of Life.

It was only then he realised he had probably just made a BIG mistake: Raben was bound to have some sort of defence mechanism attached to the dagger itself. Sure enough, suddenly a large octagonal ruby on the hilt lit up and a shrill voice inside the stone let out a piercing wail. 'Oh help! *Help!* I've been stolen by this horrible Vampire and it's all dark and wainy.'

'Shhh!' hissed Picus.

'*No I won't "shush"*... oh please, mercy, don't hurt me! Won't somebody save me from this brute with nasty long teeth and sneaky, shifty eyes? I'm so fwightened and all alone in this scary wood with this hideous creature of the night.'

'Look, I'm warning you ...'

'Ooh I *just* knew it ... threats ... and *me*, a poor defenceless piece of art-cum-history. Please won't somebody apprehend this common cwiminal, this low-life thief with terrible taste in shoes ... ooh and his breath's so smelly and his howible hands so dirty...'

'One more word, you jumped-up letter-opener –' the threat was cut short. Picus felt a cold hand grasp his throat, as unseen fingers began to scrabble at his clothes and rake his face, nails clawing at his eyes, trying to blind him. Without his sight, in this Shadow World, stumbling amongst the embittered half-dead, he'd be defenceless.

The anti-theft ruby quickly realised what was up and, more importantly, on which side its bread was now buttered.

'Oh brave and talented Vampire, save us! But first, wrap me up again so I don't have to look at that tewifying monster.'

'What monster?'

'Oh, the one that's right behind you.' Picus twisted around to look at this new threat.

'You must think I was bor – ? ... G N A R R G G H H !' Picus had turned around just in time to see a Human nearly thirty times his height rise up from the darkness at the base of the charred tree. What little remained of the creature's ravaged body was bent and broken – seemingly all that held him together were the tattered vestiges of his garments, which hung in rags from his scrawny limbs, and an ancient, ill-fitting suit of armour that ground and creaked as he lurched towards Picus. What was most disturbing was his face – or lack thereof. Eyes, nose, mouth, hair were just not there. From his shoulders down he was obviously an old Human warrior from Athens or Sparta: his corroded breastplate had once been highly polished bronze and the remains of his cloak were attached to his bony neck with a gold chain, denoting a soldier of high rank. However, his whole head was encased in puckered white skin, like that of a plucked chicken. Through the darkness Picus could see the jaw mouthing underneath the layer of clammy flesh that encased it, as if this once-man-now-creature was trying to say something.

'Quick, get us out of here you idiot!' screamed the ruby.

'You're not going anywhere, pal.' Drawing a small knife from a hidden pouch, Picus prised off the gemstone and threw it into the darkness.

'No wait, stop ... please, you can't leave me here, all on my own ... aaaargh!'

Picus actually felt a twinge of guilt but the trick worked: the ravaged fingers that had been scoring his face withdrew and scuttled towards the glowing red light of the ruby, and the warrior from antiquity lumbered off after them.

Singing another incantation, Picus parted the shadowy curtains and slipped back into the real world, away from the horrors and the dreadful sadness. That's absolutely the last time I try that, he thought as he wrapped the now silent dagger back up in the cloth.

Taking care to head in the opposite direction to where he had seen Raben go, Picus faded quietly into the night.

The Vampire, as a species, has endured since the Earth was new and its visage ran with molten rock, like rivers of blood. Somehow they survived and even flourished when the sky boiled with crimson fire that scorched to cinders all but the strongest and bravest creatures.

Chapter 2

Aliya

Peter and his younger sister, Aliya, had got up at dawn to catch butterflies at the Old Ruins. Being Human, they marched through the long grass towards the tumbledown castle making so much noise that all other creatures, both magical and non-magical, heard them coming long before they saw them and melted away into their various burrows, nooks and secret crannies.

Everyone except for Picus.

Not only was he fast asleep, he'd also stuffed his ears with thistle down, as he'd fancied a lie-in after his exertions the night before.

Peter was eleven and he held the brand new butterfly net proudly aloft as his sister, aged six, followed on behind. She was carrying a leather basket into which they planned to put whatever they caught, and it bumped annoyingly against her legs as she tried to keep up. Aliya was small for her age, with blond hair and emerald green eyes that gazed adoringly at her big brother who was telling her things as he walked along, chewing a dry stalk of grass. Aliya tried to do the same but the stalk tasted horrible so she spat it out when she hoped he wasn't looking. She still had a bitter taste in her mouth.

'When I'm older,' he was saying, 'I'm going to have a castle just like this one, except it'll probably be bigger...it'll have proper walls, not broken down ones, a moat and a whole regiment of knights in polished chain mail to protect it.' He paused to push back a mop of reddish brown hair that had fallen over one eye. 'You can come and live there too...before you get married.'

Aliya smiled happily, she could think of nothing she'd like better. 'And I'll have a big white horse but with black ears and a room just for dressing up and a marmalade cat and he'll be able to talk and say clever things...'

Peter smiled. 'Sure,' he said. He was fond of his sister, and although she came out with some pretty weird stuff sometimes, she was cute and he enjoyed her company more than he'd admit to his friends closer to his age back in the village. And she *loved* butterflies. By now they had reached the Old Ruins; Peter suddenly stopped and stared at the grass. Something had caught his sharp eyes. He rarely missed anything, and their father, the Clan chief, would declare proudly that Peter would make a fine tracker and hunter one day – the best in the village, most likely. He was staring at something in the grass. 'Wow, what's that Ali?' Even though he was older, Peter bowed to his sister's knowledge of all things in the animal kingdom.

Aliya tiptoed somewhat noisily to where her brother was and crouched down, looking at the small form he was pointing at under a mushroom.

Dragon-fly wings reflecting purple, red, green and a host of other colours she had no name for were wrapped around a small, down-covered body, no larger than her little finger. The creature seemed to be sleeping soundly – its curiously human face was peaceful and wore an expression of good-natured satisfaction. And it was *actually* wearing clothes – well tailored leather trousers, some sort of armour (Peter would know) and, for some reason, only one boot.

'It might be dangerous – shall I squash it?'

Aliya was scandalised. *Boys!* 'No, don't do that, it's … it's the most beautiful thing I've ever seen.'

Then It opened one eye and Aliya was treated to a brief but startlingly intense gaze that seemed to go right through her, like a jolt of electricity. At that very moment her brother's butterfly net went down with a muffled whoosh and the connection was severed.

'No leave him!' she exclaimed, turning around to Peter.

'Got it!' he said triumphantly, ignoring his sister. However, his smile faded as he looked at the net. It bulged briefly where the trapped being, now awake, pushed against the thin black fibres which burst open – a tiny tear suddenly appearing in the tough fabric, allowing the captive to escape. With an incredible turn of speed, far faster than Aliya had ever seen anything move before, the small creature flicked its wings and flew directly at her brother's throat.

'Ow!'

'What?' Aliya was torn by concern for her brother and a keen interest to see where the exquisite animal had then flown off to.

'Horrible little bug just bit me ... *and* it made a hole in my brand new net.'

'He's not horrible, he was beautiful, and anyway, he was probably just scared.'

'Hmm, if *he* was that scared, then why didn't *he* just fly off when he had the chance? No,' Peter was still indignant, 'that was more like revenge. If I ever catch up with it...' he rubbed the wound.

Aliya sighed and stood on tiptoe, the better to peer at the bite mark. Her eyes widened. 'Gosh!' she remarked, her young forehead creased as she studied the pinpricks of blood that welled up. She was quiet for a bit. 'He's left *two* little teeth marks,' she said eventually, 'I've never seen an insect do that. It's more like a tiny human bite.'

Before he was so rudely awakened, Picus had slept very well indeed. The storm clouds had rolled away in the night and he lay there for a long time, his eyes still closed, gently waking to the smell of warm grass drying in the mid-morning sunlight. The feather-light platinum and leather armour he nearly always wore felt warm and dry for the first time in days.

It was the year 266 AD by the reckoning of Man; no great cities, no cars nor planes disturbed the peaceful countryside. Clumsy Humans – each scores of times larger, noisier *and* a lot smellier than anything in the magical kingdom – still only covered small parts of the green and blue planet called Earth that Vampires had ruled for millions of years. He was quite alone, on the edge of Scrietch Forest.

Then two Human children appeared.

Before he was fully awake, Picus heard a noise. Opening a cautious eye he saw a child's face gawping at him. It gave him quite a shock but before he had a chance to react a net came down from nowhere and he was trapped.

Picus had very little to do with Humans but, whenever he did, over the years, it nearly always seemed to involve their children. They had a tendency to notice things the adults missed.

Ho, hum. He flexed his fingers and sent a jolt of energy at the tough fabric of the net. It tore open and Picus, still half asleep, shot out a little raggedly at half his usual speed. He wasn't going to hang about at first but the male Human with the net needed to be taught a lesson.

He'll think twice before he does that again, thought Picus, smacking his lips with satisfaction as he landed safely a few hundred yards away.

He looked back and saw the girl casting about in all directions; for a moment her gaze seemed to rest on the patch of long grass where Picus stood. Two green eyes narrowed and Picus had the fleeting but distinct impression she could see him. Impossible – you had to go a long way to find a species as unobservant as Humans. Nevertheless, the girl seemed to have something about her …

Despite the unexpected feed he'd just had, Picus was still absolutely starving. Performing magic out of the ordinary always did that to him. Taking out his knife from inside his muddy boot, he sliced off a meaty wedge of a nearby button mushroom and chewed on that whilst he took a good look around, humming to himself. A green and orange caterpillar, roughly half his size, nudged along a nearby stalk. No: he really didn't enjoy his food that colourful first thing. A light grey dove preened itself midway up an oak to his left but he didn't feel like making the effort to go all the way up there – and they always flew off just as you got your fangs in and then who knows where you'd end up. Just then a large field vole poked her head out of a clump of thyme. Ah-ha!

Ten minutes later the vole, minus roughly a thimble of blood, had gone on her way and Picus, feeling much better, smacked his lips again as he stretched his arms and flexed his wings.

He took a look around. Above him, he could make out the remains of some vast Human walls and what looked like a stone turret of some ruined citadel, now overgrown with ivy and moss. The broken stones towered above him where he stood, small and well-hidden. Seemingly impossibly tall to any magical creature, the Human-made tower appeared to be grazing the underbellies of the soft clouds that bobbed by on air currents he could not feel.

Insects hummed in the long grass as the butter-coloured sun shone down on a stretch of river to the east, making it flash gold where it bowed. The world looked incredibly good to Picus, a natural-born optimist, if ever there was one.

The warm southerly wind made the tips of his wings vibrate as it sent delicate fingers of air through the long grass. Picus sat for a while, drowsy, contented and full; feeling something like expectation slowly build inside him.

He waited until he could stand it no longer.

Then, in a sudden burst of energy, he took to the skies like a firework going off, looping through the pools of light that shone through the trees, higher and higher until he reached the leafy roof of the forest, a humming world of insects and delicate webs decorated with strings of dew, like tear-shaped diamonds. As he barrel-rolled above the green canopy, he laughed with the sheer unadulterated joy of simply being alive that morning.

Eventually he landed.

'Art the Fence deserves a visit, I think,' he said aloud, startling a fat bumblebee. 'And who knows, he might have a spare pair of boots somewhere in that shop of his.'

Magic uses up energy faster than anything on the planet. If Vampires, Weres, Wights and Faies were all the size of an adult Human, the amount of food they would need to eat every day would use up every crop field, fruit tree, herd of animals and fish in the world over in just a few months.

Chapter 3
Art the Fence

His destination was the Thieves' Kasbah, about ten leagues from where he had spent the night. Flying at full speed he could have made the journey in an hour, which was faster than anything alive – a Human on a good horse with a flat road would take over three days to cover a similar distance.

However, flying at those speeds for longer than a few minutes was exhausting, so he chose to dawdle, which meant walking for a bit, then flying a few hundred rapier lengths up in the air, then gliding – simply letting the warm currents carry his small, yet powerful frame in roughly the right direction.

By mid-afternoon Picus had finally reached the bend in the river where Art (short for Arthur) the Fence (short for total villain who made a living handling stolen goods) sold everything from rusty armour to dried Unicorn livers, stolen artefacts, and magical texts written by Vampires, Warlocks and Faie magicians Picus had never heard of.

Faies! Like most Vampires he chose to pretend they didn't unless they were in the same room. These flightless creatures were cousins of Vampires and were almost as talented with sword and the use of natural magic. Outside his professional life he did his best to avoid Faies because they were untrustworthy; plus, Picus had long ago come to the private conclusion that some of the older and therefore more powerful ones were frankly insane.

Apart from the odd rare text or gemstone, most things found in Art's so-called shop were fake or just tat; but when Picus, for various complicated reasons, had embarked on this career a few years previously, he had struck up an instantaneous friendship with Art. The old crook was sharp enough to know raw talent when he saw it and paid Picus (more or less) a fair price for the artefacts he brought in. Arthur the Fence, like nearly every other trader in the Thieves' Kasbah, was a Fiend – a clever type of Wight or magical creature of mixed origin – who traded magic texts and antiques. Vampires generally looked down their long but perfectly formed noses at such mixed-blood creatures but Picus had come to realise that most Wights were as loyal and certainly as clever as any Vampire he knew.

On the way over, Picus found himself running through the events of last night, if only to take his mind off his bootless, sore foot. He wasn't really that worried about Raben, who couldn't call on the Keep authorities because that would mean admitting he had pinched the dagger in the first place. Picus would just have to stay out of his way for the next decade or two.

Yet there was something that gave him the heebie-jeebies in spite of the warm sunlight, and he realised it was the memory of the look of pure, venomous hatred Corbeau had given him as he raised the alarm. 'Common thief!' the young Vampire had shouted as he flung the goblet and drew his childish rapier. 'How dare you come into the sanctuary of my forefathers. I will hunt you down, drain every last drop of your blood and pour it away into the sea.'[3] *Sanctuary of my forefathers!* I mean, who talked like that at his age? Certainly none of the young Vampires Picus chose to hang around with when he was still on his first set of blood teeth. Corbeau was a good-looking kid, even by Vampire standards, which generally started at stunning and improved sharply from there. Nevertheless, behind the looks, there was something cold and definitely creepy about Raben's only son. Probably some Faie blood in there somewhere. Picus had the uncomfortable feeling that he'd made an important enemy.

---

[3] [Translator's note]: An old Vampire curse. The idea being that then the Vampire's blood, and therefore his or her soul, would be mixed with salt water and lost forever. Blood to Vampires is everything.

Nothing, it seemed, had changed for hundreds of years inside Art's shop. A row of shrunken Grig heads had greeted visitors for the last couple of centuries, all grinning and leathery. ' 'Ang a few of these beauties up abowt the place,' Art liked to say, 'an' you'll sleep like a baby.' Picus privately agreed. Having even one of those hideous leering noggins in the house would almost certainly make him want to wake up every three hours crying his eyes out.

Floor to ceiling shelves filled the rest of the shop, stacked with parchments containing spells and curses, dubious treasure maps, fake gold rings and assorted bits of dead things. Right at the back was Art's *office* where all the real business went on. Picus, not being stupid, had chosen to go in the back way.

'No-one appreciates a good bit ov owd rubbish anymore,' said Art, without looking up.

For someone who'd made a living slinking about for the last three years and fancied himself one of the best slinkers in the business, the fact Picus was never able to creep up on Art undetected only increased his respect for the old Fiend. Art was looking at a large unpolished Moonstone using a pair of enormous glasses whose arms he'd attached candles to. The cheap, spider-fat candles spluttered, threatening to ignite the thistledown cap that Art permanently wore, even in bed. 'Personally, a good fake takes more effort and downrigh' inventiveness than the real fing more often than not. Look at this 'ere fake Moonstone. The goblin smith wot created this would 'ave taken about six years to get this right, plus all the slog in apprentiship before'and. Nah, any owd idiot can dig the real fing outa some mud somewhere but … coaxing this out of base minerals takes real skill. But the punters dan't want this anymore, they all come 'ere and fink they know everyfing. It's all, "can I 'ave a certificate of aufenticity for this, wots the provenance of that?" They're in the Thieves' Kasbah for Chalice sake! I might as well open a fruit stall.'

He took off his magnifying spectacles and turned to Picus. Shrewd, yet surprisingly kindly eyes took in the bundle and then studied his visitor with a mixture of pleasure and concern. His face, a mass of leathery wrinkles and some truly spectacular tattoos, broke into a gummy smile. 'Nah, wot can I do you for, you young rascal?'

'Hello, Arthur,' said Picus, more relieved than he would admit to see a friendly face for the first time in days. 'You look tired.'

※

Ten minutes later they were both sitting by the fire in Art's kitchen. Picus was blowing on his hot chocolate as Art drew on an ancient pipe that he claimed was made from part of the jawbone of the whale that swallowed Jonah. Picus did his best not to cough and splutter each time a cloud of dense smoke wafted his way. Art's tobacco smelled like dead bodies. 'Mmm ...' Art closed his eyes and let out a trickle of smoke between his wispy beard and almost non-existent black lips. 'It pongs a bit but you can't beat a good bit of Were dung baccy.' He stretched out a long bony arm and flicked open Picus' bundle with a grubby fingernail that looked like a cross between a talon and a broken tooth. Revealed in all its splendour, the dagger's hilt gave off a warm golden glow. Art's Wightish eyes shone redder than usual and he let out an involuntary low whistle. To give him his due he recovered pretty quickly. 'Get a dozen of these for a good joke an' a square meal down the market.' He snorted.

Picus smiled. 'Come on Art.'

'Tell you what, I'll give you three gold pieces and this 'ere Moonstone, an' wots more I'll never be able to live with meself.'

'You just said yourself, it's a fake! Anyway, I'm kind of off gems at the moment.'

'I *said* it woz a work of art. Now, that's the problem with the youf of today ... they don't know the value of nuffink and they never make the mistake of listening to their elders an' their betters.' Art's creased brown face did its best to assume a hurt expression but Picus was unmoved.

'I can always take it next door to The Black Widow ...' [4]

Awright, awright but you do realise this'll take some shifting.

The Eltern have been looking for the dagger for centuries – don't fink they've forgotten – and Raben's a powerful and unpleasant Vampire an' no mistake. Off the top of me 'ead, I can fink of only an 'andful of collectors who'd be interested in buyin' this and none can be trusted to keep their great big mouths shut.'

'You'll manage to get rid of it, I'm sure,' said Picus.

'You confidence is appreciated … I'll give you four bags of gold dust an' a mixed pouch of sapphires and diamonds. Final offer … take it or leave it.' Art stuck out a very long arm that might have been mistaken for the gnarled end of an old branch. Like all Fiends, long, very powerful arms made up for his short, trunk-like body and non-existent legs.

'OK,' said Picus, wincing as he felt his fingers being crushed, 'you've got a deal if you throw in a good pair of boots.'

'Wot about the last ones I gave you?'

'I lent them to a friend.'

'Oh, really? There you go.' Art flicked his grizzled head towards a shelf stacked with boots. ' 'Elp yerself.' Picus went over to look as Art took out a poker and jabbed absentmindedly at the fire. 'Suppose you'll be wanting to lie low for a bit, just like a real rapscallion … wait for Raben to calm down.'

'You'd have thought so.' Picus picked up a pair of aquamarine Dragon hide boots and held the stitching up to the light. 'This is Elvish.'

'Uh huh huh …' Art nodded then looked crafty. 'Of course, the best way to lie low –'

'I'll take it.' Picus cut in before Art could finish.

'What, the boots?'

'No, the job.'

'What job?' Art pretended to look completely innocent.

'The one you were about to offer me.'

---

[4] [Translator's note]: The Black Widow crops up in other manuscripts. She ran a fortune-teller's next door but dealt in artefacts on the side. Long ago she'd broken her leg badly when she fell down a well on a dark night (one accident she obviously didn't see coming). After that people called her the *Imp with a Limp*, or the *Fiend that Leaned*. Only behind her back, naturally.

'But...' Art now sounded genuinely exasperated, 'you don't even know what it is!'

'That's OK. I trust you.'

'Aaargh, don't keep saying that every time I'm about to offer you a job! It's an 'orrible fing to say about someone like me and it makes me want to be honest ... and that just makes me tattoos[5] go kind ov weird and itchy.'

'Well I *do* trust you.'

'Look Picus,' said Art, taking the pipe from his toothless mouth, 'you're young, so you can get away wiv saying fings like that ... but you can't trust no-one in this business, not – ' he held up a hand to silence his visitor, who'd just opened his mouth, 'even me.'

By now Picus had the boots on and was executing a series of complicated fencing steps. 'Great boots,' he said, half to himself. 'OK then. *Tell* me about the job, then I'll pretend to think about it.'

Art took another long draw on his pipe and spoke through the evil smelling smoke as he exhaled. 'It's a complex one – just the way you like it. And it's some distance, back in the old country, so you'll be out of Raben's way for a bit.'

'Sounds ideal. You know he's got a son.'

'What? Yeah, I 'ad heard, supposed to be pretty bright by all accounts. Apple of his dad's eye an' all that. Anyway all the details are in 'ere, if you're up for it.' Vampire and Fiend regarded one another across the room. Art's eyes narrowed as he held a rolled parchment in a gnarled hand. Before he could whip it away again Picus had flicked his wings, crossing the room in less than a heartbeat, and plucked the scroll from the old Wight's fist. Art was only slightly put out. 'You're getting quicker.'

'Thanks,' said Picus. 'I've been practising. And thanks for the boots.'

---

[5] Art claimed the incredibly intricate whirls and scripts in blue and red ink that covered his face were fiendishly clever charms designed to protect him from all but the most powerful magical attack. Picus privately suspected that he just liked the patterns.

'Don't mention it,' replied Arthur, a slow smile spreading across his ugly features. *Don't say it*, thought Picus desperately, *please don't say it*. 'After all,' Art was grinning from ragged ear to ear, his tattoos stretched and leering – Oh, Chalice, he's going to say it – Art was giggling now, a truly awful sight and he could barely get the words out, 'that's ... that's what FIENDS are for!'

'Oh, yes,' said Picus, doing his best to laugh at Art's favourite joke. 'Ha, ha, I get it. *Very* funny.'

'Yeah,' said Art gravely. 'I'm absolutely hilarious.'

When Picus had gone, Arthur the Wary slid open a secret drawer behind his chair and carefully stowed the priceless dagger inside. Then he turned and watched Picus amble off down the road, Art's eyes gradually going from greedy red to a sort of sad grey.[6] Of course, he knew where Picus was heading, without even asking.

Art had seen hundreds of master thieves in his shop over the centuries. He was a fence, a dealer in stolen goods and white lies and he had learnt not to judge his co-workers. But, even so, there was something about Picus that depressed him. He was a good thief, certainly, and when he was older, fully grown with a bit more experience under his sword belt, he'd make a great thief, perhaps even one of the greatest. Nevertheless, something in Art's old bones told him that Picus was out of place in his world. This was not the life for him and it wasn't just because he was a Vampire, and from one of the old Clans at that. He sensed that Picus could be so much more. It wasn't that he was basically a nice, well-brought up kid, which he certainly was. No, there was something else. Arthur had been around long enough to know when someone had a destiny as opposed to just a future. The boy

---

[6] [Translator's note]: Wights' eyes will often change colour to suit their mood. Art, being a Fiend, and therefore an unscrupulous and conniving businessman, had learnt to stop this happening over the years when dealing with others, but he allowed it to happen when alone.

had heart as well. He might just be this skinny Vampire with a talent for the old magic but then again … You're making a fool of yerself – 'e's not your kid, a mocking voice in Art's head cut in brusquely, so don't go all gooey and start worrying about him. Art shook his grizzled old head and sighed. He thought of the job he'd given him and the reason behind it. Not for the first time in his long life, he had fooled his own conscience.

He just hoped it was for the best.

As these thoughts ran through Art's mind, Picus was making his way down the Kasbah's main alley, which split the dealers in stolen antiquities on one side from the soothsayers and fortune-tellers on the other. The roadway was little more than a track so Picus slid nimbly through the crowds using his wings to hover just above the mud and puddles. A couple of folk raised a hand or claw in greeting to him but mainly he was politely ignored. Most other creatures in their world, with the exception of Faies, were at pains to give any Vampire a respectful distance. High Faies, who saw themselves as at least the equal of any Vampire Clan member, avoided outright conflict with their magical cousins simply by hanging about in different places.

Abruptly the track gave way to a neatly cobbled street bordered by some of the more 'respectable' shops in the Kasbah. These were owned by the most successful and therefore more ruthless and dishonest fences. Almost every shop window displayed piles of gold bullion, silver goblets and small hills of precious stones – mainly rubies – sparkling like crystallised blood. Weres stood guard at each doorway, chained and muzzled, their angry yellow eyes following each passer by. At night the muzzles would be removed and the chains loosened. Picus had come up against quite a few Weres when breaking into places and had a healthy respect for anything that big that could move that fast.

An especially large Were, looming in a doorway by one of the most expensive-looking shops in the street, was being teased by a group of young Fiends. Picus watched fascinated as the Were, pretending to ignore the mud pats being thrown at him, changed slowly from a shaggy wolf-like creature into a harmless looking Sprite with a walking stick and thick spectacles. The Fiends, instead of taking this as a dire warning as anyone sensible should, became bolder. 'Who's afraid of the big bad wolf, la, la, la, la, laah!' they chorused, getting closer, throwing larger pats with sharp stones embedded in the oozing mud. A chunk of mud hit the Were above the eye just as it changed back. In an instant, the harmless Sprite turned into a two-legged, greasy-haired, flesh eating, bone crushing machine. It leapt forward with a ferocious snarl as the young Fiends scattered in panic, almost catching the slowest who ran down the road with a terrified howl.

Picus shook his head – he would never get used to the speed at which those monsters could change shape, nor their ferocity. Coming to a highly polished conker wood door set back from the road, he gave it a push and ducked inside.

Food that's out of this world

Entrées
Freshly shelled Sea of Tranquillity Pink Fish
on a bed of Horror Sçop salad

~

Capricorn Goat,
brutally murdered with a tenderiser a few minutes previously,
chopped and grilled in garlic

~

Soup du jour

Main Course
Haru Spices and Dauphinoise potatoes,
in a coulis of cloud sauce

~

Liver of Jackdaw stewed in baby carrots,
spring onions and fifty year fermented blood

~

Rack of Pegasi Dragon and entrails

~

All come with a selection of freshly steamed vegetables

Sorbet

Just Desserts
A Divination trapped in sugar
and whipped to a Spiral Galaxy Meringue

~

A star cluster of fruits
frozen in stasis with a diffuse nebula of cream

~

Cheese plate

Childrens' Menu

Children

~

Chapter 4
Café du Clairvoyant

Picus studied the menu board for a bit. 'Are any of these dishes *actually* real?'

'Soup's off,' replied Fergus the owner, a gruff Wight, without looking up from the news scroll he was reading. 'What'll it be, lad?'

'Er ...' Picus looked dubious, 'can I just have an omelette?'

'Dragonfly egg or wasp larvae?'

'Dragonfly, thanks and a quart of blood Cognac, my good man!'

'You'll have honey water or nowt, nipper.'

Suddenly a door swung open and a girl, or Duchess Vampire, burst out of the kitchen, followed by a cloud of steam and an assortment of clattering noises. She was about Picus' age; a lick of black hair covered one eye, and with the other she scanned the room. Under a dirty apron she wore a red military style tunic that usually denoted a high-born Vampire from the Keep itself, and on one of her slender fingers was a very large solid gold Clan-seal ring. In spite of the smudge of dirt on her cheek and her Troll-like workman's boots, it was obvious that she was very pretty.

'Oi! Which one of you lot ordered the Imp's kidneys in gin?'

'𝔈𝔯, 𝔬𝔳𝔢𝔯 '𝔢𝔯𝔢.' A surprisingly meek-looking Troll stuck up a huge hand the size of a flagstone.

Picus, standing in the shadows, assumed he hadn't been seen. He was therefore slightly taken aback when, on her return journey, the Vampire Duchess picked up a large jug of water and poured it over his head in one swift movement. 'Oops,' she said, and shouldered her way back into the noisy kitchen.

Fergus looked up from his paper. 'Have you been upsetting your cousin again?'

Picus retreated to a corner by the fire to dry off with what little dignity he had left. Steaming slightly, he sat down and opened the scroll Art had given him. The first thing he noticed was a small ring, glued to the foot of the parchment with a generous blob of sealing wax. Picus peeled the ring away and held it up to the light, squinting as he turned it this way and that. At first glance it didn't look like anything special: just a narrow band of gold, very worn at that, and a slice of semi-precious gem. Pangean Aquamarine, if he wasn't mistaken. He rubbed it absentmindedly between forefinger and thumb.

Something within the stone moved.

Intrigued, he shifted closer to the fire, reflected flames dancing in his dark blue eyes as they focused on the gem. Something paranormal began to happen. The longer he looked, the clearer the tableau within the ring's stone became and he found he was looking out across a frozen plateau trapped within the aquamarine, whipped by silent winds that pushed the snow into sloping drifts, like silent waves.

In the middle distance, Picus could just make out a dark line of trees from where a figure, wrapped in an old shawl, emerged. The figure stopped and seemed to stare directly at Picus, who shuddered and put the ring down quickly. Now he knew what Art had given him.

Without a doubt, this was a Misery Ring. He'd heard about these, in taverns and other places where high-born Vampires weren't meant to hang about, but, up until now, Picus had privately doubted they existed. An especially powerful Vampire or Faie warlock could conjure a spell to trap an enemy, or someone they had taken a strong dislike to, within the confines of an enchanted gem. The victim would effectively be imprisoned for the rest of their lives and the warlock had the satisfaction of being able to check up on them whenever they chose. Usually to gloat over their misery: hence the name. The Vampire Eltern had pronounced them illegal a few centuries before but it was rumoured that some of the darker Clans, especially the ones who thought they were above such things, had quietly kept up the ancient tradition of torturing their enemies this way. The worst thing about the rings was that once inside it was virtually impossible to escape. Picus' heart went out to the lost and lonely figure he had seen sheltering in the trees, and wondered what her supposed crime had been.

He turned his attention to the instructions Art had scribbled in blotchy ink.

Helo Picus,
This 'ere iz a Miserye Ring, in case you haven't twiGGed all redi. It's actuali a faike.
It belongs to Count Sgi, who u've probli nott heard of on account of him bein' DED. My client – who naturali wishes to reMain anonimoose – iz the father of the poor girl trapped in the REAL RING that currentli sits on the dried up finger of this nasti old Count, (recentli semi-deceased). Your job:
Find his tomb in the Keep
… and make the switch.
(the faike you hold in your grubbi paw, is garanteed to last over 200 yrs. After that it will turn into dust. Wot you are seeing is a veri convincing replay of events inside the ring for the last 1000 days, which pretti much is exactly the time the girl has been imprisoned. (ps, I canot help finking that there must be a market for these RECORDING' contracptions).
Your reward, 1nce you have bought the ring back to me so that I can make arrangements for the safe return of the young lady to her doting father is 400 gold bars – and a nice 'oliday, somewhere warm + suni.
Yours very TRULI
ART the Honest
Ps the Count's tomb is heavily guarded by heaven knows wot. SO B CAREFUL.

'Hello, Picus, have you been in touch with your parents lately?'

He looked up, refocusing.

It was Lark, the Vampire Duchess who had drenched him and who was, as Fergus had already pointed out, his cousin. Unfortunately. She carried a flagon of fermented raspberry cordial and Picus' lunch. Picus eyed the flagon suspiciously but decided, on balance, that she probably hadn't come all the way over here to throw things at him again.

'No. What about you?'

Lark shook her head and sat down. 'That wouldn't be wise. I think your dear mother is as furious with me as with you.'

'I seriously doubt that. But if you do bump into either of them, don't tell them where I am.'

'Bump into the great Karl of Brasov and his Ducesa in the Thieves' Kasbah? It seems unlikely, don't you think? And I don't think even they would guess their only son is a common thief.'

'Less of the common. But that explains the jug of water.' Picus noted that she had the decency to look just a bit embarrassed.

'Er, yeah, sorry about that. I probably over-reacted.'

Picus smiled. 'Could have been worse. You might have been carrying hot soup.'

'Hmm, maybe next time,' Lark grinned and then looked serious. 'I wouldn't mind so much, you've been through enough back at the Keep and everyone's got to eat. Art tells me you're good at it too but it's *dangerous* ...' she chewed her lip, 'and you don't even carry a sword.'

'Come on Lark, not this again. And anyway, it's not like I need one.'

'Yeah, I know, *magic*. Art says you're good at *that* too, the best he's seen, though a bit rough around the edges.' She paused. 'But it's not exactly reliable, is it?'

'What does that mean?' Picus knew he was on shaky ground, so played for time.

'It's dodgy, that's what I mean. Everyone knows it comes and goes even if you are a natural. Sometimes it does what you want, sometimes it blows up in your face, we've all heard the stories.'

Picus shook his head. 'I don't agree, and I haven't even been stretched yet.'

Lark sighed. She decided to change the subject, and pointed at the parchment. 'What's that?'

'W-e-l-l,' Picus said slowly, half expecting more grief, 'don't get your cape in a twist, but it's another job.'

'Where's that then? I hear there's a nasty Vampire after you.'

'There certainly is, that's why the job's ideal – it's back home.'

'Are you bonkers?'

'You *know* I am,' replied Picus, matter-of-factly. 'And anyway, wench, where's my food?'

Lark only looked half-amused. 'Down the front of your shirt, if you're cheeky. It's my break in five minutes. You can tell me all about this job.'

'And you'll try and talk me out of it.'

'That's about the size of it.'

The rest of lunch passed as it always did: Lark remembering how generally uplifting it was to talk to someone whose hobby wasn't eating his own head lice (the Innkeeper) or his friends (the Troll in the corner) and Picus enjoying showing off but wishing Lark would leave the Café du Clairvoyant and go back to her life of luxury at the Keep. Then he might feel less guilty about the way things had turned out.

Her parents, like his, were one of the oldest (and therefore richest) Vampire families, or Clans, as they were almost always known. Lark and Picus had grown up together, and when Picus had been banished by his parents she had followed him without hesitation. Her excuse was that she was making sure he didn't do anything stupid enough to get himself killed; the real reason was that, knowing Picus' parents, she suspected his supposed crime was not as serious as everyone had been led to believe. So she consoled herself when things were miserable, that she'd left on a point of honour.

However, Picus still stubbornly refused to talk about what he was supposed to have done. Lark played with her food, only half listening as he told her about being chased by Raben. That was the way with all the big Vampire families: they all had their secrets. Also, she had a shrewd idea that Picus' crime had something to do with the usual Vampire hobbies – honour and violence – otherwise why would he stubbornly refuse to carry a sword?

After lunch, Picus pushed back his chair and stayed for a while longer. He was still in a talkative mood but Lark had begun to miss him before he had even left. Picus finished his acorn coffee and stood up to leave. 'Gotta go, cos.'

'I know,' she said, and kissed him lightly on the cheek. His eyes twinkled and then he was gone before she realised that her apron pocket was suddenly a lot heavier. She looked down and saw the gold and the precious stones glinting in the firelight.

And that made up her mind.

Chapter 5
hinky punk

The multi-coloured river that ran through the Thieves' Kasbah could be followed back up the valley where it flowed through Drapers Town, picking up the dyes from the vibrant silks that the local Wights coloured red, green and midnight blue. Barely more than six rapier lengths at its widest, it was too small to have a Human name but the magical community knew it as the Arco Iris, meaning *Rainbow River*. Above Drapers Town the Iris' waters started out as pure as cut glass; a dancing, chatty stream that tumbled over the miniature waterfalls and rocks high in the mountains where Raben had his stronghold.

About the time Picus left the Café du Clairvoyant en route to the Keep, Raben was to be found sitting at the end of a long table in his banqueting hall, stuffing his face whilst shouting at everybody within earshot. Eating and bellowing at the same time was never a particularly good idea for someone with the table manners of Raben. Bits of pickled sprat and Faie bread sprayed out across the table, covering the walls and priceless antiques with bits of food that mingled with the gathered dust. Stuffed Troll and Were heads gazed down unperturbed from the dining hall's high walls, while the young Corbeau looked on from the doorway, just out of range of the flying food. Distaste played below the surface of his good-looking, yet oddly sharp features.

'When I get hold of that skinny, thieving Strigoi[7], I'll nail his hide to my bedroom wall.'

'You can't do that,' murmured Corbeau.

Raben took a huge swig from a pewter tankard that bore the family crest of a Raven poised over what looked, for all the world, like a giant meatball. 'Arggh!' he threw the tankard at the

---

[7] Young Vampire, between the ages of fifty and one hundred years old.

wall, where it ricocheted off a mounted Stone Giant's head and broke a window. 'It's *congealed*! Get me another, and FAST!' A terrified Sanguine[8] ran off to the kitchens to fetch more ox blood. Raben looked at his son. 'Why not?'

'You already nailed the hide of your chief Troll guard to the wall this morning, for failing to capture the thief last night.'

Raben stopped chewing and looked momentarily confused. 'Oh yes ... so I did.' He yawned, revealing a set of badly chipped and stained fangs, the sight of which never failed to make Corbeau feel thoroughly unwell. 'Fair 'nuff ... you have to hand it to the young rascal, it was an amazing piece of burglary. Did you know, he slipped past three of my best Were guards undetected and he got clean away from me just when I thought I had him cornered?'

Corbeau suddenly went very pale indeed. 'You're not proposing that we *let him off?*'

'What? ... Oh! No, of course not,' Raben did his best to look fierce but his attention kept being drawn to a bowl of sugared firefly wings his Sanguine had put at the far end of the table, just out of reach. 'But these things are ... delicate ... mmm, yes ...' he clicked his greasy fingers at a servant and pointed at the bowl, 'the dagger ... whilst it was in our keeping wasn't necessarily ... um, so much of an heirloom as an acquisition ... yes, what is it?' Corbeau now stood before his father, proffering the bowl of crystallised wings. The look on his face was hard to read but Raben knew it well. Very well.

'Don't worry Father, I understand ... leave him to me.'

Raben studied his son's face for a few moments then giggled.

If Picus shivered at that precise moment it was probably no more than a reaction to the wind that had picked up as the early

---

[8] Sanguines were once the Vampire equivalent of a blood donor. Bred as a source of readily available food long before mammals evolved, they usually remained attached to the noble families. A sort of butler-cum-buffet.

afternoon slipped into teatime. The Iris River valley along which he sauntered at the start of his two day journey towards the Keep was still sunny, but clouds had begun to gather over the mountains to the north, so he picked up his speed. The Reeking Marsh, a thick band of foul-smelling bog, small lakes and wetlands surrounded the poppy plains that led up to the Carpathian Mountains where the Keep stood. An experienced traveller, Picus wanted to clear them before nightfall. Flying was out of the question. No Vampire would ever knowingly fly over water unless they absolutely had to.

As he crossed a small flint bridge over the Arco Iris into the wetlands, he suddenly spun on his heel and scanned the footpath behind him. A shadow had moved near some trees; but it could have been sunlight winking through the canopy. Picus frowned, shrugged and carried on. The Marshes stretched for about half a league in all directions but, being flat, it seemed much further. Picus sighed – it was going to be at least a four hour walk. Come to think of it, after such a large lunch he felt quite sleepy. He shook his head and struggled on for about another hour. By now, he was about a third of the way across, following a well-trodden track that meandered through the bog, picking out a safe path for travellers. To leave the track would be risky. Apart from the black mud that dragged even the lightest traveller down to a soggy death, the Reeking Marsh was home to a whole host of muddy beasts and malicious creatures. From what Picus had heard as a Suckling Vampire at bedtime, most were well worth the trouble avoiding.

That being said, the sun was still fairly high and the rain seemed to be holding off. Picus decided that he could probably risk stopping for a few minutes for a snooze: he really did feel very sleepy. And then perhaps he would jog the last bit; provided it was still daylight, he would be OK. He sat down, resting his back on a warm bukstone way-marker and allowed his eyes to close.

What seemed scarcely a few moments later, he opened them.

It was now pitch dark.

A light rain fell noiselessly and, to the west, Picus could make out a narrow band of dark pink, which was all that was left of the day. Briefly the clouds parted to reveal the Moon as nothing more than a fine shard of silver, the smallest it could get in its monthly cycle. Picus shivered. Superstitious Vampires saw the Moon at this stage of the month as an evil omen; even now it seemed to be smiling at Picus, but in a cold, lopsided fashion. The Thin Man's Leer, some called it. The Thin Man being the Vampires' name for all their nightmares, the evil thoughts and vile acts – the Devil, if you will…

So, with the Devil grinning down at him, as if delighted by his predicament, Picus stood up and wondered where the hell the path had gone.

Oops, he thought.

Rubbing his hands together, he pictured the sun high in the afternoon sky earlier that day and concentrated hard on that image. Instantly a ball of light appeared, burned bright for a few seconds, then turned dull orange and died. The dark around him seemed to get darker. Odd: although he had excellent night vision he could make out less and less of the countryside with every passing minute. Something seemed to be sucking all available moonlight away from the marsh, where he stood quite alone.

He tried to make some light again, this time it only got to orange before spluttering out. Hmm. He decided not to think about what Lark had said about magic being untrustworthy. This time he imagined a full Moon, high in a harvest sky. Within seconds bright white light shone out of his cupped hands across the marsh, illuminating the chalk path ahead of him like the exposed bone of some vast, long-dead creature. This was more like it. He turned his palms outwards and broadened the beam of light. At once he wished he hadn't. As the light fell across the tussocked wetlands lying off the path, muddy limbs stirred and stretched and a chorus of gurgling and moaning erupted as the moonbeams in Picus' cupped hand illuminated their shallow graves. Bad idea:

the moonlight he had conjured was simply drawing attention to his whereabouts. Picus clapped his hands together and the light vanished. The squelching and groaning noises of water Ghouls moving in the ooze went away. Picus tried to convince himself they had gone for good, sucked back and imprisoned where they lay with no light to guide them to where he now stood, quite alone and lost, doing his best not to panic.

The place was obviously awash with some kind of unpleasant curse, so much so that trying to recreate something as good and wholesome as sunlight on a spring day would not work. Moonlight worked, but woke up whatever the mud harboured in its foetid breast. Picus shuddered again. Using any light that encouraged those creatures out of the mud to flip-flop towards him wasn't an option. In any normal darkness he would have been able to see quite clearly but this darkness that surrounded him was like an inky mist, and it certainly wasn't normal.

Picus cast about in the dark, fighting a rising sense of fear that made him feel about four years old again, standing at the end of a long corridor that led to his parents' room. Usually he'd had a bad dream; and, when he got to the end of the corridor, past the shadowy alcoves and sinister portraits, he would find his parents' door firmly bolted. No amount of banging and frightened crying would get them to open up. Older, stronger Picus pushed the memory aside and took several deep breaths, forcing himself to calm down.

Then, something caught his attention.

He blinked hard into the dark. There it was again, a distant light – barely visible, even with his acute eyesight – flickering across the empty wastes. No more than a candle's flame, probably about two leagues away.

It winked off. Nothing more happened for a few heartbeats, then it flickered again, much closer and brighter this time. Picus felt shaky and slightly giggly with relief. Strangely, for a Vampire, he absolutely and completely detested the dark.

'Hullo,' he called out tasting sweat mingled with rain on his top lip. 'Hullo, hullo! Er … *help?*'

'Willow willow willow willow ...'

'What's that you said?'

'Willow willow, oh willow willow ... oh'

'Um, yes, OK ... I'm lost and I need some help ... you seem to have a candle ... of sorts ... I don't want to walk across the marsh. Obviously. And I'm worried I might fly right into spider's web or something equally nasty ... I'm a Vampire, by the way ...'[9]

'Yeesss, come to willow willow ... oh ... come.'

' ... a very powerful and ... er ... violent, ill-tempered sort of Vampire ... ' Picus had a sudden thought, '... but extremely *generous* to those who offer their help in getting me off this miserable bit of bog.'

'Come ... come, yeess ... follow the light little creature ... come to willow willow ...' The light was stronger now, dancing about ten rapier lengths from where Picus stood, squinting into the darkness. He took a tentative step forwards. His new boots met with solid ground, so he took another couple of steps.

'Who are you?'

The light grew brighter. 'I am Will O' ... Will 'O the Wyke.'

'Sorry, what? I didn't quite catch that.' He was walking slowly towards the flame, which retreated every three or four steps that he took. Picus' feet still met with firm ground but something wasn't right about this. He flexed his shoulders, getting ready to fly, even if it was risky. 'Is that your real name?'

'Will O' ... Will O' the Wisp ... many names ... none true ...'

That wasn't the right answer as far as Picus was concerned. He stopped dead in his tracks. 'Show yourself Marsh Wight!' he commanded in quite a different tone of voice and clicked his fingers, sending up a flare of silver light. The dancing flame ahead

---

[9] [Translator's note] Vampires also generally tried to avoid flying at night, partly because there was a chance they might fly INTO something but mainly for what they might fly OVER. As said, nearly all Vampires have an irrational and morbid fear, bordering on a complete paranoia, of flying over water. It's not as if they can drown. In fact, virtually the only way to kill a Small Vampire is by starvation or poison. Even if you were fast enough to catch one (which is extremely unlikely), they are almost completely resistant to being crushed, their bodies are practically fire-resistant, their limbs grow back if cut off and, if they wrap up warmly and drink good-quality blood, they can live so long as to almost be considered immortal.

of him, which had begun to burn more brightly, was immediately extinguished. The flare arced high and began to drop towards the earth. Only bleak bog met his gaze.

Nothing happened for a few moments. Then from behind his shoulder it came again.

'Will O', Will O' ... come little Vampire come you'll be safe ... you have my whispered word ...'

Picus spun on his heel but saw no-one, or at least nothing but two pale blue lights dancing just above the oozing mud.

An unseen hand tugged his wing tip.

Resisting a strong urge to scream, he turned again, heard a chuckle and felt something blow gently into his ear.

'Come ... follow the lights.'

The whispering voice was terrifying but at the same time he felt a very strong compulsion to obey. He stepped forward and his feet sank into the mud. Bubbles burst and a stench like rotting flesh filled his mouth and nose.

Two things occurred to Picus: This thing is making a fool of me! And: I can do better than this. He pointed his finger to the sky and jabbed it two or three times, seemingly at random. Instantly three bright stars appeared in the heavens, providing some light. He stamped his feet, there was a squelching noise and several rocks appeared, forcing their way up through the mud. He yanked his foot free and hopped from one slippery stone to another, using his wings to cover the distance. Instantly the distant blue lights became angry red and rushed towards him, like a wall of flame in a bush fire, the voice suddenly booming, choking with rage.

'COMMAND THE ROCK ... IN MY HOME ... POKE HOLES IN THE BEAUTIFUL BLACK SKY WITH POINTY FINGERS LIKE POINTY TEETH ...'

Picus blew into his cupped hand. A wind, starting as a low whistling from far off, picked up speed and blasted across the bog, forcing the blaze to retreat. Abruptly the flame changed course, whipping around behind him again, but Picus was ready. He whistled a tune that sounded like a small brook splashing on rocks and the air suddenly filled with jets of cold water.

The flame disappeared and Picus, grimly satisfied, let the fountains die down. Sod it, he said to himself and prepared to fly in spite of his fear. Anyway, the clouds were low and he could always fly above them for a short distance and spiral down when he was sure he had cleared the wetlands.

Just then he heard a weak cry.

At first it reminded him of a birdcall but as the sound grew louder, he realised with horror that it was the cry of a baby. The pool of unnatural darkness seemed to part and he was able to see a little way across the bog to where a naked Sanguine child lay, pale arms paddling in the gloom, its faint cries coming in hiccups from cracked lips blue with cold.

Terrified and freezing, it was obvious that she was dying.

Without a moment's thought Picus took to the air, spiralling upwards to gain height and speed then corkscrewing down towards the child. As he came in, like a crossbow bolt, the stricken infant morphed into a huge gaping maw of what looked to Picus like shaggy moss, tree roots and thousands of minute sharp teeth. He back-pedalled in mid air, despite his speed, his wing joints popping as the ligaments stretched and tore, almost dislocating both shoulders. The wings' transparent membranes ripped like delicate kites in a high wind. Picus banked, managing to turn upwards as the darkness seemed to detach itself from the sky, and he was met by a billowing cloud of black flies, each the size of his torso. Dozens settled on his wings and shoulders, their weight bringing him down towards the open mouth, which breathed hot, foetid air that made him gag. When Picus was in range, the huge set of jaws clamped around his ankles and started to suck greedily.

Mud began to seep up his legs, rising quickly until cold water gathered at his neck. Picus imagined a rope but when it appeared in mid-air it turned almost immediately into a snake that hissed venom and snapped at his grasping fingers. The soggy mouth had him by the throat now and he couldn't utter the incantation that would shrink him to half his size for long enough to wriggle free.

Each tiny, serrated tooth seemed to bite deeper into his flesh with each jerk of his limbs. He felt utterly helpless, like a moth being swallowed by a giant lizard.

As the bog closed in on his struggling body he went under, and his hearing and vision blurred. Through the murk he could make out vague shapes that looked like horribly like bones and realised with a jolt that this would be his fate if something helpful didn't happen very soon. He had been holding his breath but marsh water trickled down his nose, making him cough and retch.

'Hinky Punk, Hinky Punk!'

The voice sounded familiar.

For a few moments Picus didn't know if he had imagined it, but slowly, almost reluctantly, the soggy jaws relaxed and he felt strong but gentle hands pull him out into the fresh air.

'Fly!' shouted Lark as soon as she had dragged him free. Picus shook the water from his wings and opened them. He flew raggedly, his shoulders burning, the rips in his wings making a strange buzzing sound, but eventually he and Lark burst out of the unnatural darkness and into the normal, almost comforting night sky, studded with stars and lit by the Moon.

Some time later, they landed.

Lark looked across at Picus and felt her heart give a little squeeze. He looked absolutely terrible and he smelled terrible too. He was covered in mud and what looked suspiciously like saliva from the Will' O the Wisp. His wings were badly torn and, although like all Vampire wounds they would heal in a matter of hours, they were clearly giving him a lot of pain. Wincing each time he moved, Picus looked tired and very cross with himself.

She knew him well enough to know that his pride, more than anything, had been hurt and that this would probably take longest to heal. First, his beloved magic hadn't saved him; secondly he'd had to be rescued, and, to make matters worse, by Lark. All Vampires had their pride – Picus less than most, which was one of the things she liked about him – but still.

On the bright side he couldn't argue that her decision to follow him had been a bad one and, for the time being at least, he would have to let her tag along.

'Look at it this way,' she said, offering him a bit of cold black pudding from her pack, 'at least you're not being digested by the Wyke right now.'

Picus smiled without any trace of humour, then went back to looking very glum indeed. 'That baby seemed so real, and everything I tried didn't work as well as it usually does.'

Lark tried to smile sympathetically but he wasn't looking.

'You know, earlier this afternoon, I thought I sensed someone was following me.' He glanced at her. 'I'll give you this though, you'd make a great thief.'

'I'll bear that in mind, next time I'm looking for work.'

'What is "Hinky Punk" when it's at home anyway?'

'That's the name of the Will O' The Wisp who reigns over the Reeking Marsh.' Lark did her best not to make matters worse by looking too pleased with herself. 'They're actually very rare creatures and you were pretty unlucky to bump into such a mature, established one. The trick is to know their name.'

'Hinky Punk? That's his name?'

'*Hers*, actually,' corrected Lark.

'And how come you know it?'

'Hang around bars long enough, and you get to hear near enough everything.'

'I'll make that my motto from now on.' Picus took a large bite out of the sausage, some of his usual good-humour returning to his face. 'I still feel a bit groggy.'

'That'll be the marsh gases that float above the bog. They're toxic. As you were lying down asleep you were breathing in much more than is good for you. If you'd stayed there all night, they would have killed you. I waited about an hour, then decided to wake you up by throwing stones.'

'Oh, thanks.'

'Don't mention it.'

'Then it got very dark very suddenly and I noticed the blue lights dancing about in the distance. Didn't it seem strange that you couldn't see anything? We have better night vision than almost anything, even Faies.'

'Well,' said Picus slowly, looking sheepish, 'for a Vampire, I've always been a bit funny about the dark, as you know. Actually I convinced myself I was just panicking.'

'This is her land. If it makes you feel any better, you'd never have beaten her with your magic – hers is the really old sort and very established here. I don't want to bang on about it but a sword really would come in handy once in a while. Brute force does solve problems from time to time.'

'And it creates a whole bunch more, in my experience.'

'Have it your way.' Lark yawned and lay down, looking up at the stars. They seemed reassuring now she and Picus were clear of the marsh, resting by a sandbank that looked out across open country towards the plains.

'You know what the absolute worst thing is, though?' Picus sounded miserable again.

'No.'

'My boots! Bloody baby-impersonating, big mouth, Hinky whatchamacallit got my boots. That's three pairs in three days.'

'Good night Picus.'

'Hmm? Yeah, goodnight Lark … and … er, thanks.'

Lark closed her eyes and smiled in the darkness.

To the Vampire, blood is absolutely everything.
It is their source of strength and it is their identity —
a Vampire with no blood-ties, meaning no family
or Clan, lives in the gravest of danger.

Chapter 6
Queen Mab

Lark and Picus got up at dawn the next day and headed south. After about three hours of alternate flying and walking Picus abruptly changed direction mid-flight, without warning and for no obvious reason. Lark was puzzled at first; then she caught a faint scent on the breeze. Faies! Their odour was hard to describe but unmistakeable nonetheless.[10]

'Best avoid any more trouble, we'll have problems enough when we get to the Keep!' Picus shouted over his shoulder, turning just in time to avoid careering into a random branch. Flying low and very fast, they described a sort of half circle due north for a while, then west, and stopped for lunch on the back of a dim-looking sheep that stood daydreaming in a field.

Their precaution was well-founded and extremely fortunate. At exactly the time they were skirting the Faie's Leaf Castle, known locally as the Tussocks, Corbeau was staring out of a muddy hole that served as the Faie's doorway, overgrown with tree roots and half obscured with moss. He just happened to be looking the other way as Picus flew into view for a few moments, before he veered off sharply with Lark following.

A Faie enchantment made the Leaf Castle look just like a silver and ivory castle, perched on a grassy hilltop, its turrets flying pennants that snapped and flapped in the morning air. Any magical creature worth his or her salt would see through it immediately. Young though he was, Corbeau was beginning to

---

[10] [Translator's note] A few centuries later another Vampire from the Keep with a talent for natural magic would describe it as like smelling electricity. Erratic and dangerous. Typically Faie!

suspect that most Faie magic was more about fooling themselves than anyone else.[11]

There was a loud rumbling sound behind his back, a cross between two large boulders being ground together and a hippo with a chest infection.

Corbeau turned around to meet for the first time the huge, fat form of Queen Mab.

'So, Night Stalker, Blood Sucker, Son of Raben ...' Her voice sounded unused. 'Why do you disturb my court?'

Corbeau did his best to keep his eyes off her heavy necklace. He suddenly felt dizzy, and wondered if coming here had been a big mistake.

'Queen Mab,' he said, bowing just low enough to show respect without exposing the back of his neck. The litter on which Queen Mab's enormously heavy frame was being carried was supported by six heavily muscled Weres. The creatures, whose growls became quieter the closer they got to their prey, stood mute. Corbeau hoped this was a good sign. He was usually very good at reading faces, but this was impossible in the case of these Weres. The stories were true then, Corbeau thought with a mixture of disgust and admiration: Queen Mab had their faces bathed in acid at birth in order to wipe all expression from their features. That way you never knew if they were about to attack.

Apart from the mutilated Weres, Faies and Wights of all shapes and sizes crowded the room, leering at the slight, underage Vampire who stood in their midst.

'You have five minutes audience and then one hour's grace after leaving court. After that my children,' she waved a casual hand about the room, causing a chatter of excitement, 'will have leave to hunt you.'

Despite the threat, Corbeau relaxed a little. Being his father's

---

[11] [Translator's note] Later, he came to realise that this was only half true: the sumptuous palaces that were really no more than mouse holes, the strings of precious jewels that turned to dead twine studded with dry berries after the next full Moon and the empty gifts that became a curse were more about how Faies liked to see themselves. The delusion was not so much deliberate as second nature.

son had bought him enough time. Just. 'I have a gift,' he said, handing a leather bundle to a small brown Faie who took it to his Queen. 'From my father ... he sends his respects.'

'Yes.' Fat fingers covered in tarnished brass rings greedily unwrapped the parcel and held the blood stone aloft. 'I am sure he does. We have done good business in the past.'

Keep you friends close but your enemies closer, Corbeau was tempted to remark. 'He values your alliance above all, Majesty.' Corbeau found himself bowing again, much to his annoyance. 'The gem belonged to the Royal House of Faies who came from Persia.'

The Faie looked at him for a long while through cruel piggy eyes. 'You are young, Blood Thief,' her tongue was very red, 'you don't look stupid, so you must be very ... *ambitious* to come here. I could have had you beaten or indeed eaten on sight. What do you want in return for this bauble?'

Corbeau took a deep breath and did his best to meet her eye. 'I may have another trophy for your collection.' The Queen fingered her necklace and Corbeau couldn't help smirking.

It was a mistake: the Queen bridled. '*The Tooth Fairy!* Yes, I know what they call me. But I can hunt and kill your kind without your assistance.' The Faies lining the walls cackled and howled and began to crowd Corbeau, who finally allowed his eyes to rest on the string of teeth around her neck. All were torn from male Vampires; some were yellow and ancient, others alarmingly recent. So he moved his gaze to her jugular for a few seconds, just long enough to make a point. She had made an error, and she knew it — he was close enough to get to her before the Were guards reacted. The Queen suddenly looked uncomfortable. She flicked out a quick signal with one hand and the jeering Faies retreated, for now.

Corbeau cleared his throat – time to get back to the matter at hand. 'This one's special, a real prize. Part of the Clan of Brasov, but disowned, so he's unprotected by his Clan and there would be no retribution from them. He's still very powerful ... but I can give him to you.'

'And why would you do that?'

I've got her, thought Corbeau triumphantly. 'Oh, let's just say it's part of a lesson in respect.'

※

Blissfully unaware of the terrifying coalitions being formed against him, Picus was enjoying himself immensely. His wing membranes had healed already and the sun shone on green meadows that stretched as far as the eye could see. Flight was one of the occasions he felt truly free, and his enthusiasm was infectious. Lark found herself accelerating around clumps of corn grass to match his speed, looping, barrelling and laughing at the simple pleasure of being outside, far away from a greasy kitchen enveloped in clouds of steam and noise and smelling of stale blood beer.

They rounded the corner of a small copse that bordered a field of barley. The crop looked fresh-baked and wholesome. Picus banked into a halt and hovered there, smiling into the distance. Everywhere amongst the barley there were flashes of red, where poppies grew — a sure sign that Vampires lived nearby. The field sloped upwards into more woodland, which gave way to rocks. Picus' sharp eyes could already see their destination, perched high on a chimney of granite overlooking the rich gold and green plains. The Keep.

They were home.

※

To begin with, Vampires and their Sanguines could not have existed independently. Nowadays this is not the case, and yet they remain steadfastly loyal to one another.

Chapter 7

Vampires Keep

Beyond the wood they came to a brook that flowed from the rocks. They flew carefully, in short bursts from one glade to another, making sure that no one followed their progress, until about an hour later they found themselves on the north side of the Keep itself. They had decided on this approach as it was on the opposite side to the main gate and was normally barely guarded. Heavy woodland ran up almost to the curtain wall and a rocky path led to a smaller auxiliary gate, whose heavy draw chains were rusted through lack of use. The little-used path led to a small servants' door virtually hidden between two small towers, which were staffed at night, but usually deserted during the day. Nobody had dared attack the Vampire stronghold in a while, and these days only the main gate had a full guard.

That afternoon they prepared to enter the Keep.

'That disguise is not going to fool anyone.' Lark looked critically at her cousin. Neither of them particularly wanted to risk bumping into Picus' parents, so marching into the Keep unannounced was not a good idea: people would ask questions and might tell someone, who would then tell Picus' parents that they were back. Lark was also fairly sure that by now news of Picus' new career must have trickled back to any Keep Vampire who was reasonably important or just plain nosey.

'Rubbish, it's a genius disguise,' Picus pulled the cape's hood over his head and adopted a furtive stance.

'It just makes you look shifty and weird.'

'What about this then?' From one of his many pockets Picus

produced a small white stone, which he rubbed between his forefinger and thumb. Instantly the stone became a long tapered pipe shaped like a dolphin, which Picus put in his mouth at what he hoped was a jaunty angle. 'Art gave it to me.'

Lark rolled her eyes. 'Oh, absolutely brilliant! Now you're a shifty looking bloke in a hood smoking a comedy pipe.'

They heard feet moving through dry leaves, turned, and saw someone climbing up the path towards where they were hiding beneath an overhang.

'I know this guy! It's Bud the Sanguine,' said Picus. 'Watch this, he'll be completely fooled and you'll have to apologise.' He winked confidently at Lark and stepped onto the path, pulling the hood over his head.

The Sanguine glanced up as he drew level with the two young Vampires. 'Hi Picus. Oh! Hi Lark.' Lark glared at Picus who did his best to ignore her making see-I-told-you-faces. For a moment Bud looked like he was going to continue past them, but then stopped. He looked troubled. 'Aren't you guys meant to be exiled or something?'

'Disinherited, actually,' Picus said sulkily. 'There's a difference you know.'

'Fair enough,' said Bud happily, looking completely unconcerned. 'We're all very grate–'

'Best not to tell anyone you've seen us,' Picus quickly interrupted.

'Yes, it'll be our secret,' Lark stepped forward and touched Bud on the forearm.

The Sanguine went bright red. 'N-No problem,' he stammered, dropping and then hastily scooping up his bundle of wood.

'*Ooh, it'll be our secret, mwah mwah, xoxoxox ;)*,' Picus made a face as they ducked back behind a rock.

'Look if it wasn't for your crappy disguise ... you do remember Bud is your uncle's Sanguine don't you?'

'Yeah, but he's loyal to me. And you too now, I'm guessing, after that revolting display.'

'What? It was just an insurance policy, and anyway, he's really sweet –' Lark's eyes suddenly narrowed. 'Hang about, what do you mean "loyal to you"?'

'It's a long story,' replied Picus, looking cagey. 'Best if we just stayed here 'til dark, eh? I'm not sure I can trust you if we bump into anyone else. Ow!'

A few hours later, Picus had eventually been persuaded by Lark to consider a better form of disguise. 'Can't you just make us disappear with some of your magic?' she'd asked.

'It doesn't exactly work like that.'

'Surely there must be a *Spell of Concealment* or a *Charm of Invisibility* or something like that?'

'I don't actually know any spells,' said Picus, studying his feet.

'You what? You're joking!'

'No.'

'No?'

'No.'

Lark looked thunderstruck. 'Then how do you do all this magic?'

'I'm not really sure. Usually I just sort of make it up as I go along.'

'*What?* Rubbish!'

'No really! Look, say I need to light a fire. I just think of the sound of burning wood and the heat and the colours and, before I'm really aware of what I'm about to do, my hands are moving like flames and my mouth goes hot and when I open it these words or songs just spill out and *abracadabra* I've got lovely hot fire crackling away. I've never looked at a book of spells in my life. Wouldn't know where to begin. And, anyway, I bet it's quite boring.'

'Amazing,' said Lark, sounding like she meant the complete opposite. 'So why can't you just imagine us invisible?'

'Believe me, I've tried lots of times. But in my head, the bit of it that does the magic anyway, *invisible* seems to mean *not there*, so I just end up somewhere else, miles away and then I have to walk back, usually all on my own through dark woods. And in any case disappearing and reappearing places is risky. You might end up materialising in a cooking pot or underwater or in front of something much bigger than you that might be hungry. Worse still, you may end up slipping into the Shadow World, and believe me, you don't want that if you can help it.' Picus shuddered at the still-fresh memory of the puckered, skin-encased head.

In the end, Lark remembered seeing a washer Wight's cottage by a lake about a quarter of a league away. They'd gone back there and Lark had marched up the path and banged on the front door, peering around the side of the house at the multi-coloured rows of clothing hanging out to dry. An elderly stooping Imp opened the door, regarding Lark with suspicion through soapy spectacles. Meanwhile, Picus slipped around the back.

'Whaddaya want young man?' she yelled. Looking slightly annoyed, Lark bobbed off a quick curtsey.

'Good morrow, kind lady, I am a poor beggar GIRL, looking for honest work in return for a crust of stale bread and a sip or two of milk.'

'Whaddaya saying? I can't hear a thing, me ears are all clogged up with soap and grease. And stop jumping about, you're making me feel seasick!'

Lark, mid-curtsey, straightened up. 'BEGGING YOUR PARDON KIND LADY. I WAS JUST AFTER A DAY'S HARD WORK!' She tried her best to ignore Picus, who seemed to have a pair of grey pants on his head whilst being chased by a swarm of bees. Lark winced as the pants fell over his eyes and he ran into a tree, bouncing his head off a branch and falling backwards into the washing lake.

Meanwhile, for some reason, the old Imp had gone blue in the face with indignation. 'I'm not doing any work for you! How dare you! Can't you see I've got enough on me plate with all the washing and repairing for those fancy folk what swans around up at the Keep!'

Confused, Lark shot a worried glance in Picus' direction. It now looked like he was being drowned by a large pair of leggings. Something dawned on her. 'Oh no! I meant *I'd* do the work …

Oh! Never mind. Gotta go!' She ran off towards Picus, leaving the old lady staring rheumily after her, muttering and shaking her head.

Vampires tend to be buried with all their favourite possessions, much like the ancient Egyptians – the only difference being, there's quite a good chance that a Vampire will wake up again one day.

Chapter 8
Sigma Maze

Lark eventually managed to drag Picus out of the lake and get him up the hill, where they'd laid the clothes on a rock to dry.

'I can't believe the old witch was using killer bees to guard her clothes.' Picus shook his head: one of his ears still felt full of water.

'Well I must say, I'm very impressed with your thieving skills so far. Nearly eaten by a Will O' the Wyke, caught out by an old Imp's security measures. Breaking into the tomb of one of the most important and powerful Vampire magicians is going to be an absolute breeze, I'd say.'

'Har har. Very funny. I heard her calling you a boy. In any case, you said this was just borrowing and we'd have to give it all back.'

Lark nodded, looking prim. 'Quite so. I, for one, still have a reputation to keep.'

In the end they'd opted for two sets of low-ranking Sanguines' clothes made from rough silk and plain bumble wool, so when they sneaked in through the side gate of the Keep's outer walls, no-one gave them a second glance. It was early evening.

They had arrived in the midst of a night market, one of several that usually materialised at dusk when most Vampires came out to grab a bite[12] and then go out for some entertainment: drinking in the inns, catching up on gossip with neighbours, or, for some of the younger nobles, donning burnished platinum and silver armour to go hunting Weres through the dark forests. Vampire children ran laughing though the narrow cobbled streets, their milk fangs seeming to glow under the coloured lanterns; wings buzzing, not yet fully formed. To anyone but a Vampire they moved blindingly fast, even the smallest, rarely putting a foot wrong as they zigzagged like dancers between the

---

[12] [Translator's note] Yes, well...

adults, fighting mock battles. Everywhere there were smells of cooking: tantalising meats, and exotic, heavily flavoured bloods.

'I'm starving,' remarked Picus.

'And I've just lost my appetite.' The enormity of what they were planning had suddenly come home to Lark with a dull clunk in the pit of her stomach. Picus bought a flagon of spiced bull's plasma from a street vendor and took a huge swig, grinning macabrely at her. Despite herself, Lark had to admit that he was coping with the pressure admirably well.

'You haven't asked me what the plan is,' he said, burping discreetly.

'No, I was sort of assuming that if I did you'd tell me you were going to make it up as you went along and that would make me feel worse than I do already, so I decided to keep my mouth shut and hope for the best.'

Picus looked offended. 'I'm a professional!'

'Yes, everything you've done so far has instilled in me a deep sense of confidence in your dedication and natural abilities,' Lark remarked, more sarcastically than intended. They'd gone down a narrow side alley and stopped in front of a small door, which looked like it had been carved straight out of the ancient black granite that formed the lower part of the wall. Picus wedged the half empty flagon under one arm and ran his finger around the frame. Frowning in concentration, he whistled a short, random tune and stood back. 'OK, smart-arse, watch this.'

Lark was staring so hard at the door that she didn't notice the twisting fingers of mist seep up from the cracks in the stone flags as it curled around their legs, gradually increasing until soon they were enveloped in a thick curtain of billowing fog Picus had created, obscuring the street behind, along with all the Vampires who were still meandering about through the stalls. Picus finished his drink and chucked the flagon over his shoulder. When he was sure no-one could see them through the thick mist, he stepped forward again. 'The lock's anti-magic,' he said. 'Any attempt to open it with conjuring tricks will set off a whole bunch of alarms up in the Fast Tower. The Eltern and their guards will be down here before we make the main gate.'

'Then how are we going to get in?'

'Well, we'll ignore the lock for starters.'

'What do you mean?' Lark looked quizzically at her cousin, who was busy jabbing his finger at the rocks around the doorframe.

'Apart from the fact it's tiny, have you noticed anything odd about this door?'

Lark gave it a quick, half-hearted glance. 'No, not really.'

'So, nothing springs to mind?' Picus had the half-smile on his face he always wore when he was about to do something clever.

Lark shrugged and peered closer, mainly to humour him. 'Um ... nope, no idea ... you'd better tell me or I might be forced to give you a thump on your other arm.'

'It's obvious, really,' Picus was staring at a worn piece of stone, pressing it with his thumb. 'Ah-ha!' The stone suddenly gave a *click* and something about the door seemed to change. Lark saw tendrils of the fog being sucked in through cracks around it. 'The thing about this door,' Picus remarked by way of explanation, 'is that there are no hinges.' He smiled. 'And the lock's a fake.'

'So how does it open?' Lark pushed the door. It didn't budge.

'Well the stonework around it is a sealed vacuum, for starters. So it's almost impossible to open by force unless you want to spend a week bashing a hole through two rapier lengths of solid granite.' Picus placed both hands on the door and grunted with effort. 'But break the vacuum seal by pressing the release valve and it should just slide open.' Picus braced himself and pushed hard. Suddenly the amount of fog disappearing through the door increased as hidden runners ground into action and the rock rolled sideways, neatly retracting into a cavity. 'After you!' Picus rubbed his hands together and stepped back from the open door.

Surprisingly fresh air blew up from below. Lark hesitated. 'Where does it go?'

'Back when I was still a very young Strigoi and I wanted to get away from my parents' fighting, I explored most of the tunnels in the Keep. So I'm almost certain that this one leads to about a dozen other, much older tunnels that should take us where we need to go. With any luck, if things haven't changed, there's a secret door about sixty paces away that leads to some steps.'

'And where do we need to go?'

'To the Crypt,' replied Picus with a look of mock trepidation and horror.

'Well, what are we waiting for?' Lark drew her sword and stepped inside with as much confidence as she could muster. Picus followed her and slid the stone door back into place. All sounds from the street were immediately cut off. Picus shivered and wished he'd brought a torch, or at least a candle. Why did he always end up going to places that were so dark? They paused for a few moments to allow their acute night vision to start to work, then made their way down the passageway, ducking cobwebs and clambering over the dried remains of long-dead spiders.

Taking a right hand turn towards the Crypt, Picus immediately noticed that something was different from when he'd last been here five years ago. The air smelled less stale than he remembered and the walls were repaired in places and somewhat cleaner.

'Looks like they've been redecorating,' he remarked. But why would they bother spring-cleaning? The only Vampires that came down here were either almost or completely dead. Usually. Gradually the tunnel widened, and every ten paces or so a coffin lay in a small alcove dug into the wall. Most coffins were closed but some Vampires had chosen to leave off the lids. Picus, who'd been in quite a few crypts in his short career as a thief, still couldn't get used to the sight of a perfectly preserved, though somewhat dusty corpse, playing tug-o-war with him as he pinched its wallet. It wasn't helped by the fact that most Vampires, being very attached to their jewellery and very suspicious to boot, insisted on spending eternity with their eyes wide open.

After they had walked for about ten minutes, Picus stopped. 'OK, it's around here somewhere,' he said, 'but I still can't understand why it's so clean.'

They rounded the corner, Lark still leading the way, and

saw why. Precisely where the entrance to the personal crypt of Count Sgi had been, there was now a brand new stone wall.

'Oh good,' said Lark, running her hands along the wall, which seemed solid enough. 'Do we go back and look for another way in?'

Picus shook his head and stepped back from the wall. 'As far as I know the only other entrance is through the Fast Tower and that'll be heavily guarded.'

Lark, who had just been beginning to enjoy herself, looked disappointed. 'Got any bright ideas?'

Picus was too busy humming to himself to hear. 'The wall isn't straight,' he said. 'Look, it runs up to that pillar on the left but it's actually about half a rapier length further back on the right.'

He stepped sideways and was gone.

Lark blinked. He'd been there, right in front of her and now he'd vanished. It was very unsettling. 'Er ... Picus?'

'It's OK.' He reappeared.

'I thought you said you couldn't make yourself disappear?'

'I can't.'

'So what just happened ... hey!'

He'd gone again.

'I just walked behind a wall ... come and look at this, it's amazing!' Picus' voice was only slightly fainter than it had been.

'But how do I ... ?'

'It's a *trompe l'oeil*, trick of the eye,' Picus said, suddenly reappearing. 'Two walls overlapping, one in front of the other. 'It's quite easy to do, you just have to make sure the walls aren't too spaced apart and that the end of one wall uses exactly the same half bricks that the end of the other wall uses, so it looks like a solid row. Then you just slip through sideways ... like this.' Picus' hand appeared seemingly out of the wall next to Lark. 'But that's only the start, the Count clearly had a sense of humour ... and something to protect. Take my hand.'

As she slipped between the walls Lark realised why Picus sounded so impressed.

The chamber within was bathed in the standard vampiric

crimson glow, like blood, from candles made from spider's silk dipped in red dye. The smouldering light dimly illuminated a deep pit into which a series of walkways and stairs had been cut, seemingly at random but forming a fantastically complex spiral of passageways leading in every conceivable direction. Some twisted up, or across ways, one led down to a door. 'It looks easy,' said Picus, 'all we have to do is get down *there*.' He pointed to a stone archway at the bottom of the pit, almost certainly the entrance to Sgi's crypt. 'But I bet it's not that simple – it hardly ever is in my experience.'

'You know this somehow seems familiar,' Lark said. 'Can't we just fly down?'

'I doubt it.' Picus picked up some dust and threw it into the void in the centre of the pit. Most of it fell below, but some caught on what looked like a series of very fine metal wires, criss-crossing the gaps in the stairs and corridors. They hummed as the dust fell on them. Picus rubbed the rest of the dust from his hands. 'Thought so,' he said. 'That wire is razor-sharp, it'll slice off our wings and other tender and cherished bits before we're halfway down. No, it looks like the old fellow really wanted us to walk for some reason.'

'Isn't that going to be dangerous?'

'No, I think this is more of a brainteaser. Usually, traps where you fall into a pit of outraged spiders or when rusty spikes suddenly pop out, pinning bits of you to the floor, don't look complicated like this or dangerous, they just look like a normal bit of floor or wall. Anyway, there's only one way to find out ...' Picus put a foot gingerly on the first step. Nothing happened. Lark – who was new to all this – had half closed her eyes, expecting at the very least a cloud of bats to erupt from a hole in the wall and carry Picus off, screaming into the darkness.

And then she'd be all alone.

He took another step, and then another. 'Seems pretty solid to me.' Relieved, Lark followed. Or at least thought she did. The moment her foot touched the second step she looked up and found that somehow she'd gone the wrong way ... or perhaps

Picus had. He was suddenly standing at the foot of quite another staircase, on the opposite side of the void.

'Hurry up,' he said, 'we haven't got all night!'

'I just followed you a second ago.' She started to retrace her steps but no sooner had she gone back up the stairs than she lost sight of Picus completely.

It was now Picus' turn to look around in all directions. After a few seconds, he spotted Lark standing on a landing just below him. 'Wait up!' he shouted.

Lark turned. Tears were streaming down her face. Something was very wrong. 'For Chalice sake, Picus, where have you been hiding? I thought I'd lost you hours ago!'

'What?' Picus' mind began to swim. 'Why are you crying?'

Lark fixed him with a glare. 'I'm crying because I'm a girl ... but don't think for a minute that that means I'm soft, pal.'

'OK,' said Picus quickly. 'Just stay there, don't move a muscle! Something's obviously very wrong here.' Lark nodded. Picus saw a small door leading to the landing where she stood. He opened the door but the landing was empty. Lark, who had been there moments before, had vanished.

'Picus, Picus, PICUS!' he heard his cousin's voice, sounding increasingly panicked as the sound of her steps clattered from one walkway to another. Suddenly she appeared on the landing next to Picus. 'For Chalice sake, Picus, where have you been hiding? I've been looking for you for hours! Wait a minute, haven't I just said that?' Lark paused, and just to confuse Picus even more she suddenly grinned. 'You know, cos, I think I've just worked out what this is!'

Picus was pretty sure he knew what was coming. 'More wisdom from the hardened drinkers at the Café du Clairvoyant, I suppose?'

Lark looked put out. 'Well, yes, actually. One of the regulars, this very old Vampire who came in every day and drank cheap Cognac – really cheap – the stuff you could clean the stove with. He never bothered a soul, just sat in the corner scribbling in a notebook, mumbling to himself.'

'Yeah, I know the type.' Picus was looking around the landing where they stood, pressing bits of wall, only half-listening.

'Anyway, I once asked him what he was doing and he showed me. Turns out this old boy had been everywhere, seen this, done that, walked with Kings etcetera. Had been famous in his day as a watchmaker and locksmith, the very best, if you believed him. Drink, and years of working in poor light meant his sight had gone. But his real love was conundrums.'

Picus stopped what he was doing. 'Con-whats?'

'You know, games, riddles, puzzles ... anything that needs a bit of brainpower – I don't imagine for a minute you'd know much about that. He said it stopped him going loopy, although you'd have your doubts if you met him. On the side, when he wasn't tinkering with watches and locks, he designed some of the best security systems for some pretty big clients. All very shady and he wouldn't tell me who but he always said his proudest achievement was the 4-D Sigma.'

'You've lost me again.'

'4-D, as in 4-dimensional. Meaning it goes up, down, side to side in *space* and it also goes back and forward in *time*. And Sigma is a type of maze – what we're standing in now.'

'How can you be so sure?' Picus was sceptical.

'Well I'm not exactly, but from what I've seen so far, it fits the bill.'

Picus still looked unconvinced. 'O.........K.'

'First up,' Lark started counting off fingers, 'he was always sketching these crazy stairs and passageways that seemed to lead everywhere and nowhere at the same time, *just* like these. Secondly, he said he was the only person he'd ever met who could truly make a 4-D maze. He always said that time shifts were the hardest thing to build but that the Cognac helped. What he meant was that all buildings exist within the same moment of time or history. But knowing all that stuff about watches, he could insert mechanisms within the maze that reversed or speeded up time in different parts of the same maze. He said it was just like setting the running mechanism on a really big clock to go faster or slower.'

'That would explain why we kept going in the same direction but missing one another.'

Lark nodded. That was one thing she liked about Picus: he was open-minded. She didn't know many other Vampires who'd take seriously something like a maze that went back and forwards in time – especially if it had been explained to them by a girl. 'After that,' he said, 'the rest was easy. A Sigma maze is made up of a series of pentagons, which contain the magic. In itself it's not that hard to solve but the time shifts make it so confusing as to seem impossible.'

'Great!' said Picus looking about at the meandering steps and corridors cut into the pit. 'So how do we crack it?'

Lark's cheerful expression wavered only very slightly. 'No idea. But *you* can work it out. I know you can.' In the last few minutes, she'd really started to enjoy herself and she wanted what she just said to sound encouraging, but it came out wrong – sounding like she was talking to a child.

Picus looked very cross, which was unlike him. 'Yes, maybe if I had a week, a pen and paper *and* some food. I'm still famished.'

Lark was crestfallen. 'Sorry Picus, I didn't mean to sound like that. We're both tired. Let's take a break. I've got some marrow biscuits and some water.' She felt flustered as she pulled a bottle from her belt and rummaged in her bag, 'they're a bit crumbly but … oops!' The water bottle fell from her hand and shattered on the stone floor of the landing.

Lark stood there, mouth open. Standing there like an idiot, she had a sudden thought that she was just slowing Picus up and he'd much rather she left but he was too polite to insist. 'I should have stayed back at the Kasbah –' she began.

But Picus wasn't listening. He was staring intently at the water. Then he started to smile. 'What do we know about water?'

'It stops you getting thirsty,' Lark said miserably. 'I'll just get my things and go back the way we came.'

'What? No! I wouldn't have got this far if it wasn't for you.'

'Yeah but that was just luck, knowing about the Wyke and this maze. And luck runs out –' Picus didn't really look like he had heard. Lark felt quite cross with him again. 'Are you even paying attention?'

'Eh?' Picus turned to her and went back to looking at the puddle of water that was trickling away. 'Yes, yes, forget about all that *poor me* stuff, I've just worked it out!'

'You have?' Lark said. 'You're probably just saying that.'

'Not at all ... and by the way, that was pretty clumsy ... no, water always runs downhill. Think about it. We know that the old Wizard's tomb is lower than this floor, so we just follow the stream. It's simple.'

'What stream?'

By way of an answer, Picus lay next to the puddle from Lark's bottle and ran his hand over the wet surface. He did it again, making a sort of whooshing noise, and then once more. With each caress, more water appeared until the puddle became stream and began to flow down the slope. 'Come on!'

And so they followed the water, jogging to keep up with the flow. Each time it seemed to peter out, Picus repeated the spell and more water flowed freely, showing them the right path.

'Where's it all coming from?' Lark asked, out of breath.

'I'm just calling it from the rock, coaxing it up. These stones hold a lot of moisture, all I'm doing is gathering it in one place. Come on, keep up!'

And so they wound through the maze, across walkways, through corridors, along worn steps, sometimes on a level, sometimes even going up, it seemed, but Picus said it was just another visual trick. Mostly they traveled downwards, ignoring the time shifts that one moment made them feel as if they were almost flying from one stairwell to another, and the next that they had taken hours just to descend a few steps. Just as they were beginning to tire, the walls of the maze led to a broad corridor and they found themselves facing the stone archway. They looked up, back at the crazy steps that led to the top of the maze far above them.

'We did it!' Lark was elated.

Through an opening on a level with where they stood, she could see into a large room. Placed at the centre, on a dais, was a stone sarcophagus. Its lid was pulled back and whatever lay inside seemed to give off a faint blue glow.

They both flew towards it. Reaching the coffin just before Lark, Picus looked inside. The corpse of the old Count stared back at them, his eyes red under the torchlight – mere slits of malice – cracked lips, stained black over time, contrasting with his wizened face that was caked in a mask of white dust. It was as if he was watching them, summing Picus up, and Picus had to fight the urge to flee. He looked down, past the ancient wings, whose membranes had long-since dried and flaked, past the exquisite, intricate armour, down at his long, almost prehensile fingers.

And there it was. The real Misery Ring.

Taking great care, in case he woke the living corpse of Count Sgi, Picus slipped the ring off his dry forefinger and deftly replaced it with the fake.

This was one job he could be truly proud of – the evil old Vampire had his maze cracked by a mere youngster, hardly out of Strigoi, his carefully planned revenge ruined. Art would know someone who could rescue the girl from the ring and return her safe and well to her Clan. Pocketing the real ring, he turned to Lark with a broad grin. 'We did it!'

Then the floor shifted.

In spite of appearances, very little happens at the Keep that the Eltern don't know about.

Chapter 9
Cxkylipyr

Picus looked at his feet. The dais was moving – it was a trigger! They'd been in such a rush he'd missed the most obvious trap of them all.

Now there was a loud grating noise and a stone panel at the far end of the room began to slide open from the top down as the whole Sigma maze seemed to unlock itself and fold neatly away into the walls.

Picus looked sharply in all directions and saw a shaft of moonlight, high up in the corner of the Crypt, that had appeared when the maze had folded away … the gap was small but it was just wide enough, especially if you were slim. He checked the panel that was now about a quarter open and saw half a dozen breastplated and chain-mailed Vampire Knights, huge broadswords drawn, their wings criss-crossed with the scars of many battles and as tough as old leather, the membranes already humming. Their faces may have been expressionless but Picus could tell from their body language that they were itching to burst into the chamber.

Picus looked at Lark's own smaller rapier, which she had just drawn and shuddered: she was fast but no match for a dozen well-trained thugs. He couldn't risk it. 'Up there!' he whispered urgently, pointing to the hole in the Crypt that led out into the open air. 'I'll follow!'

Lark nodded and flew towards the gap without thinking. As she squeezed through, she looked back and was shocked to see him still on the ground, face pinched in concentration. He obviously had no intention of following her but he had no chance on his own. She turned: she had to get back in to help him. But before she had time to fly back into the chamber, several of the stones around the gap tore lose from their ancient mortar and caved in, effectively locking her outside.

On the ground, air exploded from Picus' lungs, partly in relief and partly with the effort of sealing the gap. It was risky but he'd done it – he'd got Lark out safely!

The stone panel had now lowered sufficiently to allow the armoured knights to clamber over and storm into the room. The leader, and the largest by far, was a huge Vampire with a weathered face full of creases and deep scars, his fangs tipped with iron sharpened to lethal-looking spikes. He charged straight at Picus, barking. 'Stay where you are Strigoi, if you even breath, I'll rip your throat out!'

By way of reply, Picus shrugged nonchalantly and composed himself by leaning casually on the coffin as the knights surrounded the young Vampire. They made no effort to touch him and Picus had already decided that fighting them would be useless. The panel's opening mechanism ground to a halt and someone else stepped slowly into the room.

Young, and almost impossibly ancient Vampire looked at each other.

'Good evening Sir,' Picus said politely to the Eltern, as he bowed.

꿎

Leading away from the Fast Tower, broad, stone-flagged streets, would take you to some of the largest and therefore most expensive houses in the Keep. Generally, the rule was that the older and therefore more illustrious a family you were, the closer to the Fast Tower you lived. Most of the beautifully carved walkways led to well-appointed squares, each with two or three houses belonging to the high Vampire aristocracy. The Clans. Gem-encrusted fountains in gold and marble displayed each Clan coat of arms and the only activity during the day was Sanguines bustling to and fro delivering food, firewood and expensive blood wines.

Each door was watched by a Clan gargoyle: fiercely protective creatures who didn't even get on with their own kind. Perfect for the job, as once they had found a comfortable spot, usually some vantage point overlooking the maximum area for the minimum effort, there they stayed. Sometimes for centuries. In fact it was so difficult to remove them that quite a few had, over the years, literally fossilised where they were, stuck fast by their own stubborn refusal to shift until eventually they turned to stone and crumbled to nothing but featureless rock, then dust.

Gargoyles were also generally accepted to be the most nosey, pernickety, prissy and prying species on the planet after cleaning ladies, and were consequently the usual carriers of gossip from the Fast Tower, through the swanky Clan Quarter and then down to the ordinary Vampire folk who lived amongst the many markets and on-going concerns that sheltered under the battlements.

The Brasov Clan gargoyle, Pierre, heard the latest developments at the Fast Tower early that morning from the neighbouring Drax Clan gargoyle, Chip (who had picked it up from a distant cousin who resided at the tower itself), who subsequently told Drontie the Clan Sanguine, who went upstairs and knocked on his mistress's door in some trepidation.

A cold grey eye looked up from a manuscript; a jagged finger, preternaturally long, dry and pale stopped halfway along a line of runic text.

'What is it, servant?'

'It's ...' Drontie's voice caught, as it often did, when addressing his mistress. When alone with her, he mainly concentrated on avoiding the blind gaze of her puckered eye socket. He took a deep breath and started again. 'It's your son, Ducesa.' Any light that had been in the remaining good eye instantly went dead. Drontie imagined he heard the sound of wind moaning through dry skulls somewhere far away.

'You are mistaken. I have no son.' The finger proceeded on its path through the text.

Drontie was stumped as to how to continue. Most of all he wanted to run out of the room, down the chilly, dank corridor, past portraits and mummified trophies of old enemies and out of the chaliceforsaken house, into the morning sunlight. But staying was his lot, the only other choice was torture and then certain death for desertion. He gave it another shot. 'Picus, has been arrested,' he said and inclined his head, waiting for a reaction. Killing the messenger was the norm in this Clan and the Ducesa's fangs could burn flesh like coals. For a few heartbeats there was no sound in the room.

'Thank you. I will inform the Karl.' Her one good eye now blazing, she looked up at Drontie who was fumbling with the door. 'LEAVE!'

***

As the sun came up Picus, standing in the Inner Chamber of the Fast Tower, in the heart of the Eltern's palace, couldn't help wondering why he wasn't languishing in quite another part of the Keep – notably in some cold dungeon somewhere. With spiders. He looked around at the guards who seemed to be doing their best to ignore his friendly smiles and yet keep a close eye on him at the same time. Then he studied the face of the Eltern in front of him. The older Vampire's features were lively for his age and his dark green eyes met Picus' gaze with a cold force, so that within seconds Picus felt like a Milk Imp who'd been caught steeling nectar from the Fast Tower kitchens. He studied his feet instead.

Picus hoped Lark had done the sensible thing and had got as far away from the Crypt as possible, as soon as she realised he'd made the stones collapse to shut her out. She'd be furious with him, of course, but he couldn't risk her putting up a fight in there and getting badly hurt or even killed. He tried to feel guilty about letting her come along but realised that, if he was being honest, he was glad she had – right up until the trap had been sprung on them, that was.

He turned his attention away from his thoughts and looked about the room. Most of it was fairly nondescript: just an octagonal chamber, stained black over the millennia from tallow candles, and at one end a large pine-needle fire that crackled and spat. At the other end of the room, a heavy moleskin curtain hid something from view. Through a chink Picus saw the end of what looked like a clear, diamond-plated screen. Whatever was behind the curtain must have been very valuable indeed. Nothing, except a larger and heavier piece of diamond, could break through the highly polished viewing pane.

The Eltern cleared his throat. 'The ring please, young man!' The voice was old but contained power. This Vampire was almost certainly a Nosferatu, which meant he was well-over a thousand years old.

Picus must have looked dismayed.

'Don't worry,' the Eltern added, and suddenly his tone was almost kindly. 'We will return the girl, as planned, to her family. You did us a favour, actually, Count Sgi's maze had us all running around like idiots for months. As soon as we found out about the Misery Ring – they're illegal, as you are no doubt are aware – we tried to break in. You should be proud of yourself, young Strigoi, some of our best Nosferatu haven't been able to crack the maze. Incredible, really...' he paused, his eyes now positively twinkling as he studied Picus, his old, cold exterior gone. 'I assume the fake is in place? It was very costly – our mutual friend Art is quite right, you know! Sometimes a fake shows more artistry than an original and therefore should have the greater value. Thank you,' he said with great politeness as Picus dipped his hand awkwardly into his pocket and fished out the ring. 'My name, by the way, is Duke Limitri van Lud but you can call me Orielle.'

Picus nodded. 'Delighted to meet you.'

The Vampire Eltern became brisk now. He waved a hand airily in Picus' direction. 'Art has an eye for raw talent. Never known him to be wrong!' Picus was confused by the sudden changes in the Nosferatu's tone, whose mood seemed to go up and down in an instant, as well as by what he was saying.

'Sorry, I must have be bumped on the head by one of your henchmen,' Picus said. 'I thought Art was a wanted Wight. He always claimed there was a price on his head at the Keep.'

Orielle paused in what he was doing, which was fiddling with the long sleeves of his gown, and looked faintly amused, although his gaze had just regained all of its sharpness. 'Things are never that straightforward. I would have thought that, young as you are, you may have realised that by now.' He studied the ring briefly, holding it up to the light, and then nodded as if satisfied. Taking a long key from his belt, he drew back the curtain and inserted the key into a lock.

Something cup-shaped, the colour of molten lead or a winter's sky, shone dully from behind the clear diamond glass. Picus stared open-mouthed as he felt a sense of vertigo wash over him.

'Is that what I think it is?'

'If by that you mean *by golly Mr Very Important Vampire, is that the Chalice?*, then yes!' Orielle made a show of peering more closely at it. 'Looks quite ordinary though, don't you think?'

'I suppose so,' Picus was forced to agree. He'd seen more expensive-looking Hollow Night decorations.

'There are those who say that it's not safe here and must be moved ... but I am not entirely sure I agree. The Chalice belongs with us. You see, it is the greatest of our treasures and its home is the Keep.' Orielle peered at him over his spectacles. 'Now, I suppose you are wondering what all this is about?'

'You're not going to have my hands chopped off for theft, then ... and I'm going to get a present for returning the ring?' Picus dared hope.

'Not so fast Strigoi. You're not out of the woods yet. Not by a long way.' The temperature in the room had just gone down by several degrees. He's using his voice to control me, thought Picus, Like magic. As long as he's calling the shots he's happy to be this charming, eccentric old Vampire but if I step out of line I'll get no mercy. Picus inclined his head formally, to show respect.

'Sorry.'

'In fact, you're still in a lot of trouble. Your family have declared you an outcaste officially for ...' Orielle paused, 'well, let's just say a *family matter*. And I have it on good authority that Raben's spies are combing the Thieves' Kasbah and surrounding areas for you. Worst of all, by *far*, I should add, is that we, the Eltern, are also quite keen to have a chat.'

'About what? Er, *Sire*,' Picus added after a moment's hesitation.

Orielle seemed to be looking for something behind the curtain. 'Ah, here we are,' he said cheerfully, back to his usual self. 'Well, firstly we need to talk about your regrettable habit of pinching things. Stop it, there's no future in being a thief. And secondly, during the course of our discussions with our mutual friend, Art the Stooge, it seemed like you might just be what we are looking for.'

'?' looked Picus.

'You're an honest thief,' Orielle said, 'and a jolly good one at that, by all accounts and from what we learned about you last night.'

'How do you know I'm honest?' Picus hoped it didn't sound like a challenge: he was actually warming to the old Nosferatu.

'As I say, I've known Art for centuries, and I trust his judgement. He says you still have honour, which a rare commodity in your business ... very rare.'

Picus didn't know what to say, so, for once in his life, he said nothing.

'Right,' continued Orielle, 'to business! Gentlemen?' He looked at the two guards who still flanked Picus. Without a word, one produced a key and opened the padlock on the shackles he'd been roughly clapped in all night, and then both guards left the room, moving surprisingly quietly given their size, even by Vampire standards. Picus made a mental note of this – the elite guards in the Fast Tower rarely mixed with other Vampires and he had often wondered if they were as dangerous as everyone made out. Silent – yes. Deadly – most definitely.

When he was satisfied that they were quite alone, Orielle gestured for Picus to approach the curtain, and then pulled on a drawstring. The heavy cloth fell away. Picus saw seven pure diamond-plate cabinets in a backlit alcove. Each contained a single item or artefact, with the Chalice at the centre. Picus recognised the platinum chain mail shirt belonging to Prince Vladimir, the last Wandering King and founder of the Keep; in another cabinet, a pair of Vampire wings, whose importance Picus couldn't place immediately; and a jaw he was certain belonged to the legendary warrior emperor, Dracul, gaped at him. Incisors as long as Picus' finger, and as still sharp as razors, shone in the light. He shuddered.

'The Seven Treasures!' Orielle exclaimed, 'only …'

Picus pointed at the cabinet on the far left. 'It's empty.'

'Exactly. And that's why you're here.'

Half an hour later they were sitting on a balcony with a truly spectacular view overlooking the rest of the Keep and the surrounding forests, which stretched down to the golden fields dabbed red by poppies.

It was a breezy morning but Orielle and Picus were comfortably sheltered by a thin screen of sharded amber as they tucked into a late breakfast of wild strawberries and elderflower champagne.

'The Humans are growing in confidence. What they lack in magic and all our other Chalice-given abilities, they more than make up for in willpower and sheer inventiveness. Just look at this!' Orielle took a tiny leather pouch from one of his voluminous coat pockets and tipped the powdery contents onto a small marble-topped table. With impressive dexterity he produced a flint, seemingly from nowhere, and a strike-stone of the sort used by Sanguines everyday for lighting the great fires in the Clan houses they served. He jabbed the flint across the face of the stone and instantly the innocent looking black powder flashed white-hot, gave a *whump* sound and scorched the top of the table. At this wholly unexpected turn of events, right in the middle of breakfast, Picus started backwards and fell off his chair, whilst in the middle distance, a crow changed direction rapidly and disappeared down the valley with an indignant squawk.

Picus was impressed. 'Where did you get this?' he asked, picking himself up off the floor.

'From one of our wandering cousins, lately settled in China.'

Orielle looked terribly pleased with himself. 'They call it *Gone Powder*.'

Picus regrouped. 'And what's it actually for?'

'Well, for the time being at least, the Humans are making fireworks out of it, but something tells me they're going to find less playful things to do with the stuff eventually … and that's not all. Did you know, they've actually invented the clock mechanism? Quite without our help as well. And something called mathematics, although I can't see that catching on, it's all to do with everything being explained by numbers, when every race halfway sensible knows it's all in the planets and the stars …'

Picus knew a pet subject when he heard one, and changed it. 'But I still don't see what it's got to do with me?'

Orielle stopped, two green eyes focused back on Picus. 'The Seventh Treasure,' he said, 'the one that is missing from the Inner Chamber. We lent it to the Humans nearly a hundred years ago and they never gave it back.'

'And you need me to get my hands on it for you,' Picus had begun to suspect as much as soon as he had heard it was Art who had recommended his skills.

Orielle raised a powder-blackened finger. 'Not just *us* – we need it back for everyone. Every Clan member, faithful Sanguine, Vampire child, Faie – yes, even them,' he added firmly when he saw the look on Picus' face, '… every Wight, Pitscie, Puck and Dragon. Every member, however small and un-regarded of the Hidden Kingdom.' He leant forward. 'Our magic is deserting us. You may not know it but you, my fellow, are becoming something of a rarity – a Vampire who can do natural magic – and one who achieves this without any training in the Lore! Although, from what I hear, you seem to practice Faie magic, which is interesting in itself.'

'But I still don't understand why you need the treasure so badly. Is it worth a lot of money?'

Orielle looked exasperated. 'Money's got nothing to do with it! There are those of us – and I count myself as one of them – who believe that if we can gather the Seven Treasures together then we can begin to work on restoring the magic that is slipping away from us. Our magic. Our birthright! Without it we will be defenceless against our enemies, including the Thin Man. Conflict always arises from shortages and we are running short of our most valuable commodity.'

Picus was puzzled. 'What's that?'

'Our natural powers. Our magic. There is going to be a war, before too long – in my view it will start as a civil war between our kind who disagree with what we replace the power with – brute strength, like this noisy and possibly extremely dangerous powder here – or can we recapture our old ways, the magical Lores. I believe that we need to show the Vampire world and every creature in this Hidden Kingdom of ours that magic can still work! Reuniting the treasures is the only way we can do this and so perhaps prevent a terrible conflict!'

He's pretty persuasive, I'll give him that, thought Picus. He took a long gulp of his champagne, playing for time, burped (he hoped) discreetly through his nose and looked enquiringly at the venerable old Vampire.

'And so what is this treasure that I have to steal back?'

'Exkylipyr, Picus. We want you to retrieve the Sword of Kings!'

Picus was enough of a student of destiny to know when life reached one of its rare tipping points; where a decision, either way, would change the course of his own existence forever. So as soon as Orielle mentioned Exkylipyr he was aware that this particular moment was a biggie. As a keen student in anything valuable in his world he knew that the name 'Exkylipyr' was made up of three words: 'ex' - *out of*, 'kyli' - *cup* and 'pyr' - *fire* together meaning *forged from the cup of fire*. Legend had it that that cup the sword was forged in the belly of the Chalice itself. Some even went as far as saying that some of the metal from the Chalice had mixed with the ore being smelted and this was why the sword was so powerful. Many Vampires held it in as much awe as they did the Chalice itself. One thing was for sure, this would be a career high for Picus if he actually managed to pull it off.

'I don't exactly do swords,' he said without much conviction, looking up from the table. Orielle had just enough time to arrange his features into a bland screen of concern for Picus' feelings, but Picus could see quiet triumph behind the mask. He saw that Orielle knew Picus would say yes. Eventually.

'So I heard. Some members of your family, the more vocal ones anyway – including your own mother – brand you a coward for this.' Orielle paused to give emphasis to what he was about to say, '*I myself do not agree.*'

Picus struggled to keep focus, as he nearly always did whenever his mother was mentioned by anyone other than Lark. 'Thank you,' was all he could say, eventually.

Orielle ploughed on. 'Of course, we are not asking you to use the Sword. Though you are of almost royal blood, it is highly questionable that it would allow you to make full use of its powers in any case. However, the Eltern are satisfied that you are sufficiently well-born for it to allow you to become its temporary guardian, to transport it. The important thing to know is that Exkylipyr will shrink or grow to the size of the individual, be they Man, Vampire or Beast who uses it for good and who uses it for the good of a royal bloodline.'

'Whose royal blood would that be, then?'

'Whoever is the rightful heir at that time.'

'And who is the rightful heir to the Vampires? I thought the nobility stopped at Karls, since the Wandering Kings died?'

'Quite so, quite so,' Orielle looked faintly embarrassed. 'Well, we're not completely sure, but once you have the sword in your hands, we rather hoped that you being a Count and therefore a Vampire noble with at least some of the Wandering Kings' blood flowing in your veins, would do the trick.'

This isn't going to be straightforward, thought Picus. 'OK, assuming you are right, how do I get my hands on it?'

'You need to go to the seat of all natural magic. To Angleland, Picus. Exkylipyr has been there for decades, languishing in one of their long barrows.'

'What's a long barrow?'

'It's where the Humans from that part of the world bury their dead.'

'Is it heavily guarded?'

Orielle shook his head. 'Not at all, as far as I know.'

'Is it hidden?'

'No, it should actually be in quite a prominent position once you get down there.'

Picus was thoroughly confused. 'Then why do you need me?'

'Good question!' Orielle seemed unnaturally delighted, as if Picus was a clever student. 'First of all, as I have mentioned, you are of almost royal blood, so that means you can actually handle it; secondly, Art vouches for you, so it's unlikely you are going to run off with this potentially very dangerous heirloom and use it for your own purposes. And ...' Orielle paused.

'Thirdly?'

'Yes, that's it – thirdly, we're not taking any chances. It might be easy enough for any Vampire to lay their hands on the thing but getting out of there and back here is another matter entirely. For that we need someone with your particular set of skills.' Orielle smiled broadly, 'So there you have it in a nutshell: we need a high-born, honest thief who owes us his allegiance in return for not being thrown in a dungeon for the rest of his life, having been caught breaking into the Crypt to steal things ... now, young Vampire, how many of them do you know?'

Picus paused for a long while. 'Me?' he said eventually, in a very small voice.

An hour later Oie, the guard, considered the agile form of Picus from a distance as he made his way up into the hills that surrounded the Keep and wondered if his master, Orielle, hadn't made a ghastly mistake. Like most guards, he spent a lot of his day standing dead still in one place and this gave him a lot of time to study the comings and goings of his fellow Vampires.

And a lot of thinking time, too. Over the years Oie had become a student of Vampire nature. It was something of a hobby and it certainly helped pass the time.

His wife, Swan, said he probably thought too much but she also said he worked too hard and should eat more fruit and wear warm socks in winter. Oie liked thinking about his wife; and apart from sore feet from standing up all day, he generally saw himself as a lucky Vampire who was generally happy with his lot. He was a very good judge of character and he wasn't entirely sure about this young thief.

Orielle had offered Picus an armed guard all the way to the Sleeve Sea, where he would make the choppy and dangerous crossing into Angleland, but Picus had politely but firmly refused an escort beyond half a league from the Keep, saying he preferred to work alone.

'Right,' said Picus brightly, as he and Oie finally reached the Keep borders, just where the forest began proper, leading up through darker, more dangerous mountains. 'Cheerio, then!'

Oie merely nodded and watched Picus as he headed north, picking his way lightly though the huge rocks and boulders. Stepping quietly into the shadow of a large fir tree, Oie then watched Picus, as he was almost out of sight, check over his shoulder and abruptly change direction, away from Angleland and his mission. It looked like the young thief never had any intention of keeping up his end of the bargain.

Oie shook his head sadly, as if to say, *I knew it*.

Contrary to popular belief, Vampires rarely, if ever, feed from Humans. It is a curious fact that Human and Vampire blood tastes remarkably similar.

Chapter 10

Lark was absolutely furious with Picus. As usual.

After Picus had tricked her into flying out of the Crypt without him, thereby saving *her* but leaving *him* at the mercy of the Vampire Knights, she had enough presence of mind to realise that she should probably lie low for a bit. Going back to her parents in the Clan Quarter was out of the question. After running off with Picus, she wasn't sure they'd have her back just like that and, even if they did, there were going to be too many awkward questions.

Instead she had pulled the cape firmly over her striking features and simply walked out the main gates just as the sun was rising. Dressed as she was, in rough, stone-coloured work clothes, the sleepy guards, who had been up all night watching empty streets, barely glanced at her twice, assuming she was just another lowly Sanguine on her way out of the Keep on a dawn errand. She was relieved to be away: skulking about was not her style and she'd had enough of tunnels for the time being.

Lark had a vague plan to head back to the Thieves' Kasbah and the Café du Clairvoyant. It had its own very sophisticated information network, and news of Picus' fate would filter through to her there faster than most places she could think of. If he had been captured and taken to the Fast Tower, there was very little she could do by staying at the Keep anyway.

An early morning mist had rolled across the poppy fields like soft, fluffy bedding. Lark used the cover it afforded to return at least some of the clothing borrowed from the Imp crone, then followed the river bank for a time until she came to a doe otter lying half asleep in a pool of sunlight, its soft white underbelly rising and falling in time with its breathing.

Having drunk her fill, Lark dabbed the otter's blood from the corner of her mouth and found her own sunny spot close by. It had been a long night, and she fell asleep almost immediately.

⁂

The sound of a dry twig snapping brought her awake, sword drawn, in a heartbeat.

A little way off stood a young Vampire about her age. He was dressed expensively, although looking a little old fashioned, in black leather armour and a light mail shirt whose silver links were interspersed with gold, forming an intricate wave pattern. He regarded Lark warily through heavy black lashes. His own sword remained undrawn at his side, one hand resting lightly on the pommel, the other raised, palm facing her, in a calming motion. 'I'm sorry if I made you jump,' he said in a soft but self-confident voice. 'You're quite safe,' he added sincerely.

Lark said nothing at first, but studied his face, looking for any trace of deceit. She saw conflict in his features but put it down to that sense of occasion experienced when two complete strangers meet unexpectedly in a potentially risky situation. Especially when they both instinctively liked one another. She smiled wryly. 'Well, you would say that.'

The young Vampire now looked surprised, as if he wasn't used to people making jokes and wasn't quite sure how to react. Lark turned up her smile a couple of watts and eventually he smiled back, if a little hesitantly.

Lark relaxed, sheathed her sword and held out her hand in its place. 'I'm Lark. Pleased to meet you.'

The good-looking Vampire stopped smiling, stepped forward and took her hand very gently in his. 'And I am Corbeau,' he said solemnly.

⁂

Barely an hour later they were strolling across the poppy field, Lark saying she was headed south but careful not to say where exactly, Corbeau feigning surprise that this was exactly where he was going too!

Corbeau was congratulating himself for the skill with which he was able to fool Picus' cousin. However, he was slightly disconcerted by the suspicion that this was not the only reason for his uncharacteristic cheerfulness. A lot of it had to do with Lark. She walked slightly ahead of him, completely at ease now, chatting airily about this and that as they wove a path between the barley and poppies that towered overhead like a huge floral forest. There was something about Lark that made him feel unreasonably happy, but not having much contact with anyone his age – especially a Duchess Vampire – he couldn't find a basis for it.

After leaving Queen Mab's burrow, he had made straight for the Thieves' Kasbah, picking up three of his father's Trolls on the way for protection. Not that he needed it for himself – though still a Strigoi Vampire, thanks to some expensive tuition and a strong natural talent he was already more than a match for most fully grown, adult Vampires with a rapier in his hand. However, a backdrop of these lumbering thugs, he had learned, was helpful to show people that you meant business.

Fergus at Café du Clairvoyant had been tortured. Regrettable but necessary and Corbeau had been fascinated by the Troll's methods. Within a few hours, he found out from the broken innkeeper that Lark had left shortly after Picus and headed north, towards the Reeking Marsh. That road only led to one place – the Keep – so he had set off at full speed, wanting to catch up with the cousins before they reached the protection of the Vampire stronghold.

In their haste, his party had crossed the wetlands carelessly and one of the Trolls, missing his footing, had been sucked under the stinking black mud before they could pull him out. The three remaining travellers, Corbeau included, had merely shrugged in the gathering dusk, silently looking on as the last remaining evidence of the unfortunate Troll – a few bubbles – expanded and burst. They then continued on their way.

Picus and Lark were moving fast, so Corbeau changed plan and decided to wait until whatever business they had at the Keep was done and he would hopefully catch up with them on the way back. He sent the two remaining Trolls, Disk and Tools, to the east and west of the Keep, in case they left that way, and set himself to cover the southern exit.

That morning his patience was partly rewarded when he came across the sleeping form of Lark. Luckily he had spotted her from a distance, before she awoke, and recognised her immediately by the Clan ring she wore on her left hand. She was sleeping deeply by the stream only a quarter of a league from where Corbeau was camping.

Soundlessly, Corbeau had crept up upon the sleeping Duchess Vampire. For a moment, he considered ripping her neck out with his teeth, then rejected the idea as uncouth – even if highly satisfying – and instead drew a long, sharp dagger that tapered like a needle at its point. Poised to stab her through the heart, he suddenly hesitated. The girl's lips were parted, revealing just the tips of her blood teeth, as she made soft breathing noises and her eyelashes moved. She was dreaming. One hand, cushioning her head, exposed a slender, incredibly pale inner arm. A vein pulsed slightly at the wrist, her neck arched like an invitation.

Whatever he had been planning to do, Corbeau found he could no longer go through with it.

He told himself, for now, that sparing her meant he could find out where Picus was.

Taking a few paces back, he snapped the twig on purpose to wake her.

'So, where are you from?' Lark turned and smiled at Corbeau, who found himself smiling back yet again. He made a mental note, there and then, not to grin like an imbecile each and every time she addressed him. Smiling used muscles in his face he wasn't used to using and it made his face ache. 'You never know,' Lark went on, 'we may have friends or family in common. Sometimes I think that half the Clans are related anyway.'

Corbeau felt a sudden burst of panic. She was right, he was going to have to be careful not to give too much away. 'My parents, Count and Countessa Arad, have their estates twenty or so leagues from here.' He plucked a name out of the air – Arad was a common enough name amongst Vampires. She was assuming he was noble – not just the only child of a rich crook – and he saw no reason to put her in the picture. For now.

'Oh, I think I've heard of them,' she replied a little vaguely.

Corbeau smiled at her white lie – he had guessed rightly that she would be polite. Her sort always was. As soon as she had told him Picus' whereabouts, he would kill her and move on. But even as he thought this, he knew it didn't sound convincing, even to his own ears. 'What about you?' Corbeau drew level with her, noticing just how beautiful her slender fingers were.

Lark shrugged, her wings hunching, catching the light and refracting it in a rainbow of colours. 'Oh the usual. Stuffy Clan family, mother unable to move half a league from the Keep without having a panic attack, father obsessed with politics – which noble is in favour with the Eltern, who's got their teeth into whom ... we've got estates in the country and even a castle or two but we never seem to go there.' She turned and touched Corbeau ever so lightly on the hand, a gesture which he wasn't sure was purposeful or accidental. He felt like he'd received an electric shock. 'I envy you,' she went on, 'growing up with all that fresh air, all that freedom. Sometimes the Keep was ... is so oppressive.'

Corbeau thought of his brutish, controlling father, who bullied everyone he met, and of his mother who remained on her own in her bedroom most days, drinking, sleeping or simply staring into space. He'd lost count of the times he'd gone to see her as a child for comfort or just some attention and found her sitting there crying for hours over some nameless fear or sorrow. Unable to get through to her, he'd stay there for a bit and then slip away, usually unheeded, always unmissed. 'Yes,' he said very quietly, 'it was lovely.'

Then he looked up and saw she was looking at him intently, almost fondly. Suddenly, alone with her on this beautiful morning, his mother's illness and his father's violence didn't seem to matter so much any more. All he was aware of was the moment, and that he was exactly where he wanted to be, here in this field with this pretty Duchess Vampire. They were just coming to the end of the poppy field and Corbeau felt a small sense of victory: he had suddenly realised why he was feeling like he was. His father used brute force and money to get where he wanted and Corbeau was accustomed to dealing with that fear and even hatred that this brought in his dealings with other Vampires, Faies or Wights. Lark was the first member of the Hidden Kingdom he had spoken to in years who seemed to actually like him. He frowned, as it dawned on him that things weren't going to plan.

As they wandered along a bright green beech hedge that bordered the field, they came, without warning, to a Human cottage. It had been built in a haphazard fashion, its thatched roof leaning this way and then that, eventually sloping down on one side to a large wooden wheel that turned slowly, pushed by the force of the same stream where they'd met earlier.

'Wonder what that is,' remarked Lark, pointing at the wheel.

Corbeau had a strange look on his face – if Lark had to guess she would have said he looked intrigued. This was an unusual reaction since, in her experience, most Vampires, confronted with anything Human, tended to be off-hand, disinterested or just downright disdainful. 'It's a vast machine of some sort.' He wandered forward seemingly without any fear, although he was crossing open ground now. 'The water pushes the wheel and there's probably a mechanism inside that does something or other...'

Lark dredged up her minute experience of Humans. 'Do you think it's a weapon of some sort?'

'Hmm,' Corbeau shook his head, 'I doubt it ...' Just then there was a piercing scream and both Vampires took to the air, drawing their swords in unison. The sound was awful – like something foul-tempered being strangled, badly. 'Aarghhh!' said Corbeau shaking his head as if to drown out the sound.

'Ahhh!' said Lark as her features assumed a sort of soppy expression that, in Corbeau's eyes, girls reserved for fluffy toys or young deer. 'It's a *Baby*.' Ever since she remembered she'd loved reading books with illustrations of Human babies. She flew down to where the dreadful noise was coming from – a sort of wooden crib by the back door of the cottage. They were sooo pink and squidgy and they had the coolest expressions ...

'Don't go anywhere near it,' warned Corbeau, now hopping in agitation from one foot to the other from some distance away. 'It'll grab you with one of those pudgy hands it's got and squeeze you to death.'

Lark rolled her eyes. 'Nonsense,' she said, sheathing her sword and performing a graceful handstand on the edge of the crib. The scream was immediately replaced by a pregnant silence and then a gurgle as Lark executed a perfect back flip and then a twisting somersault on the wooden rim. More silence that built into a sudden peel of laughter whilst Lark flew at speed around the baby's head and landed on lightly on its nose. 'Oh! I wish I could take you homey womey,' she said in a silly voice waving her finger.

'Well, I am quite peckish,' said Corbeau from a safe distance.

Lark glared at him. 'You'll do no such thing ...' she turned back to the baby. 'Oh, would the nasty Vampy wamy bite you ... well, not unless he wants his butt kicked,' she grinned at Corbeau who suddenly felt another one of *those* smiles breaking out.

'Kick my *what*? You and whose Troll?' He made a show of rolling up a sleeve. 'It's time baby was treated to a display of real Vampire agility...'

'Oh yes?' Lark opened her wings and went into a looping dive, under the crib and into the shadows. Corbeau followed, trying to pick out where she'd gone. A wild peppercorn zoomed out of the trees, hitting him painfully on the back of the head. Corbeau momentarily veered off his flight trajectory and flew straight into a spider's web. The silk was old and had lost its stickiness but Corbeau still got a mouthful of musty, foul-tasting thread. 'Caah,

caah, blaa, gaarh,' he coughed.

'Ha, ha. All mouth and fangs, just like all the other Strigoi I know!' shouted Lark, spiralling up to the tops of the trees and disappearing into the forest. Instead of feeling foolish and angry, like he would have with anyone else, Corbeau found himself easily entering into the spirit of the game.

Both Vampires spent the next half hour happily weaving at almost supersonic speeds through the woodland, trading insults and mock ambushes.

Finally, Lark noticed a small clear pool fed, presumably, by the stream where that ran past the Human mill. 'I'm boiling,' she announced, and without hesitation dived in.

Her trajectory was so steep, her wings folded back and fully streamlined, that she hardly made a ripple as she entered the water. Just a few bubbles fizzing to the surface at intervals, marked her passage under the surface. Corbeau was reminded of the last traces of the Troll they had lost in the Reeking Marsh, and quashed the image as Lark surfaced noisily at the far end of the pool. She burst upwards, wings opening briefly, giving her just enough height to somersault back down, almost but not quite belly flopping. She bobbed up again, laughing and coughing. 'Come in!' she shouted, 'it's so refreshing, and you look like you're going to explode in all that armour!' She grinned and looked at him under wet lashes. 'I can assure you my intentions are *entirely* honourable.'

Corbeau shrugged in mock self-pity. 'I'd love to but I'd sink like a stone.' In truth he could swim – just about – but he had a Vampire's horror of water. He couldn't quite work out how Lark seemed to have got over hers. 'I didn't think our kind were supposed to go in water. You swim well,' he added rather stiffly.

'Picus taught me,' she replied. 'He's my cousin, he says all Vampires should learn to swim, it's very liberating.' She shook her head in the dappled light, treading water.

This was Corbeau's opportunity! If he wanted to find out where he was, now was his moment – she had just introduced Picus into the conversation, without him having to do anything.

It would be easy enough to bring it around to his whereabouts … but he found he couldn't get the words out. He knew that as soon as he got his information the moment here with Lark, and this feeling, would be over and he didn't want that. Starved of friendship for years, he was just getting used to it again and it would be a long time before he had his fill.

A noise like a hob-nailed boot scraping against rock snapped his attention away from Lark. Mechanically he drew his sword, bringing it around to face the direction of the sound as his father's Trolls – Disk and Tools – came into view. Lark turned too, just as recognition was forming on Tools' face.

It was then that Corbeau made a decision that would affect the course of his life. He flew towards Tools in a blur.

'Master – ' was all his father's servant had time to say before Corbeau cut his throat.

Disk, who was standing behind Tools, started to speak. 'Wait! It's –' then he saw what was coming and started to bring up his heavy two-handed axe. He didn't even get it past his waist before Corbeau sank his teeth into his Adam's apple and bit out all sound and life, then turned in mid-air flicking back to stab the dying Troll in the heart, leaving the priceless rapier vibrating in the huge torso as he landed on the bank next to Lark.

She stared for a moment at the scuffling feet, the blood on the dead leaves and the lifeless eyes staring into space.

'I've never seen anyone move that fast,' she murmured, 'not even Picus. But …' she turned to him, a shadow passing over her eyes, 'why did you do that? Not all Trolls attack … we could have tried talking to them … and I dunno, one of them seemed …' She swung her gaze around to face Corbeau, gazing into his eyes, a flash of realisation dawning in hers. Corbeau felt his soul flinch. 'I can't believe it,' she said, 'did you actually *know* them?'

Corbeau took a long juddering breath. 'We need to talk,' he said and flew uphill, away from the carnage.

And so he told her everything.

He told her about the night he had heard a noise in the corridor along from his private chambers, his encounter with Picus and his rage. He told her about his meeting with Queen Mab, the Tooth Fairy, and the deal he had done with her court to deliver Picus to them.

He *tried* to tell her about how he had felt meeting her, he wanted to open his heart to this beautiful Duchess Vampire, but when it came to that part of the conversation, he found he didn't have the words. Corbeau did not have the vocabulary of love, or even like, because no-one had ever spoken those words to him. Instead he left his reasons for killing Disk and Tools hanging, hoping that Lark would somehow guess them. He suspected, though, that she would merely think it had been done to trick her all the more into a false sense of security, just another strategy to gain her confidence.

When he had finished, Lark had merely nodded and walked away. He went to find her about an hour later and discovered she had buried the two Trolls as best she could.

For the remainder of the day they travelled together, continuing to head south. Once he had tried to touch her arm, just as she had done to him earlier that day, but she flinched away as if burnt.

'I did it for you,' he blurted out.

She stared at him coldly. 'You murdered for *me*?' she said, her voice rising at the end. She took a deep breath, as if to control herself. 'Why?'

And Corbeau had no answer.

They camped that night on the edge of the wind-blasted Reeking Marsh. The breeze coming off the water was cold but Lark refused a fire and Corbeau's offer of his cape. As he lay there listening to the sound of her breathing, he wanted to cry in self-pity. To stop himself, he bit down on his knuckle, his razor-sharp teeth drawing warm blood that flowed freely down his hand and wrist, soaking his shirt sleeve.

Eventually he must have drifted off, because when he awoke

just before dawn, damp and depressed, he saw she was gone. He wasn't surprised.

Some Humans have a surprising connection with Vampires and Faies alike, so perhaps they have a common ancestry after all?

Chapter 11
aliya revisited

Corbeau may have lost Lark but, as she left him sleeping just before dawn, someone else peeled away from the quiet shadows under the wet willows and crept after the Duchess Vampire through the half-light.

The young Human girl, Aliya, had been thinking a lot about the strange and beautiful creature she had found with her brother a few days previously but had assumed that she was unlikely to come across anything like Him again. That night at supper, ignoring hard looks from her brother, she had mentioned what happened at the ruined castle. To begin with, she assumed that no-one had been listening because no-one said anything – that often happened – so she repeated the story. ' – it was really cool,' she finished, '*and* He bit Peter.'

'Aliya!' Peter had gone red. 'You don't need to tell everyone everything *all* the time.' He chucked a lump of stale bread at his sister's head.

'Boy!' his father barked. 'Go to your room!'

'But ...' then he saw the expression on his father's face. Gorlag wasn't head of the village for nothing and Peter was right to fear his temper. He sloped off to his room, muttering under his breath.

After a few moments Aliya's mother got up, two spots of red appearing at her temples. 'I'll go and see to him.' She looked upset about something.

Aliya's father watched her mother go and then turned to his daughter. He gave her a stern look that made her feel about half her age and lasted longer than was comfortable. 'Now listen to me carefully, young lady,' he said eventually. 'You may be sure of what you *thought* you saw but most likely, in the morning mist, you were still half asleep and what you saw was closer to imagining than anything else.'

Aliya opened her mouth to say something, thought better of it and closed it again.

'Wagging tongues cause more harm than good,' her father continued, 'and now let that be an end to it ... go and put your brother's supper by the fire to keep warm until he's sorry and then come back and finish yours. You can speak when you're spoken to for the rest of dinner and when you do, let's hear no more silly talk about made-up creatures!'

Later she was sat by the fire, sulking, when she chanced to look up. Aliya had long since got used to her granny just sitting there not saying very much. Most of the time she seemed to be in her own world. Right now, though, she was staring at her granddaughter intently.

The old lady hawked and spat into the fire. Aliya wished she wouldn't do things like that. 'So you've seen a bit o' the Hidden Kingdom, my girl?' Her voice sounded like an old door opening. 'And thems that rule it – the Vampires – you're not the first ... but one of the few, I'll grant you that. I remember we'd know them by the golden trails they left when they flew. Threads of magic that hung in the air, like spider's silk. Some could see it, others couldn't and so denied it ever existed. But my cousin, little Em, she could see the threads right enough, I know 'cos she picked up a good trail once on Pall's Hill an' we followed it all day until we came to Them. There they all were, hovering in the forest, caught in a beam of light. I'm ninety now my girl, older than most'll ever be, an' my sights dim – like looking through a dirty window – but I'll never forget what I saw that day. It was the most beautiful thing I'd ever clapped eyes on and ever likely to. Just a few seconds before they sensed us and disappeared – but I felt the priv'ledge of it.' She lent close to her granddaughter and pinched her cheek gently. 'Don't listen to your Dad – he means well but he doesn't know everything – sees less – men!'

A few days later, Aliya had been babysitting for their neighbours who owned the Mill nearby. She had spent most of the afternoon daydreaming but a sudden cry from baby Horken snapped her out of it. She went over to the window and caught her breath.

As the creatures flicked and flew their way around Horken's crib, she lost sight of them momentarily. She scanned the area around the front garden and was about to give up when something glinted in soft the morning light. It looked like a thin wisp of coloured smoke, hanging in the air. Aliya felt her chest go tight and a little burst of excitement. It was just as her grandmother had described it – catching the sun's rays, it resembled spun gold as it twisted and floated high over the tops of the trees.

Aliya took a deep breath and followed.

Chapter 12
ruby

Barely half a league away from where Lark and Corbeau spent their wretched night, a Faie child was running for her life.

Legs pumping and lungs burning, she tore through the tangle of wild grass that sliced into her skin like dozens of deep paper cuts. Her goal was the relative safety of the hills in the distance – it was further from home than she'd been in her life but it was her only chance of survival. Some way behind her, she could hear the hunters closing in. Not yet five, her ill-formed and uncontrolled magic spat and shot out sounds and images at random: a wail of terror, more a symptom of her state of mind than anything else that she smothered, lest it give her away; images of home, her mother's apron, a fire burning in the kitchen hearth, her favourite teddy – all appeared in the air about her before she burst through them. She tried to think of something practical that could help her or discourage the hunters but her mind was scrambled with panic.

Out collecting sugar from cowslip blossom in the early morning mist, she had been attacked by a group of Grigs – small brown Faies who were well known for taking other Faie children as slaves. She had run but they had simply followed close by, herding her deeper into the mist, getting closer, close enough to scratch and bite before falling back, to herd her once more, further and further away from home.

She was lost and confused, nearing the end of her endurance when she saw the rocks rising above the fog in the distance: the start of the mountains where the Keep's territory began. Grigs were unlikely to follow her there, past the telltale poppies, into Vampire dominions. It was a risk, but the only chance she had.

Before Picus went to Angleland – he thought as he doubled back – he was going to find Lark and make sure she was safe.

He was careful not to pass too close to the Keep, moving silently through the trees, descending the small range of mountains that rose up behind the huge citadel. Even so, he had the nagging feeling that he had turned too soon. The guard who had escorted him to the edge of the Keep's territory showed every sign of not trusting Picus one bit and the young Vampire sensed he had seen what he was up to.

Not only did he feel a pressing need to find Lark, he also wanted a word with Art. Or two. Orielle had been persuasive, but since his exile Picus had developed a natural aversion to doing what he was told by his elders and supposed betters. Especially if he suspected that he hadn't been given the whole story. Things hadn't exactly gone to plan recently and he was finally learning to be cautious. So, upon tracking down Art, he had every intention of checking out Orielle's story about this sword, Exkylipyr. *Then* would he decide what to do.

His mind was on this when the Faie girl blindsided him.

She was small – tiny really – but she'd been going so fast she knocked him clean off his feet. He hit his wing on a rock as he went down. 'Whatwo'ah ... *hey!*' was all he had time to say before the girl, who had ricocheted off his shoulder, was up on her feet, eyes staring blindly forwards in fear as she made to continue up the hill.

Without thinking, Picus grabbed hold of her arm, prompting a shower of magic from the girl, like sparklers going off in several directions at once. She made as if to pull away but he held onto her easily. He noticed then that she was still a child and that she was bleeding from almost every part of her body: her hands, legs, arms, face were all lacerated. Her breath came out in terrified gulps.

'Stop ... *stop* ... it's alright ... whatever it is ... *was*, you're safe now,' Picus said. Only then did he think to look around in the rough direction she had come to see if what he said was strictly true. Even over the clatter and confusion of the collision, he had heard the sound of several pairs of bare feet running after her, but whatever they were, her pursuers had faded away, back into the fog that covered the valley floor. Whoever it was, they had stopped when she had crossed into Vampire territory.

For an instant a face seemed to peer out of the fog. Picus had a brief impression of pointed features full of wickedness and then it was gone with a mad giggle and the pad of feet quickly moving around and behind him.

Picus, looking intently at Ruby, put his finger to his lips and listened hard. One, two, three … he counted at least four separate footfalls. Safety in numbers, ha! They must have thought there were enough of them to go up against an injured Faie and an unarmed and immature Vampire.

Picus closed his yes and concentrated hard – waiting for just the right moment. When it came he flicked his wings and flew in a tight circle, gaining momentum, spiralling down, judging his trajectory to outflank the hidden attackers who were trying to get behind Picus and attack them both. He caught sight of four blurred forms through the fog, running at speed, just before they split up. They were about half a dozen rapier lengths from him. Picus landed softly, making no noise whatsoever and sent out four bolts from his open palms in quick succession.

Startled yelps came from the hunters who had suddenly found themselves the hunted, and four sizzling backsides disappeared into the mist in search of a pond.

Picus returned to the Faie kitten as quickly as he could, just in time to catch her before she ran back in the direction she had come from. 'It's fine, you really are safe now,' he repeated as gently as he could. He relaxed his grip. Realising she couldn't get away, she had gone limp, and now looked at him with large, round eyes.

'You're a Vampire,' she whispered, close to tears and made as if to bolt again.

On impulse, Picus knew that letting go of her was the best way to calm her down. When he did, she moved a couple of paces, but didn't turn and run, as he thought she might. Picus sat down very deliberately on a rock, letting the girl study him. 'Who were you running away from?'

There was a long pause. The child's eyes slid behind him, back into the fog. 'Ggsss,' it sounded like to Picus, who made an enquiring face at her. She tried again. 'Grigs.'

'Who?' Picus had not heard the name. Knowing something he didn't seemed to give her more confidence and she visibly relaxed.

'They've got scratchy nails and they steal children to take away and they make them work for a hundred years until they are old and nearly dead and then they eat them all up, except their buttons and shoes. Grigs are smelly.'

'Oh.' Picus did his best to digest the information. He looked at her and she stared back at him. He made a show of flexing his injured wing and wincing. 'You're stronger than you look.' This almost raised a smile. 'Still, you did the right thing coming here. The rocks were your best bet to lose them and I am a powerful and terribly fierce Vampire.' The Faie child looked alarmed. 'But only when it comes to Grigs,' he added hastily.

She did smile then, and bit her lip. 'My name's Ruby,' she said, suddenly deciding he wasn't a threat, 'and I've got a teddy and he's called Teddy.'

'Pleased to meet you Ruby, I'm Picus.' He held out his hand in mock formality. 'You're hurt,' he said, 'let me do something about those cuts.'

Trustingly, she lifted her hand to show him a larger gash on the soft flesh under her forearm. Clearly it was the one causing her the most pain. Picus assumed that Faies were similar to Vampires in that they healed very fast indeed but he sensed it was the sight of her own blood that was distressing her more than anything. To take her mind off what he was about to do he conjured a small Merry-go-round of prancing Unicorns and blue-green Mermaids who pirouetted to music as it spun in the air. He took her hand and blew on it. The bleeding stopped instantly. He then did the same with her other arm and finally the small gashes on her face. He placed a cupped palm on each of the cuts in turn and felt a burning sensation and knew that her pain was ebbing away.

Pleased, Picus stepped back, breathing slightly heavier than usual, as if he had been flying hard for a few minutes. 'There!' he said. 'Though I'm sure your parents will want to give you a hot bath and a change of clothes when you get back.' The Merry-go-round faded and so too the music, drifting off on the morning breeze. 'So which way is home?'

Ruby pointed east, in the direction of the Tussocks.

Corbeau lay in the dark cellar, his legs, hands and wings roughly bound with wire that cut into his flesh each time he moved. As he drifted in and out of consciousness his mind ran through the savage beating he had just received. He'd seen his father like this before: incoherent rage expressing itself in violence – ranting, clubbing his heavy fists – usually beating senseless some servant who'd made a mistake or a merchant who owed him money. But the rage had never before been directed at Corbeau – his own son. In fact Raben had never laid a finger on him before that evening when Corbeau had come home and confessed he had fallen in love with Picus' cousin and that he'd killed Disk and Tools for reasons he still couldn't quite fathom.

His father had always supported him, even against his mother – no – especially against his mother, in the early days when she had still been able to express an opinion without shaking or stammering uncontrollably, or weeping. Somehow he'd imagined that his father might be disappointed but he would understand, even sympathise a little with how he'd messed things up.

When he'd got back to his father Corbeau had still been distraught about how things had turned out with Lark, and probably wasn't thinking clearly when he decided to confess all. That made two confessions in one day, two bouts of uncharacteristic honesty that had turned his world upside down, and destroyed everything he cared about.

There was a lesson in this.

His father had been calm at first, helped by an afternoon of drinking, but gentle admonishment had quickly given way to shouting. The Sanguines, sensing what was going to happen, had melted away. However the first slap, when it came, had taken Corbeau entirely by surprise, so much so he thought it was a mistake and almost laughed. This enraged his father all the more, who began to rain down blows on his son as he dragged him down one of the winding turret stairs to the cellars.

The thing that had hurt the most, more than the punches or kicks, had been what he said.

'She's made a fool of us, you scrawny imbecile! She's probably with Picus right now, laughing at you. She tricked you and you fell for it. That's all these aristocrats are good for – lies and making people like us know their place! Why would she go for you, a snot-nosed whelp in last century's armour that doesn't even fit? She's seen it all before, the wealth, the glamour. You wouldn't seem impressive to her. Just a joke! SHE SAW YOU COMING! And you took the bait like a wet-arsed puppy running after a ball. I thought you had some nous, lad! Instead you make me sick.'

And his father was right.

Lying alone in the dark cellar, Corbeau's worst fears and paranoia stalked him. She probably had known who he was all along, he thought bitterly as the cold remorse crept into his joints. He tried to stand, managed to get to his knees but, virtually hamstrung by the wires, he fell back, cracking his head on a wet flagstone. The flash of pain gave him a sudden vivid picture of her by the stream where they had first met. Except now she was sitting with Picus. They were giggling as she mimicked Corbeau's awkward manners, his sullen looks and monosyllabic answers.

She *had* known.

She'd been bait and trap in one and he'd fallen for it. Because of her he'd lost the respect of the one person he could count on – his father. A small, sane part of him ruefully commented on how quickly love could turn to hate but the rest of him raged now at

Lark. Fury spread from his stomach as bright flecks of red burned in his dark eyes.

He was no longer cold. His rage and lust for revenge would keep him warm now. It would be his comfort.

As Raben staggered drunkenly up the cellar stairs, a heavy key dangling on an iron chain at his side, he congratulated himself. He loved the boy more than anything, except perhaps himself, but it had to be done. Raben was satisfied he'd taught his only son a valuable lesson in life. *He'll thank me one day*, he thought.

Drunk though he was, Raben had the wily brain of a Vampire used to winning his battles by any means necessary. He had spies everywhere, not least the Keep, and they had told him that Picus had been released earlier that day, having been arrested in the Crypt. He was last seen heading north.

Raben had pondered on this for a long time, turning the matter of Picus' arrest and surprising release over in his mind. Eventually he had come to the conclusion that the young Vampire had been let off in order to provide some service to the Eltern. Raben didn't live in the Keep; not being a Clan Vampire, he would never have enjoyed the freedom he currently enjoyed in his lair had he chose to live so close to the Eltern, but he knew how things worked. It was typical of the Eltern, to let Picus off to carry out some errand, he'd warrant, and get him on their side.

Truth be known, Raben actually quite liked and admired Picus but the game had changed beyond mere revenge. As the Blood Cognac wore off, Raben had a sudden flash of clarity. If Picus was employed by the Eltern it could only be for one thing: the activity he was best at: burglary! And whatever the Eltern were after it wouldn't be some trinket.

Then there was this girl Lark. He had a contact – a very important one he'd been saving for a special occasion – who could help secure her. And Picus would, by all accounts, follow his cousin to Hades and back if necessary. If he let it be known that he had the girl, then there was a good chance that Picus (and, more importantly, his prize) would go to save her *before* he went to the Eltern.

Raben chuckled. He just had to get the girl, and in so doing, he'd get his hands on Picus and the prize the young thief was securing for the Eltern. Raben was a big believer in simply letting the good things in life come to him.

⁌

Fifteen leagues away Picus was amusing the Faie child, Ruby, with a succession of (what he thought to be) hilarious apparitions: extremely fat Sprites who flew for a few seconds and then landed heavily in muddy puddles, Weres sporting fluffy pink bows and silly haircuts, and a bewildered-looking Dragon who blew fire out the wrong end.

He had guessed correctly in that her injuries seemed to be healing well already, but she was filthy and looked very tired. After half an hour she let him pick her up and he flew the rest of the way as she dozed.

Picus wasn't stupid; he knew that Faies wouldn't usually let him waltz into their burrow, unannounced and uninvited. However, he was pretty sure that his act of kindness would be viewed benevolently and he might just get a good meal and a bed for the night. In his experience, Vampires and Faies generally, when not at outright war amongst themselves, pretended that the other lot didn't exist. It had been a couple of centuries since the last pitched battle between Faies and the Keep,[13] and so whilst Picus had heard of the Tussocks, he wasn't sure what to expect.

Coming upon the series of burrows and muddy scratchings, he was unimpressed, if not a little disgusted by the dirt and gen-

---

[13] [Translator's note] The Battle of Four Bridges, AD 04. Unusually this was not over who controlled the bridges themselves - that right had long been ceded to a family of Trolls who collected silver bits from travellers in exchange for safe passage - but over fishing rights. History seemed to dictate that Faies and Vampires went to war over the stupidest things. The battle was a magnificent victory for the Vampires, who don't even like fish.

eral air of squalor that surrounded him. Faie Lords and Ladies[14] paraded down a muddy thoroughfare that ran between the hovels, dressed in silks and furs caked in dirt, wearing priceless necklaces and tiaras that had long since tarnished or lost gems. Like Corbeau, he had immediately seen through the magical smokescreen that made the Tussocks look like a wonderland of cobbled streets and quaint cottages with an ivory castle on a hill.

Oddly, no-one seemed surprised that he was there at all – a lone Vampire carrying a Faie child who was drowsing in his arms. In fact he was largely ignored. Once in a while, one of the Lords would bow regally, though without really looking at him, and his Lady would curtsey. However, after a few minutes, a group of young Faies about Picus' age, who were standing outside a smoky-looking inn, stopped talking in order to watch him pass. Picus noticed that one sloped off down a muddy alleyway.

Ruby was still muzzy with sleep in his arms but he managed to get her to show him roughly where she lived. After some searching, he eventually came to a hole in the ground, about half his height, with a tuft of grass for a door and a harassed-looking Faie female sweeping dirt from the doorstep.

'This is it,' said Ruby without much enthusiasm, and slid from his arms. She went indoors without glancing back, ignoring the Faie who stopped her sweeping and looked fearfully at Picus. Picus stood there feeling a bit foolish. When she saw he wasn't armed, she shrugged and continued with her housework.

Picus was stumped. 'Um, is this your child?'

'That's our Ruby yes. 'As she been bad then?'

Picus was not that shocked at her apparent indifference. He had heard that Faies were notoriously careless with their own children, though strangely kind, if they had a mind to be, with the ones they stole.

'No, she hasn't been bad at all,' Picus sounded indignant to his own ears.

The Faie woman looked back down. 'Why are you 'ere then?

---

[14] [Translator's note] Their equivalent of Vampire Karls and Ducesas.

Do youz want to buy 'er?'

'Not especially,' Picus replied. 'She's been attacked by Grigs. I brought her back. She's got cuts ...'

'Yes, I saw,' the woman interrupted, 'thems'll heal but I don't know the magic that'll stitch her best frock up as new, do youz?'

Picus thought about it. 'No, I don't. But hadn't you better have a look at her? To see if she's alright?'

'She's walking, she's fine,' Ruby's mother said curtly.

Picus rummaged in his pocket and pulled out a nugget of gold he'd been saving. 'Here, this will buy you all new clothes ...'

'No thanks.' If she swept that spot anymore, the stone would wear away.

'Oh.' Picus stared at the nugget, turning it in his hand.

Realising that he wasn't going away, the women stopped what she was doing with an audible sigh and looked him in the eye for the first time. Picus immediately saw the resemblance with Ruby; she had once been a pretty little girl with favourite toys who liked games. She put a rough hand on her hip and arched her back with a grimace. 'Look, Mr Fancy Vampire, I am't sure what's been going on but it seems to me that you've helped our Ruby out of a spot of bother and I'm grateful for that, I really ams but I'se got fourteen other children to worry about as well as that girl an' if she keeps running off in'ter woods alone, then that's 'er lookout.' She paused. 'But thank youz anyway and sorry for your trouble. Little missy will be staying put for the next few days, so she won't be bothering you again. I'd offer you something to drink but we've got nubbit but rain water.'

Picus immediately stopped feeling cross with the woman and felt sorry for her instead.

'Look,' he said, holding out the nugget again, 'I can afford it, I really can ... and I'm sure it will help.' He stepped forward and put the gold in her hand before she could react.

'Ahem!' someone cleared his throat behind Picus, who turned around slowly. 'Blood Thief!' a large Faie in stout boots stood close by jabbing a stubby finger in his direction. Behind him a troop of guards carrying an array of mis-matched swords at the ready fanned out left and right, blocking any escape.

'Yes?' Picus arched an eyebrow and did his best to keep his features neutral.

'The Faie Queen Mab requests your immediate presence in her court. Come quietly, or I have orders to clip your wings … and to hit you with *this*,' he added after a moment's hesitation, holding up a large club that looked like it had once been part of a Troll's arm. He waved it about a bit. Picus looked around. He knew he could probably fly straight up and make for the safety of the trees, but he wasn't sure if one of the Faies was carrying a bow.

He shrugged. 'Certainly,' he said, bowing slightly. 'Lead the way, chaps!'

Queen Mab, slumped in her litter, was dribbling slightly – something she always did when she got excited. A servant stepped forward and attempted to dab her chin with a cotton hanky but she pushed him away impatiently and fell back to gloating.

She couldn't believe her luck.

The Vampire before her was a fine specimen, a very fine specimen indeed – young, good length of limb, well-developed wings but – best of all – those teeth! Ever since she was a girl she had loved the sight and the smooth feel of teeth. Long teeth. Vampire gnashers.

More dribble. She wiped it away herself, only half succeeding in stifling a girlish giggle. 'What,' she did her best to sound imperious, 'did you say your name was again?'

'Er, Picus,' replied Picus, looking coolly around the chamber. He noted the pile of gold and precious jewels at her feet, some court Faies lounging around the outer fringes of the room and a group of Pigsies – some sort of embassy, he assumed – watching the proceeding disinterestedly with bloodshot, drunken eyes. 'I am Count Brasov.'

So it really was him! The exiled Vampire! What a turn up. And he was hers and no one, least of all the Clan he was from, would look for revenge if that Corbeau Strigoi had been telling her the truth. A disgraced Vampire, cast out, had no friends and – importantly – no one to avenge him. She hated the Blood Thieves though she had a healthy respect for them and feared their revenge. But she'd got this one without any help from Raben's sly son. After she got those teeth he could have him. And Raben would then owe her for this and she'd make sure he paid up in full when the time was right.

Queen Mab, the Tooth Fairy, nodded her head to where two of her lieutenants stood by the door. They dashed forward, and one made a show of whispering in her ear while she pretended to listen. She turned back and glared at Picus who met her gaze levelly. 'Why are you here?' she demanded.

'One of your kind, a Faie child, was being hunted by Grigs. We, er, bumped into one another. I thought it only right to escort her to safety, back here, amongst her own. I apologise if my arrival has caused any upset. I crave your good graces and without further ado, I'll be on my way.' Picus turned as confidently as he could but found his way out of the burrow blocked by a sea of silent Faies. Queen Mab tutted.

'Oh, no no no nono. That won't do, won't do at all, no no *no*.'

Picus turned back to face the litter where she slumped her immensely fat form. 'But I have saved one of your own, and now I wish only to be on my way.'

'I have news from the Faie kitten, Ruby. Before she died of her wounds, just a few minutes ago, she accused you of being her attacker! You attempted to feed from a defenceless child, then bought her here to claim a reward for saving her! Is there no end to the evil Vampires do to peace loving Faies? So what say you Picus, *Count Brasov?*'

Suddenly Picus stopped feeling his feet and in his ears a strange buzzing sound started up. He tried hard to concentrate, despite the shock of what he had just heard. Ruby dead!

'I'm waiting,' the Queen drummed a dirty fingernail on the arm of her throne.

He knew in an instant that he wasn't going to get out of there alive unless he did something immediately. He whispered the Song to himself and prepared to slip into the Shadow World. He knew he'd sworn not to, but desperate times meant reckless solutions.

Nothing happened.

He tried it again. This time, in the corner of his mind he heard a heavy door slam. Picus tried to conjure up a flock of crows. He'd heard that Faies were terrified of these birds. Far away, across the empty fields that surrounded the Tussocks, he heard a squawk but that was it. The Faies crowded around him and, as if in on the joke, they all started to make crow noises, screeching in silly voices, flapping their wings, pretending to peck him. Picus looked up and saw a half-smile on Queen Mab's face.

'Child, you attempt your conjuring tricks here! You use our Faie magic against US? What next, a white rabbit? Saw yourself in half! Oh, I don't think so. The only person doing the sawing will be ME! But first I'll have your teeth, those lovely gnashers will look perfect dangling from my delicate ears.' She made a show of looking outside. 'It's late. He is guilty of murdering the kitten Ruby, and will be punished. Take him away. The ceremony will start at sunrise and I need to prepare! I need a bath and something to eat … Grig liver pie and a dove's coddled brains, I think …'

Queen Mab was raised up on her litter with great difficulty and carried out of the court, as the rest of the Faies crowded in on Picus, binding his wings and arms, pushing, biting and scratching until he fell to his knees. A heavy blow fell on the back of his head, stunning him just as Queen Mab was carried by. She smiled and waved coquettishly as another blow was dealt and he blacked out.

It felt like he was falling down a deep well backwards, arms grabbing at thin air. The last thing he saw, as if looking up at the world through a long tube, was the Queen's leering face. His vision blurred and, as he slipped into unconsciousness, her face morphed – eyes first, then hairline, nose and finally teeth. Mother.

It was as if his years in exile had never happened and he was back in the Gathering Room.

She stood before him – her narrow Vampire face, fashionably caked with chalk powder, lips rouged and livid. 'Do it!' she screeched.

'Steady on my dear.' Picus turned his head, re-remembering each detail of the scene. 'He is too young.' It was Picus' father, dithering in the doorway to the cellar, wringing his hands and hardly daring to meet the Ducesa's eyes.

'You stay out of it!' she whipped around with a snarl. 'If you don't have the stomach for this, then why don't you scamper back to your precious books!' His father momentarily looked like he was going to bolt, but in the end stayed put. But he refused to meet Picus' imploring look. His father had never stood up to his mother's rages before, either for himself, or, indeed, his only child. It was hardly likely he would do so now.

Picus turned his attention back to the needle-sharp rapier he held in his shaking hand. The handgrip was encrusted with diamonds; intricate silverwork depicted a dragon's face, its wings half-spread, making up the rest of the hilt and hand guard. The dragon's eyes were pinprick rubies and now they glowed red in the torchlight. The blade was thousand-year-old platinum, already slender at the base, tapering to a fine needlepoint at the tip.

The point of the sword currently rested on the neck of a heavily perspiring Sanguine named Becasse. The Ducesa put her face against Picus' ear, so close he could smell the stale metallic odour of her last blood feed. 'Do it,' she hissed.

Picus looked into Becasse's eyes. He'd known the elderly Sanguine since birth, had played on his knee as a child, and had accepted sweets and occasional advice from him as he got older. Very early that morning, in the slate grey light of dawn, Becasse had been caught trying to leave the unhappy household where he had been a servant for the last three hundred years.

Desertion, dereliction of duty, escape – call it what you like – was punishable by death and Picus' mother had decided that Picus, Becasse's favourite, would be the one to pierce his heart and so allow him to bleed slowly to death in the Gathering Room, where blood was harvested. It would be drunk that very evening – still fresh – by the other Clan members.

The point of the sword pricked the exposed flesh just above Becasse's heart. An orb of blood immediately welled up and tricked down onto the stone slab where the old servant lay, untied but paralysed with fear. Picus pressed the blade harder and the blood began to flow freely. Out of the corner of his eye he saw his mother begin to smile triumphantly and step back a pace in order to drink in the whole scene.

This would be Picus' only chance.

He lashed the sword around, intending to throw it into a corner of the room – in protest. However the hilt, slick with his own sweat, slipped from his hand, leaving his grasp too early and slicing across his mother's face. She fell back, clutching her eye with an ear-splitting scream.

Picus had no time to think, and only moments to react. He grabbed Becasse, forcing the old Sanguine, who still seemed petrified with fear, off the slab, and dragged him towards the cellar stairs. He just had time to register the indecision and panic on his father's face as he pushed past his flapping hands before both Sanguine and Vampire were out of the house, clattering down the cobbled road.

※

Picus' head began to clear and he awoke, drifting slowly back away from his unhappy memories to the reality of his situation. He must have been out for just a few moments, as he was only just being pulled from the gloom of the Burrow Court, coming out into the midday light.

Laughing, the Faies hauled him along the wet stony ground and tied him to a wooden post outside; where they left him, guarded by the same lumpish Faie who had arrested him, bleeding and shivering in the rain.

Picus forced his brain to start functioning and had a good look around. He wasn't beaten yet, not by a long margin. But, for now, he waited.

≻∞

Back in the hovel where Ruby's mother had so assiduously been cleaning the porch earlier that day, there was an argument in progress. Normally it was the type of disagreement that was decided by the sort of family democracy where the people who can shout loudest get their way. This time, however, a small but insistent voice prevailed.

≻∞

As it began to get dark, Picus' patience was rewarded. From out of nowhere, two small Faie children ran up to his guard. 'Quick, quick,' they chorused. 'The Queen has broken her nail! She's asking for you!' The guard looked panicked.

'What? Why me?' he blustered.

One of the children, who appeared to be the eldest, rolled his eyes as if it was the stupidest question in the world. 'How should we know? We're just kids. But she's furious,' he added as an afterthought, 'you'd better hurry before she gets even crosser. She said that if you didn't come immediately, she'd let the Vampire drink your blood before she took his teeth away.'

The guard's eyes widened with fear and he shot off as fast as he could.

The boy untied the gag around Picus' mouth. 'That's a really rubbish cravat,' he remarked.

'Very funny. What happened to Ruby?' Picus recognised similar large, round eyes.

'She's fine, the Queen was lying,' her brother whispered. 'Ma sent us to see what we could do. She said to untie you, then we're to hide in the forest.' He jerked a grubby thumb at the retreating rump of Picus' ex-guard. 'Ned won't remember who he talked to anyway. It could have been any kids, we're always playing tricks on him. He likes to hit people with his club and steal their food, so it serves him right.'

'What's your name?'

'I'm Tom and this is Jack, he's got head-lice, so I wouldn't get too close.'

'Thank you both,' Picus said sincerely as Tom loosened his bonds and Jack glared at his brother.

'No problem,' Tom added. 'You saved Ruby. And anyway, we think Vampires are cool. They're our favourite game!'

'Oh,' said Picus, slightly surprised, 'thanks.' His wings were free now. He glanced around the deserted street. 'You two should make yourself scarce. I'll wait until you're out of sight and go the other way, so if they do chase us we won't all be caught. Anyway, they'll follow my scent, not yours.'

'OK!' the boys said in unison, and looked like they were having a great adventure.

'Give my best to Ruby!' Picus added. 'I won't forget this.' But the boys had already gone. Picus flexed his wings. He had one thing to do before he left.

Flying into the audience chamber at full speed, he was relieved to find that the Weres had gone. Instead, a couple of Faie knights dozed either side of the pile of treasure. Clearly Queen Mab had decided that other Faies were far too scared to steal from her or else she would have had someone better guarding it. He selected a large diamond and a couple of emeralds.

He was already out of the audience chamber before the Faies reacted to his presence. He was free! Shooting up, over the hovels and away from the Tussocks, he felt the cool wind on his face and an enormous sense of gratitude and relief.

Queen Mab would be apoplectic about the theft of her precious jewels and the fact that her great prize had got clean away with all his teeth where they should be. He couldn't risk trying to find Lark now, not with Raben and the Tooth Fairy on his tail. There was only one place he could go.

He turned north, towards Angleland.

Angleland is the seat of all natural magic and a lot more besides. Too long have Vampires been absent from its shores.

Chapter 13
Camelan Castle

Picus stood on the beach looking at the sheer white cliff that rose up from the shoreline like a gigantic crust of icing sugar.

It had taken him nearly three Moon cycles to get to the shores of Angleland and the worst bit, by far, had been the crossing. Drifting through squalls for nearly a day on a small fishing boat was appalling. At first he'd been terrified for his life, then he just wanted to die. Eventually, the Trollish fisherman who'd given him passage had threatened to throw him overboard if he was sick once more. Picus had looked at the freezing, greenish sea and kept his mouth clamped firmly shut for the rest of the voyage. The fee had been the smaller of the two emeralds.

Dry land felt fantastic, or at least would do as soon as he stopped feeling quite so queasy.

According to the basic map Orielle had scribbled on the back of what looked suspiciously like an old shopping list, Picus still had about three days travel ahead of him. However, he wasn't holding his breath, as the directions and the distances shown had all been the old Vampire's best guess.

That was one thing Picus could never quite figure out with the Eltern: for all their supposed eccentric ways and lack of attention to detail, they still ran things very successfully. The Keep hadn't been invaded, or even seriously threatened for over a hundred generations and they somehow contrived, without seeming to try, to make sure that none of the competing Clans actually got powerful enough to start a civil war.

And other species seemed to have long since worked out that you crossed Vampires at your peril. For all their guards who fell asleep on duty and left the gates open at night, the Eltern were surprisingly – and habitually – quick to react to a real threat. Picus had lost count of the stories of large Faie invasion forces running through the woods in fear of their lives, having coincidentally bumped into an elite group of Vampire Knights out on an evening stroll before the invaders could get a decent attack off the ground. Once, the Keep had awoken to find thirty heavily-armed Rock Giants lying dead at the foot of the curtain wall. When quizzed, the Eltern had looked faintly bemused and put forward the frankly preposterous theory that they had all cut themselves shaving and bled to death.

Whatever the truth, the mild-mannered old Vampires you saw bumbling around town could react swiftly and decisively to any security risk with startling ferocity. To dispatch a brigade of Stone Giants without anyone noticing took some doing, so most Vampires tacitly agreed they were the best people for the job and left it at that.

Angleland was quiet, green and leafy.

Picus decided he rather liked it as he flitted from one hedgerow to another, occasionally checking his map, always heading due west. It was a couple of hundred years before the discovery of Memory Exception Crystals[15] but the birds and insects generally left him alone. He didn't look or, indeed, *smell* like any food they knew about, so mostly they assumed he wasn't especially edible and ignored him.

Once or twice a silent but heavily armoured ant would block his path, waving its antennae in mute warning, but each time he would avoid a fight by simply flying around it. As for beetles and caterpillars, they all moved far too slowly to be much of a threat; you just had to make sure you didn't fall asleep on a leaf and get nibbled by mistake. Spiders, or at least their webs, were tiresome and the spiders themselves could move relatively fast. Most Vam-

---

[15] [Translator's note] M.E.C.s were first discovered by Boris Gorky who was hopelessly lost, far below the surface of the frozen tundra in Siberia, busy digging for salt. They work in the following way: If you hold the crystals in your hand or around your neck any insect will see you but within seconds of doing so, will promptly forget you are there. Each time it does remember that there is a soft, squashy Vampire to eat in the vicinity, it suddenly remembers something like one of its million or so aunties' birthdays, or that it better make the most of the day as it was going to be dead of old age in half an hour.

pires, by the time they reached their first decade, had learnt that spiders were creatures of habit who always hung out in the same places. If you avoided these, then you were usually safe enough.

As he got closer to his destination, Picus came across more and more Human habitations. This was not the first time he'd seen a house or a fort that had been built by Humans, but he was usually left speechless just trying to take in the sheer scale and vastness of the colossal buildings. Many Vampires laughed at the idea of these beings lurching about with no more magic in them than your average rabbit. In Vampire terms, it seemed as if they'd only climbed out of the trees last Tuesday and quite a few of the magical creatures, besides Vampires, assumed that anything that big and unskilled would die out soon enough, much like the other great-but-doomed-beasts, the Terrible Lizards.

Picus – when he actually got around to thinking about it for any length of time – wasn't so sure. It was pretty much true that Humans were basically baboons who'd remembered to shave but they had achieved a huge amount in a short time and, having made their first contact with Faies and Vampires three thousand years previously, they'd recently shown every sign of being able to get by on their own, without any help from members of the Hidden Kingdom – and very nicely too, thanks all the same.

Picus had a pet theory that the Vampires and Faies who laughed the loudest at these huge booming creatures – these naked apes – were the ones most put out by the fact that their pet project had outgrown them. Picus wondered whether taking back the Sword of Swords, namely Exkylipyr, had almost as much to do with pique as with the practical necessity of restoring the Treasures. That bringing all the Treasures together could restore magic was, after all, just a theory; whereas removing a thing of true power from the Humans did have the advantage of getting one up on the talentless upstarts.

They certainly could build, though.

After two days of fairly hard going, the young Vampire was skirting along the edge of a town near some hills that Orielle had marked as Chillton, or Chillturn, or *something* – he couldn't quite see, as the Eltern had left a jammy thumb print right in the middle of the word. Apparently, the whole area belonged to a local King – a Human called Uffa – and slap in the middle on a flat-topped hill stood a giant citadel made entirely of chalk blocks. To Picus it seemed to rise from its flint foundations almost into space. The castle's stupendous size was only outdone by the way the huge white expanse of soft stone reflected the changing light. Picus had first seen it the previous evening, the town nestled in a soft green hollow between two hills, the castle sitting proud above it. The sun was sinking below the horizon, setting in a fantastic display of graded colours from pale orange to blood red. The castle and its pennants, flapping in the breeze, glowed reflected pink. Picus had never seen anything remotely like it.

Now that he was closer, the following morning, it blazed headache white in the sun, so much so that Picus, with his highly sensitive sight, was sure he'd go blind if he stared at it much longer. He turned away and saw that far up on a neighbouring hill, facing the castle, someone had carved the outline of a prancing horse. The craftsmen had removed the grassy turf and topsoil, cutting down to the chalk. It was at least fifteen hundred rapier lengths long and a thousand high. To achieve the same feat would take Vampires thousands of years, and even then he wasn't sure how they got the proportions so accurate or the horse so realistic.

In short, he was impressed.

Picus was startled out of his reverie by the thunder of real horses as a phalanx of Human knights rode by. By now, he had crept through the long grass that grew around the castle walls and was keeping out of sight between two small rocks edging the road that led to the main gate. The Humans made their customary racket – a tremendous din of chain mail, brass buckles, iron hooves on flint and barked orders. The portcullis of the castle ground open as the descending drawbridge covered the moat. The sound of horses' shoes took on a hollow, wooden quality as the riders disappeared inside, leaving Picus clutching his ears and reeling. Suddenly, his quiet world of the Hidden Kingdom seemed assaulted from all sides by Humans. He had to get out of here.

Not far away, several sets of malevolent eyes watched. They tracked Picus as he flew low, away from the castle and the small town, tracing the curve of the road that ran between the tops of the two hills towards what he thought was the safety of a hollowed semi-cave in the rock.

Faies had long been in Angleland and the Blood Thief's incursion had been noted almost as soon as he landed. For good measure, the Troll who had given him passage was captured and tortured for information as to where Picus might be heading. It wasn't long before news of the Vampire noble who had strayed far from home reached the ears of Queen Mab.

In fact, she was already on to him. After he escaped, the Queen's Weres had spent days and nights tracking Picus, sniffing out a faint scent that grew stronger until they were certain of the direction in which he was heading. Then they sent word to the Queen. Without hesitation she followed, taking with her a small force of Weres and four of her best Faie swordsman. She *would* have those teeth and her revenge for the theft! But also, the closer they got to the Sleeve Sea the more curious the wily old Queen became. Like Raben, she suspected something was up. Picus' route wasn't the route of a Vampire in exile, or one trying to avoid capture. There was something deliberate in it. Yes! The Abomination was on a mission and Queen Mab planned to find out what – shortly before she killed him horribly just for having the cheek to run off like that, spoiling her fun and stealing her bright things.

She had landed on the deserted shoreline with its towering cliffs a few days after Picus. The Weres quickly picked up his scent whilst she negotiated safe passage with some local seafaring Faies in return for a small bag containing what looked like bog-standard house dust. In fact, the 'dust' was the charred and ground remains of a mermaid's heart – a handful of which would calm the most dangerous seas. The Sea Faies were delighted with the bribe and offered her provisions for her journey (which she declined when it turned out to be four heavy barrels of dried fish) and a soft bed for the night (which she accepted with poor grace).

The next morning, well rested, yet making a mental note not to touch dried fish again as long as she lived, the Queen took her small hunting band of Faies and Weres after the unsuspecting Picus. They finally caught up with him at Uffa's castle, tracking him for the first time by sight alone, as he made his way to a vantage point above the town.

They bided their time, waiting their chance to spring a trap. He was clever and dangerous but they had surprise on their side and numbers!

Thousands of leagues away Lark was in a hurry, and she was also confused.

She headed back towards the Keep as fast as she could fly, taking a zigzag route that was far longer but would hopefully put Corbeau off her trail if he was stupid enough to try and follow her when he awoke. There was a good chance that Picus was still in the Fast Tower and she had to get to him, to warn him about Corbeau and the Tooth Fairy. From what Corbeau had confessed to her after he had murdered the Trolls, Picus was in more danger than he could possibly imagine. She'd heard tales of Queen Mab in the Café that would turn a Vampire's hair white. She knew that it would be a risky strategy for her to return to the Keep but she didn't especially care.

However, she was confused because she couldn't shake the feeling that she had been too harsh on Corbeau. The massacre of the Trolls was horrific and uncalled for but as she slipped away into the night, alone save her thoughts, she could see the twisted logic to his actions. Admitting what he had done had taken some courage. And he had lovely eyes. Surely no-one with eyes like that could possibly be all bad?

Picus was equally confused. For starters he wasn't quite sure how to go about finding Exkylipyr, secondly he had an unsettling feeling that he was being followed. Once or twice, in the heat-hazy blue distance, he was sure he'd seen one or several figures slide quickly out of sight as he scanned the horizon from where he sat.

Of course, there was movement all around him: a rotund ladybird making her way up a blade of grass that bent and bridged a small puddle, several bumble bees, as big as Picus' head, weaving their way through the meadow where he sat and the never ending bustle of the Human traffic below. However, none of them actually shied away from his gaze. The very fact that the unknown figures were aware he was looking at them from that distance meant they were Vampires, Faies, or at the very least, some sort of Wight with a spyglass. Picus looked about again and decided that, for now at least, if they came any closer he could easily outrun them.

Picus shrugged and lay back on the cool moss, the better to ponder the problem of Exkylipyr's whereabouts. Orielle had said it was buried in a barrow near Uffa's town. So far, so good. Looking about, though, there seemed little general indication as to where this barrow might be or, specifically, what the thing even looked like. He had the vague idea that the sword was going to be under a lot of earth and that it was going to be leagues from anywhere. For now he was tired and there were too many insects about for his liking, so he dozed through the heat of the day, all the while keeping an eye on the line of trees in the distance where he had seen the movement before.

Sometime after noon, as the strength of the sun diminished, he stirred, forcing himself awake in an instant, and darted like a firefly into a swarm of midges. These billowed upwards in panic (at the news that something with big teeth had just flown into their midst) and then the swarm darted downwards with Picus firmly in their midst and all but invisible, towards a pond bordered with rushes. This was Picus' chance. In the confusion, he peeled off into the rushes and hid amongst their felty tips. The midge cloud, still boiling this way and that in alarm, continued to head off down the hill towards a distant riverbank.

The ruse worked. On the horizon, Picus saw at least half a dozen figures move fast, following the direction the midges had taken.

Confident he'd shaken off his mysterious trackers, Picus, feeling pleased with himself, grinned and headed in the opposite direction to explore at his leisure. During his rest, he'd noticed that the majority of the Humans who left the castle headed along the flint road that ran along the crest of the hills towards a copse of beech trees. Something about the age of the trees and the way the Humans quickened their pace as they approached made him decide to look here for the burial ground. It was a fair way off and hard to fly, thanks to a strong headwind that had begun to blow in hard from the west, carrying the faint briny scent of a vast, distant sea. The last half league was made much easier by the fact that he threw his scruples (and sense of smell) aside and hitched a lift on a passing mule. It was pulling a cart driven by a weather-beaten looking man wearing what looked like a jacket made out of sticks, mud and crows feathers. He also took the opportunity to have a late lunch from the mule's rump.

And then, there it was.

'Wayland's Smithy – cursed place,' muttered the old man to no one in particular and he quickened the mule's pace to a brisk walk. He spat twice and touched an iron amulet on his arm for luck as Picus patted the mule by way of thanks and hopped off.

In front of him, half-hidden by the towering trees, was a long mound covered in grass. Beyond the trees, edging the road, were fields of wild flowers (though not one poppy, Picus noted). Under the trees grew yellow and white primroses; but it was odd how they stopped abruptly in a perfect orb around the pod-shaped mound. On top of and around the mound grew thousands of small grey mushrooms and red toadstools, spotted white. Picus shivered. He understood the Humans perfectly and their desire to pass this place as quickly as possible: there was something twisted lingering about this place; it lurked in the darkness that pooled beneath the trees. The air temperature was unnatural, as if the corpses below the soil demanded coldness.

At first he thought it was another trick of the shadows, the sudden dimming of the ambient light in the copse. Then he looked up and realised that the strong headwind had carried with it a summer storm. The darkness came tumbling across the hills and valleys under bruised clouds, as a few spots of early rain found their way through the green awning above. The ancient burial area and its sinister secrets became unbearable.

Finding Exkylipyr would take courage but, for now, Picus looked about for a way out of the heavy rain that would surely come.

The hunting party left the shelter of the woods. Queen Mab, who had the sharpest eyes in the group, had been first to notice Picus try and make good his escape in the cloud of midges. 'He's seen us!' she cried, shooting an acid glance at the Faies who seemed to crumple under the unspoken accusation that this was probably their fault. Growling with the effort, the Weres picked up her litter and broke cover, running towards the distant cloud of insects. The cloud changed direction and the hunters swerved too, following its swirling progress down the hill to a small river valley.

They had been running for nearly an hour before the Weres began to tire. 'Slow!' commanded the Queen. They only needed to keep the cloud in sight. However, the Queen was beginning to suspect the worst. 'How do we even know he's still there?' she asked no one in particular and therefore received no response besides brief, panicked glances between her Faies. The Weres eased up to a jog, their acid-burned faces remaining as impassive as ever.

One of the Faies, Jack Farr – the most experienced Faie there apart from Mab – shrugged. 'I could always catch up, flush him out?'

'Ha!' yapped the Queen. 'By yourself he'd kill you in a heartbeat. I'd almost let you for the sport of it but I need you all together. We hunt the Blood Thief in a group. They work alone, so packs confuse them.'

'My lady?' It was Tom, the youngest of the Faies and the Queen's current favourite.

'Yes, kitten?'

'Look,' Tom pointed west. No storm clouds were yet visible on the horizon, but the Faies could sniff out the water-laden clouds better than any creature. Then a gust of wind dispersed the midges and the hunters scrutinised the whirling insects as they re-grouped. They looked at each other in mute agreement: the bloody Vampire had given them the slip.

'Damn his teeth! We'll wait out the storm up there.' She pointed savagely to a group of trees on the hill above the valley where they were. 'Once it has passed, we will split up until we find his trace.' She lashed at the nearest Were with a silver chain, barbed with tiny razors at the end. The beast grunted as its blood welled through a deep gash in its hide that was already heavily marked with a latticework of half-healed scabs and white scars. 'GO!'

Queen Mab could never understand the caring ruler. She loved her subjects with such fierce passion that any betrayal or mistake, however slight, would be met with instant white-hot fury. Violence was how she showed she cared.

A while later, they were nearing the trees. It was raining in earnest now; fat-bellied clouds cut out the sun, and thunder, sounding like heavenly indigestion, echoed across the landscape. The leading Were, unable to help himself, suddenly lifted his head and howled at the storm in defiance and in terror. The tempest continued to roll in as the hunters moved deeper into the copse where the trees were thicker. In the centre, in a clearing, was a Human burial mound. The Queen looked at the mound and the profusion of fungi growing there and noted how it wasn't just the storm that was making everyone uneasy.

It got darker as the rain fell harder and the thunder battered the clouds into flight. Suddenly a flash of lightning illuminated the stand of beeches. Jack, who happened to be watching his Queen at that moment, saw her face break into a broad grin.

※

Picus had been sheltering from the rain for about ten minutes, when he felt his whole body stiffen. He detected the faint magical discharge the moment they entered the copse. Faies, at least four of them, and Weres too.

Another flash of light lit up the trees like the skeletal remains of giants. Across a few rapier lengths of grass, through the sheets of rain, Picus saw her.

Queen Mab, showing a blackened set of gums, grinned horribly back.

So that was who had been following him. And he'd underestimated them too, tracking him here to this terrible place, when he was sure he had lost them. He felt his stomach lurch but steeled himself for a fight.

Picus, who was usually at his best when acting alone, using just his instincts, immediately thought of the lightning – imagining the jagged light and the white-hot fire and clapped his hands. Instantly, a bolt of light shot from his fingertips, zipping towards Mab. The horrible sneer vanished in an instant and she ducked just in time as the bolt burnt a black gash in the tree behind where her head had just been.

Picus saw two Weres, their burned faces emotionless and their jaws hanging slack. Without a sound they peeled off to try to outflank him. He concentrated on the storm again but this time only sparks fizzed from his hands as he staggered and fell to his knees, suddenly more exhausted than he had ever felt in his life. Creating something similar to lightning took far too much energy; he had to think of something else. Fast! The Weres now blocked any escape; in the gloom you didn't need to see them, a reasonably good sense of smell was enough. The Faie hunters approached from the front and sides. Queen Mab was holding back, a huge squat figure – like a toad – gloating from her litter at the sport that was unfolding. From where she sat, she had no doubt that Picus was well and truly trapped. 'Still trying to use our magic to defeat us. What's wrong with Vampire Lore? Or has it finally deserted your kind for good?'

Summoning all his strength, Picus now sprang, executing a complicated back flip over the heads of the Weres. They attempted to morph into spiders, mandibles and front legs elongating from their wolf-like features, stretching up to catch him. They were fast but they didn't quite pull off the transformation in time; Picus cleared them, using his wings, corkscrewing gracefully over their snapping half-wolverine, half insect jaws, to land on his feet. He now stood on top of the mound, with a height advantage over his attackers.

But his elation was very short-lived.

One of the Were spiders hurled a large rock at his legs, catching him unawares. He heard a loud crack as his leg snapped just below the knee. Picus cried out in agony and frustration. But with no time to recover, a wall of pure magic hit him square in the face, like a giant lead hand.

He'd stepped into the circle of toadstools but he'd realised his mistake too late. No wonder the Queen looked so confident: Faie rings! This was as much *their* place as a Human burial site. With a supreme effort of will, he tried to drown out the cacophony of magic that now surrounded him. *It was like being blinded, deafened and suffocated at once.* Picus blinked very hard, thought of Art, Lark, and – strangely – the Faie child, Ruby, came to mind. Slowly some clarity returned to his sight as the pandemonium in his head abated. Through tunnel vision he made out a door in the side of the mound, a small glimmer of hope. However, as he half-ran, half-limped there, his leg sending jolts of white-hot pain through his body, he realised that it was sealed. Although Human-made, and therefore huge, there was no crack around the stone frame or keyhole through which to squeeze. It was impenetrable.

He turned to see Mab looking annoyed that the magic circle had not knocked him out cold, as she was probably expecting, and then triumphant as soon as she realised he had effectively trapped himself. The four Faies advanced on him, swords drawn. A perfectly balanced throwing knife flicked out of the shadows and lodged in his shoulder. Picus cried out and summoned just enough energy to conjure a large tree root that swung in the air and hit one of the Faies smartly in the face, before Mab clicked her fingers and the root became a cloud of broken splinters that made straight for Picus. Right, thought Picus, and bared his teeth for the first time at his attackers.

All four Faies stopped dead in their tracks, unwilling to be the first to advance on a cornered and therefore extremely dangerous Vampire. The Queen made a tutting noise and the splinters switched direction and made for the Faies. Picus, one leg and an arm useless, made as if to fly over their heads again, hoping that none of them carried a bow. However, just as he took flight he saw that the Were spiders had been busy and now a large, badly made but effectively sticky-looking web bowed and sagged in the downpour above their heads. It looked like a funeral shroud.

Picus did a rapid calculation. He'd get at least two before they got him, possibly even three, but he knew with a terrible sinking feeling that he'd never manage to get his teeth anywhere near the Queen. Oh well…

Just as he prepared to fight for the remainder of his relatively short life, another bolt of lightening came from the heavens, shredding and setting alight the amateurish web, scoring a direct hit on one of the Faies who immediately erupted in flames. Faies are as terrified of fire as Vampires are of water and, in the confusion, a gap in their ranks appeared. A chink of hope.

Picus saw his only chance to escape. As he took to the air, one of the Weres' arms shot forward and grabbed him. Picus shouted in pain as the broken bone ground against muscle and he kicked out, losing his assailant but also yet another boot in the process.

He shot away from his assailants, and out into the storm.

The friendship between Wink and Picus marked a change in Vampire-Human relationships that would one day save both species.

Chapter 14

Wink

Copper-coloured sunlight poured through the stained-glass window onto where the sickly Human child lay in bed. Propped up, thanks to several well-plumped pillows, he could see out over the gleaming white walls of his father's castle, down the lush green slopes and all the way to the river that ran past the thatched cottages lying snug in the valley far below.

He had been *dreamsailing* that morning. *Dreamsailing* was his own private name for dozing somewhere south of real sleep but just drowsy enough to blank out almost all sounds and light around him. The trick was to let your mind wander (easy enough when you still had a high fever) and thereby flit from dream to dream, as if he was a traveller in his own head. For someone who felt a virtual prisoner most of the time, confined by his sickness to his chambers high up in the Eastern Minaret, this was as close to a true sense of freedom as he was ever likely to get.

Wink was a fragile child and recently had spent a lot of time either ill or very ill. Though his mother and father loved him more than all their lands, their riches and even this beloved castle, Camelan,[16] he would never be the great warlord his father was, nor would he ever have the natural grace of his mother. But he had been born with his father's clever grey-blue eyes and his mother's smile and to this inheritance he had added a charm all of his own. Even if it were not for his father's wealth and power, he would have been popular. Wink had that rarest of gifts – more precious than gold, power, good looks, good health or any of the other

---

[16] [Translator's note] Camelan, meaning 'crooked'. The name was given to the chalk castle by the locals because the Central Tower leant heavily to one side. The reason was the foundations: namely, there were none. Legend had it that the hill upon which it was built had been hollowed out by two dragons whilst engaged in a fight. Both died, their flesh turning to ash and now it was nothing but their massive rib cages that acted as a buttress in holding the hill (and Camelan Castle) up.

things people often think will make them happy. For everyone Wink met instinctively liked him. It was a sort of magic in itself.

Right now he was waking slowly, feeling the fever gradually lift for the first time in days. The white walls and turrets of Camelan stood out noble and strong against the dark blue backdrop of the sky. It had become a symbol of hope in these dark times, whilst the Romans with their legions and their laws seemed to be deserting them – drifting away, back across the troubled seas from where they had come hundreds of years before.

He was still very weak, wan and exhausted by his recent illness. Turning away from the chalk-white brightness outside, he lazily allowed his eyes to follow the clean line of the window frame, all the way down to its ledge. Around the edges, the glaziers had used their cheaper glass. Full of bubbles and minor imperfections, it bulged in places creating a sort of magnifying lens.

Something caught Wink's attentive gaze.

Enlarged by the glass, lying on the worn stone ledge, was a figure of breathtaking delicateness and beauty. Black, mole-like down covered most of its lithe, well-formed body, only turning pale cream around the tummy. Arms outstretched, a pair of dragonfly wings fanned away from its shoulders catching the sunlight in colours of oil on the surface of still water. The creature's face resembled almost precisely that of an exquisite young Human. A pair of eyes, deep blue in blue, snapped open and regarded Wink with sudden knife-like intensity. The two stared at each other for a few moments.

'Hello,' Wink said by the by. 'Are you an angel?'

Picus struggled to collect his thoughts. The Human boy, looming up through the window, was actually talking to him, using the ancient Faie tongue. Come to think of it, Picus had heard somewhere that the Faies had taught their tongue to the Druids who inhabited this isle – in return for certain woodlands to be left wild, a kind of sanctuary for the Faies. Even through the window, though, the sound of his voice was booming. Mentally he turned down the volume.

'What are you?' the boy modified his question to something more sensible Picus thought.

The injured Vampire winced and groaned as he struggled up. He'd been badly battered flying through the storm and the knife wounds hadn't yet had a chance to dry out and heal properly. 'I am hungry, that's *what* I am. I feel as if I've been chewed by someone's pet dog. I probably look as bad as you,' Picus added. 'Are you ill?' He actually used the Faie expression for, *sad because something ails you*. This was because Vampires rarely, if ever in their whole long lives actually got ill. Hence they didn't until recently have a real word for it. The whole concept of *well versus unwell* actually fascinated Picus.

Wink frowned. He could see the angel's tiny mouth moving but he couldn't hear a thing. Then he had a bright idea. Ducking under the bed he rummaged around and eventually pulled up a sort of brass funnel-cum-trumpet that one of his doctors had left. It had been used for listening to his rattling lungs.

Putting it to his ear, he opened the window, nearly knocking Picus off the ledge in the process. Picus, who regained his balance by fluttering his wing tips, looked at the trumpet and nodded: he got the idea. 'HELLO-UP-THERE-MY-NAME-IS-PICUS!!'

Wink reeled back and fell off the bed. 'Alright, alright, no need to shout,' he said looking delighted nonetheless as he clambered back over the goose-down duvet. 'My name is Wink. I am son of Uffa the Warrior King, Lord of everything as far as the eye can see.'

Picus looked around, impressed. 'What, he's King of those clouds over there?'

'Er, actually, no.'

'What about the Sun then?'

Wink looked a bit embarrassed. 'Um, everything on *land*.'

'Is he King of that river?'

'Yes.' Wink nodded enthusiastically – he felt he was on surer ground here.

'And all the fish in it?'

'Yup.'

'But he can't stop them swimming away to the sea?'

Wink struggled with himself for a moment. 'No, he can't,' he was eventually forced to admit. 'Unless he catches them.'

'So he's King of just the stuff on top of a few hills and theoretically some dead fish, then?'

Wink narrowed his eyes. 'How would you like it if I just flicked you off that ledge?'

'Sorry.' Picus knew when he'd gone too far. 'I've just never been able to get my head around this Human ownership fad.'

'Dad said being King is more of an administrative thing. Lots of paperwork.'

'Paper what? Oh forget it.' Wincing through the pain in his shoulder, Picus drew himself up to his full height and bowed. 'If your father is a King, then you must be a Prince – so I am honoured, even humbled to meet you. As said I am Picus, Count Brasov, Vampire. I am at your service.'

Wink's eyes opened wide. 'A Vampire! You can fly about the place at night?'

'Yes sirree.'

'Drinking maiden's blood?'

'That's us – in a nutshell.'

'You can make the sky go dark, read minds, kill giants with your bare hands and go invisible?'

Picus paused. 'Um, not really, no.'

Wink looked disappointed. He held up two fingers. 'So you *can* fly and you *do* drink blood?'

Picus nodded.

'You're sort of like a mosquito then?'

Picus felt stung. 'Now look here –'

'OK, OK, I was only joking!' Wink laughed and Picus got the strong impression that it was something this pale boy hadn't done in a long while. He found himself grinning back, instinctively, liking his new companion.

'May I come in? I notice you've got some bread and chicken

soup you haven't touched and I really am hungry. Obviously, I promise not to drink any of your blood.'

༺

Ten minutes later Picus relaxed on the soft mountainous folds of Wink's bedding as he polished off the first decent breakfast he had eaten in weeks. Wink sat at the other end of the bed, being careful not to lose sight of the Vampire who was his new friend.

'So you could see me through the window, magnified?' Picus said. 'Extraordinary. That's the second time in just a few Moon cycles I've been seen by a Human. Some Vampires go their whole life without talking to a single one of you.'

'Well, I was as surprised as you were. What were you doing up there?'

'Long story,' said Picus. 'Very heroic, though,' he added. Best to change the subject, nevertheless. 'The window pane, then, that's not diamond is it?'

Wink laughed. 'Are you kidding? My father's loaded but not quite that rich. No, it's glass, of course.'

'Glass?' Picus sounded like the word stuck to his teeth.

'Yes. It's made by heating up sand.'

'Yeah, right.'

'Seriously, I've seen it being done. Has to be jolly hot.' Wink shifted his left leg, which was going to sleep, and Picus had to stick out his injured arm to stop himself slipping down and being lost in one of the deep folds of cotton. He yelped in pain.

'You're injured!' Wink looked suddenly concerned.

Picus grimaced, as if to say, *Oh 'tis just a scratch*, then realised that the Human probably couldn't see that from where he was. 'Just a bit,' he conceded.

'Don't worry,' said Wink, 'my dad's personal physician, Ambrosias, is going to be here in a bit to check on me. She's very old and rather clever, I'll bet she could help you too.'

Wink correctly translated the silence that followed. 'It's OK, I'll *order* her not to tell a soul about you. Not that Ambrosias listens to anyone's orders in general. But I've got a funny feeling you two will get on.'

Just then the door burst open and a tall, quite stupendously wrinkly old lady, marched briskly up to the bed. The hair on her forehead was shaved and she wore a silver skull-cap that covered the rest of it. Here and there, she had also tied small animal bones, bits of jewellery and what looked like random lengths of string into the grey ringlets that grew long at the back.

She looked at Wink briefly and tapped the side of the bed with a long, worn staff she carried. 'Appears y' better, young man,' she stated shortly, 'and in consequence, and by that logic – if you are damn fool enough to set anything in store by logic – I've wasted a trip. Ninety seven steps,' she said, 'at my age. Could have done for me!' she gave Wink a sudden shrewd look. 'Seeings I'm here … I'm parched! Got any meade[17] under yer pillow?'

'I thought you'd given up.'

'Balderdash!'

'You said it gave you a dicky leg and your left eye went funny.' Wink smirked.

'Nonsense! What imbecile told you that?'

'You did!' he giggled as the old lady pretended to rummage around under Wink's bed with her staff. 'You said it made one leg shorter than the other and you could only see round objects out of your left eye. Everything square, oblong or triangular was invisible.'

She stopped what she was doing under the bed, stretched back to her full height and looked at her patient with the kindness and wisdom of ages. Picus thought of Art. 'So you really are better. Good! Now,' she said clapping her hands together, 'aren't you going to introduce me to your friend?'

'Who?'

'Why, the Strigoi, of course.'

Bloody hell, thought Picus, Might as well hang fairy lights

---

[17] [Translator's note] Fermented honey, widely drunk before beer took off in a big way. Sticky headache juice.

around my neck. So much for the *Hidden Kingdom*.

She pointed her finger at a spot on the bed. 'My eyes aren't what they used to be but I'm guessing he's sitting right there. He has an injury or two, if I'm not mistaken.'

'Yes, although he was going to be a surprise. And he *is* hurt,' Wink was excited. 'Mum's right, you're not just an old conjurer! How did you know he was there?'

Ambrosias (Picus had guessed as much by now), smiled faintly. 'Oh, well, it's been a long time since our paths have crossed but one never forgets.' She bent down. 'So, how's the Keep keeping, Vampire?'

Up until now, Picus had been uncharacteristically speechless. 'Fine,' was all he managed to say rather faintly.

'He says "fine",' added Wink, thinking he was being helpful.

'Yes, yes! My eyes might be bad but my hearing's still pretty good, thank you.'

'Can you make him better?'

Ambrosias waved a wrinkled hand dismissively. 'Oh, they may be small but they're amazingly robust, practically immortal compared to us. Someone really should find out how they do it, but they don't seem to like being dissected. Anyway, he'll be fine in an hour or two I daresay.' She turned back to her patient. 'Now let us bend our combined intellects back to the whereabouts of this meade.'

Mab squinted up at the towering white walls and snarled. 'Are you sure he's really there...?' Tom trailed off as he saw the ferocious expression on her face. The Blood Thief was in there right enough; she felt it in her marrow.

'What do we do, Majesty?' growled the Alpha Were, now reverted back to his wolf-like form. His voice was so low it sounded more like a distant avalanche than actual speech.

'We wait.' Was Mab's brief reply. She was annoyed that the Were had dared address her directly. She would have to reassert her authority before too long. She turned to Tom, who took an involuntary step back under her glare. 'Do you have the remains of John Baggs?'

Tom shuddered at the recent memory of collecting up his friend's partly charred, medium rare remains under the Queen's supervision. Like all Faies, the thought of being electrocuted to death by lightning made him feel sick and weak all at the same time. Mab was still glaring at him. 'Yes, it's all here.' He hefted the sack into view.

'Gooood,' the Queen purred. 'The sweetmeats can be our supper, the rest we will grind to make magic stronger than the little weasel has ever dreamt of. When he eventually skulks out of the Human citadel, we'll be ready. I'll peel his skin off bit by bit; before he perishes he'll give me everything. I'll have the prize he has come to Angleland for, my jewels *and* his teeth!'

Sickness for Vampires is only really self-inflicted, for example having too much Hot Todd (strong Cognac laced with blood – presumably from someone called Todd). Picus wasn't alone amongst other members of the magical community in finding coughs, colds and tummy-aches a faintly ridiculous concept that just went to show how weak and generally rubbish Humans were. Even their pets didn't get ill as much as they did.

Chapter 15

Waylands smithy

Lark was beginning to suspect she'd made a terrible mistake.

In under an hour of her arriving at her parents' house, dishevelled and dirty from days on the road, they had dispatched a Clan Sanguine to announce her arrival – not to the Fast Tower, but to Picus' parents, the Brasov Clan heads. She'd barely had time to wash and change out of her leather armour and into some hastily cobbled together court robes before she was also dispatched to Vanquish, the house where Picus had grown up, *Seat Majeur* of the Brasov Clan they both belonged to.

Picus' father – supposed Clan head – stood by the window, hands quivering, mumbling to himself, whilst his wife – Lark's aunt – stared into the unlit fire, seemingly ignoring her visitor.

She stirred. 'In danger, you say girl?'

'Yes, your son's life is being threatened by the Vampire Raben and a Faie – Queen Mab.' Lark kept her voice low and level, her gaze likewise.

'And why should this concern the Karl!'

Picus' father gave a little start and stuttered something that sounded like an apology.

The Ducesa glared at her husband before turning her attention back to her niece. 'Our son is of no concern to us! You have told me yourself that he is held in the Fast Tower – charged as a common thief.'

'With respect, Ducesa,' Lark hardened her eyes to show that the respect in question was strictly limited, 'I believe that it is in your ... *our* best interests to care. Picus is your only heir and will one day head the Clan. If he is in danger, then he should be warned. Let me go and tell the Eltern myself. If he is guilty of common theft, as you say his is, then they would have announced it by now, at least to you and the Karl. No such thing has happened.'

The effect of Lark's words was immediate. 'Impudent slip!' the Ducesa shrieked, the chalk that whitened her face cracking alarmingly around her rouged lips. 'You presume the Eltern. You presume the Karl! I will have you whipped and your parents punished for this.'

'Oh, I'd leave my parents out of this if I were you.' Lark surprised even herself.

The Ducesa briefly looked like she would have dearly loved to scratch Lark's eyes out, but gained control of herself. Just then a Sanguine stepped forward and handed the Ducesa a note. She scanned it, and smiled. 'Well, young lady, it so happens that you are less value to *him* than he appears to be to *you*, as is so often the case with foolish young girls.'

Something about the tone of her voice made Lark's guts go cold. The Ducesa's cold eyes showed satisfaction. She tried to read the note where it lay on the table but the scroll had rolled back into itself. 'How so?' was all she could say.

'It appears that Picus has embarked upon a fool's errand without you, but one which will most probably, if played right, be of some benefit to us all. I intend to see that the game that is now afoot is played with consummate skill.' She turned to the Sanguine. 'Bring our friend in!' she ordered. She turned to Lark with a sickly smile. 'As usual, Picus is off chasing riches that do not belong to him. This is clearly intelligence that he has avoided sharing with you, his supposed friend! There have been rumours lately from the Fast Tower that the Eltern are seeking to unite the Seven Treasures. They are fools, of course.' The Ducesa's voice raised an octave or two. 'Magic is no longer the currency of this miserable ball of mud and rocks, this beleaguered orb, our Earth – but Cunning and Wealth, for only these two lead to real power. The Humans show us this daily. I have cunning enough for everyone in this Clan. If this treasure is what I suspect it is, then we will soon have the wealth to topple those old men, the Procrastinators, those fools up there on the hill!'

Lark, who had been staring at her feet, was still trying to come to terms with why Picus had run off without her and she barely registered the treason against the Eltern that the Ducesa was advocating. What was obvious to her was that after he had been released, he had not even sought her out to make sure she was alright. She raised her head, blocking out this uncomfortable thought for the time being. Her aunt's words eventually sank in. 'What are you planning?' she whispered, horrified.

The Ducesa wagged a long finger playfully across the room. Lark noticed, with a certain amount of distaste, that the nails had flakes of what looked and smelled like dried blood on them. 'All in good time.' She almost trilled. There was a heavy tread at the door and everyone, even the Karl, turned around. The terrible old lady's features morphed into a mask of charmed delight. 'Raben, Sir!' she cried. 'How splendid of you to join us!'

Yes indeed, thought Lark miserably, as Corbeau's father clumped into the room. She *had* made a terrible mistake.

Ten days had gone by.

Picus' leg and arm had indeed healed in no more than a day but Wink was still convalescing, getting better by the faintest degrees, that even his mother found hard to measure. To pass the time when Wink rested, Picus had been spending large chunks of his days with Ambrosias. The old woman had an extensive knowledge of Vampires, which surprised Picus, but she would become vague and a bit cagey whenever he pressed her for details of how she had come to make such a firm acquaintance with a species who generally shunned Humans and all other clumsy creatures hundreds of times their size. In turn she quizzed Picus on generalities, such as the state of the Vampire Nation, current affairs of Faie-Wight relations and so on but seemed entirely disinterested in what had bought Picus to Camelan.

Picus was, at present, sitting in the chamber that Ambrosias called her den, browsing through a scroll on practical magic. It was a long and rather boring account of the incantations, the fiendishly complicated and (most probably) unhygienic ingredients needed to make someone fall in love with you. If you didn't poison them first.

Over the past few days of using Ambrosias' library, Picus had formed the opinion that most *spells* relied on one part magical ability to ten parts pure showing off. Some of it wasn't even magic at all, just common sense; like the stuff for curing diseases using herbs that would probably work even if they weren't harvested during a full Moon, with a golden sickle, by a grown man wearing nothing but a long beard.

After his second unsatisfactory encounter with Faies, Picus was deeply troubled, so he asked Ambrosias if she had anything to counteract Faie magic, especially when it was practised in the confines of the Faie burrow. Picus' pride was still smarting over the fact that Mab had defeated him so easily on two occasions. He had even found himself secretly agreeing with Lark: he still had a lot to learn when it came to magic. For instance, he still didn't understand why his magic still had more to do with Faie enchantments than strict Vampire Lore. Happily, by the sort of stroke of blind luck that followed Picus all his life, quite a bit of that knowledge seemed to be contained in this chamber, right here on dusty shelves stacked with parchments made of Bheulach[18] hide, jars of trolls ears in brine (good for clearing up constipation – all that wax), delicate phials of Vampire blood (the nerve of it!), the thigh bone of the first Dragon supposedly to have broken through the Earth's crust, like an egg, to lord over the continents of pre-history and spawn an army of reptilian monsters. Pickled Phoenix eggs, a collection of ill-matched eyeballs in aspic, some jewellery that Picus had cast a professional eye over and pronounced near enough worthless (very much to the old woman's annoyance), and Ambrosias' packed lunch that

---

[18] [Translator's note] A monster or demon spirit, commonly found on the deserted Isle of Skye in Scotland. Sometimes this creature took the form of a man and sometimes that of a hairy beast in search of blood. Horrible to see or hear, it was thought to be the ghost of a murderer or a murdered soul. Either way, like Weres, they had thick hides that Faies – at times brutally practical – made good use of when covering books.

she'd filched from the kitchens earlier. Picus reflected that Art would have loved this place.

Art and Lark! Both had been in his thoughts a lot lately; they would be worrying about him and he had wondered if Ambrosias might know a way of getting a message out – at least to Lark, to let her know he was fine. Art could sweat it. Picus still hadn't forgiven him entirely for tricking him back to the Keep.

Apart from getting back to Lark to make sure she was OK, Picus was in no hurry to move on. He knew that Queen Mab would almost certainly be waiting for him to poke his head out of Camelan Castle, plus he hadn't forgotten his mission. With this in mind, he had a shrewd idea that Ambrosias would know how to get her hands on Exkylipyr. If not, its whereabouts might well be written down somewhere on one of the shelves Ambrosias was rifling through right now. It was just a matter of finding it.

'My material on Faies, y'say? I know it's here somewhere,' Ambrosias was muttering as the chair she stood on began to creak ominously. 'I was looking at it only last Michaelmas … *Minoan Love Poetry*, sounds ghastly, *Cooking Unicorns*, *Trollish Cuisine* hmm, doesn't seem to have got past the title on that one, *Incantations for Dummies* … *Coming to terms with being Sacrificed* … *The Dark Ages Enlightened* … bingo!'

Picus looked up hopefully. 'You found it?'

'Hmm, what's that?' Ambrosias peered down at him. 'No, of course not – I simply said *"Bingo"*, it's a stupid game, rots the mind, very dangerous in my view. I've been trying to suppress it for years but it'll catch on sooner or later I daresay. Ah-hah! Here it is.' She looked very pleased with herself as she held up a crystal casket in both hands. There was a faint hissing sound when she flicked the hasp. 'The library of the late John Thistle, a very august and learned Faie indeed.' She rummaged around and took a pair of silver tweezers from a fold in her robes. Carefully stepping down from the chair, she prized open the lid and used the tweezers to extract an ancient bound tome the size of her fingernail. Perfect for Picus.

'Never been able to get into it myself. But I imagine you'll be able to find what you want.' She gave Picus a piercing stare before disguising it with a benign smile.

Picus was still amazed that Ambrosias managed to communicate with him, apparently with no difficulty at all. However, when Picus had asked how she could hear him, Ambrosias had immediately launched into an indignant but not very convincing tirade about old people never being given a moment's peace, treated like bumbling fools, and Picus was forced to drop the subject. He flew up to the rim of the giant crystal casket. There were hundreds of books neatly stacked horizontally, so when the casket was on its side it acted like a beautifully carved crystal bookcase. The leather covers smelled slightly musty but it was all surprisingly dust free.

Ambrosias seemed to read Picus' thoughts. 'After my dear friend John Thistle died, I sealed his library in a vacuum, the better to preserve the books.'

More Human ingenuity, thought Picus. He read some of the spines in gold-leaf lettering that he recognised. 'It's Elvish,' he said.

Ambrosias nodded, 'Uh huh huh.'

Picus gave her a funny look. 'Why do people keep saying that?'

Ambrosias looked innocent. 'Saying what?'

'Nothing.' Picus shrugged and turned his attention back to the text. His Faie Linear was rusty but he wasn't in a hurry to leave whilst Mab was still loitering outside. Learning more about Faie magic was one thing, he reminded himself, but the goal was still Exkylipyr. Something told him he should keep quiet about the Sword for now – even to Wink.

Time passed and the summer peaked – days fat with sun. The flower heads in the castle gardens were heavy, drooping in the heat, each one a miniature explosion of colour that contrasted with uniform beige of the dry grass. Picus now spent most of his time in the relative cool of Wink's chamber, away from all the insects. Wink was on the mend. The more the two chatted, the more they came to like one another. Whilst keeping the boy company, he was also gradually ploughing through the library. For the first time in his life, Picus was actually learning something on purpose. The more he read, the more he wanted to read. Books and pamphlets were devoured with increasing speed as Picus got to grips with the ancient language. Wink was impressed, and did not seem to mind if all the studying meant he saw less of his new friend.

As Picus' knowledge grew so did his confidence at the thought of facing Mab again.

After a few weeks Wink had actually got up from his sick-bed to be with his school friends, but for some reason no-one – not even Ambrosias – had been able to fathom, he'd suddenly fallen ill again; going off his food, his lungs filling with fever. Picus did his best to keep his spirits up but could see that Wink's latest infection had weakened him almost to the point of being critical.

Even Ambrosias was worried.

No one said anything, but on everyone's mind it seemed doubtful that Wink would make it through the long, cold winter if he did not recover soon. Twice a day, morning and afternoon, his mother and his father would visit him, entirely unaware of the Vampire's presence as he watched them from the rafters. Fear and worry for their only child had affected them almost as badly as their son. Uffa, though clearly a robust man not given to sentimentality, looked drawn and almost ill himself. His mother did her best to be upbeat when they came but Picus, though no great expert on Human facial expressions, could see that these days she smiled only with her mouth. Her eyes already grieved for what seemed inevitable.

Like almost everyone, Picus had grown fond of Wink in a very short space of time and took comfort that Ambrosias, for all her eccentricity, knew what she was doing. If anyone could cure the boy it was her. Then, just as Wink seemed to be making a slow but steady recovery once more, everything suddenly changed.

It was late evening when the boy sat up in bed, sweating profusely, his eyes staring, slightly glassy. He vomited what little supper he had eaten and then fainted, crumpling sideways, as he fell out of bed onto the stone floor of his chamber.

Picus flew out of the room to get help; touching the speed of sound on the straights, weaving through the labyrinth of corridors and oubliettes all the way to Ambrosias' study in order to wake her. When they got back to Wink he had vomited again. This time a thick, green mucus whirled with dark blood. Ambrosias called a nurse, who helped lift Wink's frail body back onto the bed, and then she ordered the King and Queen to be summoned.

Their only son was dying.

Whilst waiting for them to arrive, Ambrosias paced up and down the room tugging at her hair, wringing her hands. 'This is not normal,' she kept repeating. 'Something missed ... in all my investigations ... a turn for the worse, so pronounced, he *seemed* better ... not normal ... not normal *at all*.'

Picus was already finding the combination of powerlessness and anxiety to save his friend almost impossible to bear. 'Let me help,' he said.

The sorceress continued her pacing. 'No, no, Vampire, you care for the boy I know but what's to do that hasn't already been done? But ... *I don't know* ... I've missed something, I feel *sure* somehow.'

'I don't understand.'

Ambrosias stopped and turned to Picus, who stood on the window ledge. 'I've long feared that the Prince's condition is manufactured.'

'How so?'

'I don't know, and that's the truth of it!' Ambrosias exclaimed, throwing her bony hands into the air. 'I've tested for all common sorcery and some of the more uncommon ones too – magic leaves an aura, as you well know, and there's none on the boy. But this sickness, it's too violent, too unpredictable to be down to a mere disease.'

Wink is the son of a warlord who must have his fair share of enemies, thought Picus, as he looked on. If they couldn't get to the King, then what better target than his only son? His death would break Uffa and leave Camelan without an heir. No one to continue the work establishing a kingdom and rule of law in Southern Angleland. The island would be sucked even further towards the abyss where the rule of terror and superstition held sway.

Wink uttered a low moan as the nurse mopped the boy's fevered head, seemingly oblivious to the one-sided conversation the sorceress seemed to be having with thin air. Ambrosias went over and held her patient's hand, staring intently at his face. 'The infection waxes and wanes for no reason, it moves around his body, displays different symptoms on a daily basis, reacts well to one treatment one day that harms him the next.' She stroked Wink's hand softly and said, almost to herself. 'He'll die if I don't get to the bottom of it.'

Picus stood at the window, lost in thought. Something Ambrosias had said flicked a switch somewhere in the hidden alcoves of his thoughts. *Waxes and wanes*. He looked out at the late evening sky, at the slowly revolving canopy of a million tiny pinpricks. It was a muggy, breathless night; the few clouds were dark shadows contrasting with bone-white light from the full Moon.

Waxes and wanes ... its an odd phrase really, wanes and waxes ... never that way around ... funny – Picus felt his mind wandering, something like the *dreamsailing* that Wink had described to him. He recalled a snippet of a childhood song that his mother in a softer, far off time had sung to him. It was called *The Tides*:

> 'All alone, all alone,
> The Moon is made of dragon bone.
> If he is to wax, then I must wane.
> The Countenance will rise again ... '

The Countenance was the old Vampire word for the Moon ... something to do with it resembling a face if you looked at it in the right way ... Picus started out of his daydream. Something had just gone *click*.

'THE MOON!' he shouted it so loudly that even the old nurse, hearing Picus for the first time, turned her head sharply in the direction of the unexpected noise.

'What?' Ambrosias was startled out of her own thoughts.

'The *Moon*. It waxes and it wanes with the tides.'

Ambrosias looked sceptical. 'So what?'

Picus took a deep breath, forcing himself not to gabble. 'I've been reading about this in John Thistle's library. It's very basic magic, practised by Sprites, Wights and some of the more bog-standard-type Faies. Even Humans can master it with a little practise. You just need an item belonging to the person you want to harm, a decent off-the-shelf curse, and the Moon does the rest. You wouldn't have picked up on it as it's not magic, as such, no more so than wishing someone bad luck or walking under a ladder, or seeing a black cat. But I've read that it's very effective, as long as the person uttering the curse has a great enough sense of grievance and a bit of patience. Somebody must really hate Uffa.'

Ambrosias looked grim. 'Hmm ... unfortunately that doesn't narrow things down. Uffa's trod on a lot of important toes to get where he is today. As I did to put him there.' As she said this, she dashed to the window to look at the Moon, ran back and gently peeled back one of Wink's eyelids. She shook her head and felt briskly along the length of the boy's body, all the way down to his feet, then sat down heavily on the edge of the bed, counting rapidly on her fingers. Slowly her expression changed.

'You might well be right! The Moon cycle. Every twenty or so days the boy seems to get better. Just when everyone starts to hope he is finally getting well, his condition worsens as the Moon gets fuller and exerts more influence on the Earth. It's been under my nose all this time ... I am a stupid old lady and you are a clever, clever Vampire! I only hope we've still got time to save him, but we cannot afford any mistakes, even of it is possible to reverse the curse before he dies. Let me think,' she stared at her hands, speaking rapidly, almost to herself. 'All of this Base Magic is just superstition but the cure must fit the curse and, most importantly, the cure has to be believed by everyone. Now, let's see. The Sun consumes, it requires a flesh sacrifice; the Moon controls the seas. It demands liquid.'

'You mean we sacrifice water?' Picus did his best not to look too incredulous, now that there seemed a glimmer of hope.

'No no, no! Much more potent than that. Something that your sort should know a lot about. B L O O D.'

'Whose?'

'Who cares? No wait, it's actually rather important, the blood must be of the best quality, pureblood, magical, from a living entity. Dead blood is absolutely useless. Can't be a sheep or one of the lower mammals...' She stopped in mid flow and grabbed her staff. 'I'll be back in an hour, no more!'

'Wait, you can't leave!' Picus felt panic rising.

'Keep him hot!' Ambrosias almost yelled at the poor nurse. 'Cover him up, no matter how much he protests. The Moon is cold – we have to counteract its effects with heat if we are to keep him alive.'

'W-Where are you going?' the nurse looked like she was about to burst into tears.

'The Smithy!' the sorceress cried, already halfway down the stairs. 'I have something of the utmost importance to ask of Wayland.'

Over an hour passed and the King and Queen had arrived only a few moments after Ambrosias had left the tower.

The Queen, Matilde, was unable to hold back the tears as she stood at the head of Wink's bed. Uffa, on the other hand, was furious. Like a volcano, he threatened to erupt at any moment. Even his colossal guards were clearly in awe of him. Pacing up and down the room with the heavy tread of a soldier, he slammed one fist into a mailed glove on the other hand and swore. 'Where is that blasted witch? Damn her, she should be here!'

The bedroom was now crowded with the addition of two of

the Queen's handmaidens, a Christian priest and Uffa's personal bodyguard who stood half in and half out of the doorway.

'Where did she go?' Uffa barked at the nurse for the third time.

Terrified almost to the point of passing out, all the nurse could stammer was, 'The Smithy. She said to keep the boy warm and that she'd be back in an hour.'

'She's needed here!' raged Uffa, 'by my boy's sickbed.'

Wink was looking clammy and grey. Covering him up had briefly seemed to help, and his eyelids had flickered open. In a faint whisper he had asked for water but the moment he had taken a few sips he'd choked horribly, falling back on the bed, seemingly in a coma.

Picus, who had flown up to a wooden rafter when the King and Queen had arrived with their entourage, viewed the scene from above with increasing panic. If Ambrosias didn't hurry up he feared the worst. His friend was fading fast: Wink's lips had now gone blue with cold, although thick blankets covered almost every inch of his body. It was as if he had been drained of blood in the last hour. The full Moon peered in at the window, like a silent assassin.

'I can't feel his heartbeat,' his mother's voice was hardly a whisper, but what she said cut through the noise in the room, silencing the priest and Uffa. 'He is gone from us.'

'NO!' And every head in the room turned to the doorway to see who had just spoken. Ambrosias! She stood there looking utterly exhausted, her hair wild, robes splattered with chalk mud.

In her right hand she held the most beautiful sword that Picus had ever seen.

Barely an hour earlier, Ambrosias had jumped from her mount and stood facing the ancient burial mound. A little further away, three sets of eyes watched her with keen interest. They twinkled, as only Faie eyes do when caught in the Moonlight. If the old woman saw them, she decided to pay them scant attention – she had more pressing matters at hand.

The Smithy was the oldest thing in the landscape by far, older even than the Standing Stones that congregated, as if in conversation, a few leagues away in the west.[19] Ambrosias did not possess Picus' sharp senses but she knew, without any doubt, that untold quantities of Human blood had been spilled here over the centuries in the name of a pick n' mix of gods. It was as if the trees and the grass that grew here fed on it. In Ambrosias' firm view, the Smithy was not a nice spot for a picnic.

Enough! She had a job to do.

She marched up to the stone doorway where Picus had stood a few weeks before, fighting to save his own life as the storm raged. 'Esgusodwch fi!' she called out more confidently than she felt. There was no sound from within. Ambrosias rapped her bare knuckles three times on the stone portal, her hands showing up in the Moonlight, deathly pale, like those of a corpse. 'Deffro hen ffwl!' She cried much louder this time, 'Stir yourself.'

The sorceress listened at the door again. Just as she filled her lungs to repeat the ancient words in the long lost tongue, she thought he heard something. She lent her ear against the stone and listened intently.

From deep within she heard the sound of something shuffling; the eerie drag of rags and bones and dust. 'Hurry up for Pete's sake, I haven't got all night!'

The shuffling sound continued before something metallic chinked against stone. Ambrosias started back from the door. From behind the thick stone there came a low moan, quite possibly the most bereft sound she had ever heard. The heavy door slowly swung open and darkness actually flooded out into the glade.

She fell back, trying to master her fear and uttered the final incantation. 'Lubire este un fel auÁi da.'

---

[19] [Translator's note] Wayland (sometimes known as Volundr) was an ancient smithy, or metalworker, who could not refuse any job, however hard it was, so long as he was offered payment. It would make sense that the job of making Exkylipyr would fall to such a man. Apparently he had also made Beowulf's mail shirt.

Shortly afterwards, Ambrosias, galloping back down the hill on one of Uffa's fastest horses, couldn't rid herself of the feeling that she was actually fleeing.

Wayland – the old blacksmith – had stood at the door of his grave, his body loosely swathed in rags with just his mouth and hands remaining visible. If there was any reluctance on his part to hand over the Sword in his care, he did not show it. In any case he had no choice, Ambrosias knew the command and she had spoken the words precisely. The cadaver's mouth, showing a dry pair of lips and a toothless maw, made a hollow moaning sound, as fresh air from outside was sucked into the stale tomb. He held up his fleshless hands, nothing more now than dry tendons and bones. In his grasp he held the finest object he had ever beaten out of iron and steel. Exkylipyr. The greatest sword in the world.

Ambrosias kicked the mare, urging her to go faster. She knew she had been gone far too long and that it was very likely that the boy was dead. But she'd had no choice, this was the only way he could be sure of saving him! She was now at the castle gates. 'Open the gates this instant or I will draw down a curse from my black arts that will shrivel your heads like dried apples!' she commanded. The guards – recognising the voice and, more to the point, taking the threat seriously – set the great wheels in motion as the drawbridge came crashing down whilst the portcullis thundered up.

Ambrosias skidded to a halt on the cobbles outside the Minaret, flung herself off the horse and dashed up the stairs, carrying the sword wrapped in its shroud from the tomb. The wretched thing weighed a ton in her hands but she hoped that it would behave differently for the one who would eventually wield it tonight.

As she flung open the door and saw the tear-stained face of her Queen, and felt her whole body turn to water. 'NO!' she cried.

Uffa moved forward, his face contorted in anger and grief, but before he could say anything Picus flew down and landed on the hem of Ambrosias' mud-splattered robe. 'Wink's still alive!' he yelled. 'It's very faint but I can hear a heartbeat and his blood moves still ... bloody hell!'

Ambrosias drew the sword and held it aloft in the candlelight. For one heart-stopping moment Picus thought she would use it to defend herself against Uffa who looked murderous, but mercifully stayed put. 'Take the Sword, Vampire, I know that it is what you came for anyway – smelted from the Sacred Cup you call the Chalice by Wayland for the Nosferatu, it belongs to you truly – but in return I ask that you heft it tonight to save this boy.'

Picus reeled. Everyone else looked confused. 'Of course,' he blurted out, 'but I don't know what to do.'

'Take it,' ordered the sorceress, her voice a thundering command magnifying around the chamber 'Quickly! We've no time left.'

Remembering what Orielle had said back at the Keep about the sword's allegiance to a royal blood Vampire, Picus flew up and laid a trembling hand on the pommel of the great sword that soared up in Ambrosias' hands like a huge steel shaft. Instantly his whole world seemed to tilt forward. It must be the magic, he thought, and then came to his senses. The world really was tilting, the weight of the sword had overbalanced him and he was plummeting to the ground.

Suddenly Picus felt the sword go light in his hands and yet to everyone else in the room it looked as if Ambrosias had made Exkylipyr disappear into thin air.

It had shrunk to his size, just as the Eltern Vampire said it should! Picus flicked his wings and banked gracefully upwards, marvelling at how light the huge sword had just become, how it flashed in his hands, perfectly balanced, *exquisitely deadly.*

Ambrosias' commanding voice broke into his thoughts. 'You have the sword, by which you can cure this boy prince. Take it, open a vein and let him drink of your antediluvian blood, for doing so will break the curse on this boy that is killing him!'

Picus didn't hesitate.

He'd suspected all along that Ambrosias had guessed why he might be there and since the first mention of blood he somehow knew, at the back of his mind, that it would be his. In one fluid movement he flew up towards the rafters once more. As he reached the apex of his climb he flourished the sword, letting its keen blade kiss the inside of his arm. Instantly blood sprang out of a perilously deep cut in his wrist and cascaded downwards. A huge glut, that immediately shaped itself into a falling teardrop and, perfectly timed, fell downwards into Wink's half open mouth.

The effect was instantaneous.

Wink's back arched and he let out a piercing scream, as if in pain. A cloud passed over the Moon and something subtle changed in the room, as if it had just moved itself to a warmer part of the castle. Then sweat appeared on Wink's brow and his colour went from blue-grey to ruddy for the first time in months.

The moment his scream faded it was replaced with a series of short sharp breaths, like a swimmer breaking surface on a lake, and then a long sigh as he fell back onto his pillows. After a few heart-stopping seconds he opened his eyes.

Wink smiled wanly at his mother and father and almost everyone burst into tears.

Ambrosias took a step or two sideways, away from the jubilant throng around Wink. 'Pretty showy,' she said gruffly to Picus who was back on his rafter out of harm's way. 'But very effective, I must say!'

The main difference (apart from size) between Humans and those creatures who loosely make up what is known of as The Hidden Kingdom, is an awareness that everything that exists can be spoken to. A Human would no more think of conversing with a cloud or a flower than he would think of sprouting a pair of wings and flitting about in the trees.

Chapter 16
battle at the glade

'Amazing!' (the King was saying), 'tiny little creatures no longer than a child's little finger with wings and pointy teeth! Intelligent, you say?'

Ambrosias cleared her throat. 'A sort of mean intelligence, a native wit if you will, rather like a well-trained chimpanzee.' She glanced sideways at Picus who was currently standing with his so-called friend in the throne room for his first and last interview with the great warrior King.

Luckily the King wasn't really listening or Picus would have found some way of biting the old witch. Uffa frowned. 'Well, I promised this Vampire anything he desired for saving the life of my son and I will keep my word. But you and I both know that this sword is probably more trouble than it is worth.'

Ambrosias appeared to sigh inwardly. Uffa had gained power by brute force and now kept hold of it largely through a fearsome reputation and a smattering of diplomacy. Truth be told, he had very little time for magic and magical objects. For a while Exkylipyr had been useful, it was a sword after all, but it worked in ways that Uffa could never fathom, so he'd never really trusted it or used it to the full extent of its powers. He usually preferred a nice heavy axe these days. When she had approached the Vampires for a loan of the Sword, all those years ago, Ambrosias had known it would be more of a symbol than anything else, a rallying point for the various small armies and miniature kingdoms that Uffa was trying to consolidate into one.

Meanwhile, Uffa tried to keep a look of satisfaction off his face. Frankly, giving up the sword Exkylipyr was a small price to pay for his son. He'd known people demand whole realms for less. On top of this, the Sword was a constant reminder of the debt he owed Ambrosias. Worse than that, people always expected it to sort out their lives for them: as if Uffa marching about the kingdom holding it aloft would make the crops grow, fences mend themselves, nasty children behave. Uffa was a big believer that people had to learn to do things for themselves.

Granted, it *had* been useful for a time, a sort of mascot, just the talisman he needed. But he could no more perform magic with it than he could sprinkle fairy dust and play the harp. His warriors, battle hardened though they may have been, were as superstitious as old ladies. Having this supposedly deadly sword that had been forged by the gods was good publicity, nothing more – just like this castle, in fact. Camelan was hopeless for all practical purposes. Whoever heard of a stronghold made entirely of chalk stone, one that a mere child could crumble with his or her bare hands? As usual it had been Ambrosias' idea, easy to build the thing with such soft rock – nice and high on a hill for show. He had to admit on sunny days it did look pretty impressive, all white, a blindingly obvious symbol of goodness; but on rainy days he feared half of it would be washed away. In just a couple of generations Uffa supposed that the whole lot would have eroded to no more than a few earthworks and a legend. That nag carved up on the hill would be there longer! But for now it served its purpose – a beacon of beauty in this savage, lawless world that Uffa had made his life's work to civilise … What was that? The old conjurer seemed to be saying something. Again.

'Picus, the Vampire, relays to me that you have earned the friendship of the Keep for your generosity, Sire.'

In response to this, the King bowed – somewhat ironically. He couldn't for the life of him see what these little creatures, smaller than field mice, could do for him. He supposed they must be something like these Faies the common folk made up stories about. His great-grandfather, Uther, had apparently parlayed and made truces with the elfin folk, but he'd never really bothered much with them. If there were any of the little blighters about these days, then they had clearly decided to keep themselves to themselves and that suited Uffa just fine.

'Tell the little fella that if there is anything I can do for him, then he need only ask. The Queen and I owe him our happiness and the future of the Kingdom.' Uffa meant this sincerely.

Ambrosias tutted. 'Tell him yourself, he does speak Anglish you know. His people invented it.'

'What? Yes, of course ... so you've said ... where is he?'

'He's down there.' Ambrosias rolled her eyes as if her patience was being stretched to the very limit by a badly behaved puppy, then pointed at the spot where Picus stood, holding Exkylipyr.

Uffa nodded, faintly embarrassed, in the general direction the old woman had pointed. He'd better be there, Ambrosias could simply be making a fool of him, inventing imaginary magical folk. He wouldn't put it past her. Uffa smirked at a priceless story he'd heard about the sorceress: she'd once persuaded a rather pompous ruler of a neighbouring kingdom to walk about with no clothes on for a week, not a stitch, and in the middle of winter! She had convinced the poor man that he was wearing a magnificent suit of ermine and silk that only very clever or wise people could see. Uffa wondered what this king had done to offend Ambrosias. For his part, he'd always been very careful to treat the old woman with respect.

Behind him a courtier coughed politely. Uffa looked up from his musings. Everyone seemed to be waiting for him to say something. He stirred himself. 'Ahem, humph ... yes ... YOU MAY LEAVE! GO WITH A KING'S BLESSING AND A FATHER'S GRATITUDE!'

As Ambrosias left, presumably with her little friend in tow, Uffa sat back in his throne with some satisfaction. That last bit had sounded rather good.

Cheerio, Wink!' Picus hovered a few rapier lengths from the boy's nose, pleased to note that most of the colour had now returned to his friend's cheeks.

Wink looked downcast. 'Will I see you again?'

Picus shook his head. He badly wanted to say yes, but he didn't like to make false promises. 'You will, if I have any say in the matter ...' was the best he could do. He paused. 'But I really don't know when. I've got quite a few things I need to do when I get back.' For some reason he had a panicky feeling about Lark, as if she was in trouble. He kept telling himself that she could easily look after herself, better than him, but the nagging feeling in his gut wouldn't go away and, if truth be known, he was itching to return. He'd learnt to rely on his instincts over the last few years and something was telling him that he was needed urgently back home.

Wink turned up the corners of his mouth. 'We'll miss you,' he said. 'Um, *I'll* miss you.'

'Well thanks for not squashing me on your window ledge.'

'Thanks for making me drink your blood! I still shudder when I think of it but I guess it did the trick or else I wouldn't be here.'

'Don't be so squeamish. A second cousin of mine once bit into a boil by mistake. Apparently he still gets nightmares.'

'Goodbye Picus. I have a feeling our paths will cross again.'

'Well, I hope so!' the Vampire called out, circling the room one last time before darting down the stairs, his wings a blur.

Picus found Ambrosias waiting for him at the foot of the Minaret. He hadn't seen her for a day or so, but he'd half expected she'd pop up before he left Camelan.

'Be careful of that sword, young Vampire!' Ambrosias said sternly. 'In Human hands it's a mere bauble most of the time, but it was forged for Vampires and I strongly suspect it will work quite differently for you. Get it to the Eltern as soon as you can!'

Picus nodded, 'I will,' he said, and he meant it at the time.

Ambrosias nodded, as if satisfied. 'Do you know why they let me have it?' She asked suddenly. 'I'll tell you. It was to get it out of the way. They're a wise old lot those Eltern and I think even they recognised that it's a dangerous tool – too potent for them until the time is right. Well, I only hope that the time is right and that their need justifies combining the Seven Treasures. For that is what they are doing, is it not, small Vampire?'

'Um,' Picus squirmed, 'if you know so much, then you probably know I can't say.'

'Hmm, yes, I suppose you have been sworn to secrecy and a lot of other rubbish besides. Well, good luck!' she said stoutly.

'Thanks, Ambrosias, thank you for everything ... but,' Picus couldn't help himself, 'can I ask you something?'

'Of course.'

'How come you know all this stuff about us and ... er, a lot more besides?' he finished, rather lamely.

At this the old witch stopped looking so serious and laughed. 'I suppose you've a right to know! Well, now, there's no mystery. It all seems so long ago. Not for you but for a Human I am very old indeed: I was the youngest daughter of a rich senator, a true Roman, and servant of the Empire. We travelled widely and I met many people and saw many places before I was your age. And everywhere I went I noticed things. Strange things, odd people, *odder* creatures that I quickly realised that my parents and my siblings could not see. I had a gift of sorts but I also had the sense to keep it quiet until we came to Carpathia and I met my first Vampire. We are entering into a period where Humans who possess any magic, particularly women, I'm afraid to say, are considered a dire threat and risk persecution for it.'

'Who was this Vampire?'

'Hibou was his name and a kinder truer friend I will never have. He recognised my ability and travelled with us for two years. He taught me everything I know. When my parents died of fever I slipped away and went back to Carpathia and spent more time living near Vampires from the Keep, conversing in secret with your Eltern. They, at least, recognise the value of the universal language that speaks to everything. Most call it magic but it's just a form of conversation. When I left I wandered for a bit and eventually found myself on this beautiful yet flawed island, this jewel in the sapphire sea, just as it was being deserted, left to mayhem by my former countrymen. I said to myself, I can do something to help them! So I went back to the Keep, borrowed the Sword and used it to do the first bit of good I think that lump of steel has ever achieved since it was cast in the belly of the Chalice!'

Picus took a while to process what she'd just said. 'I guess that explains a lot,' was all he could think of saying.

Picus thought that he would have a better chance of avoiding the Faies if he moved under the cover of darkness. This was, of course, assuming they were still there. Part of him hoped they weren't but he had learnt a lot from the Faie, John Thistle's, library and he was also quietly confident in his newly learned powers should he bump into them.

It was mid afternoon when he left Camelan via a concealed exit that Ambrosias showed him at the base of the Southern Tower. She had offered to escort him as far as Uffa's boundaries but Picus had politely refused. He needed to get back quickly and planned to go at full speed. There was no way his ancient friend would have been able to keep up unless she had a broomstick handy. In fact, even though he was not sure they existed, if they did, Ambrosias was one of the clumsiest people he'd ever met. He'd been watching her preparing concoctions for weeks and had witnessed first hand most of the ingredients ending up on the floor for the cat to taste. It must have been the most magic-resistant cat in the world by now. He shuddered to think of the damage she'd do to honest folk's property (and sanity) flying about the countryside on a domestic cleaning product. All things considered, he was better off on his own.

As a precaution, Picus waited for nightfall in a stand of oaks, noting, with mixed feelings, that the cloud cover was thick and what little light there was stopped dead under the foliage where it was dark as a cave. He shivered, wondering, and not for the last time, if he'd ever learn to relish the night the way his kind was supposed to, before steeling himself to go out into it. He flitted across country so silently that he startled a bat out on her evening rounds and weaved a path through a group of oblivious rabbits nibbling at the young grass that grew at the edge of a field.

Before long, Picus almost forgot his anxiety in the dark and found himself enjoying being out and about in surroundings that suited his size. If he was being honest, he'd begun to find living at Camelan oppressive – everything Human was so large and imposing – almost daunting. Human faces had most of the same expressions as Vampires but just the sight of someone that huge laughing, their massive nose wrinkling and a giant red mouth drenching you with spit and bits of their last meal was pretty revolting. He'd long since learnt that watching Humans eat close up was a big mistake.

An intermittent breeze lifted his wing-tips and he thought seriously about flying. He'd planned not to until he got well away from the castle, and he was able to travel by day, but it was tempting and the conditions were perfect. The trouble with flying was that it took a lot of attention and Picus wanted all of his for looking out for any traps that Mab may have set. More importantly, it left a magical trace that hung about for days, which any other supernatural creature could pick up follow as easy as a piece of silk thread floating across the countryside.

Instead, he crept slowly through the pitch-black landscape feeling free and happy.

'Death comes.'

Picus, spun on his heel, looking this way and that. Who's there! He was tempted to shout out into the night but no earthly noise disturbed the fields and copses, save the passage of the breeze through the long grass. 'DEATH COMES!' this time the voice was more insistent.

> 'The Elfin folk will stalk your homes,
> Steal your shadow and twist your bones.'

Picus ran towards a hawthorn hedge, the voice now booming in his head, over and over. 'Death comes, death comes, death comes, death comes, death comes death comes, death comes, death comes, death comes, death comes, death comes, death comes, death comes, death comes, death comes, death comes, death comes, death comes, death comes, DEATH COMES, **DEATH COMES, DEATH COMES, DEATH COMES, DEATH COMES, DEATH COMES!**...'

Something over the noise and confusion in his head told him to look up. As he did so, he saw a large black and yellow spider on her web. It hung in haphazard fashion between two stray barley stalks, a couple of holes in its fabric suggesting it was an old web or perhaps just badly made ...

The voice in his head was a warning!

Picus had turned just in time to see the spider dart towards him, its thick bristled legs a blur as a set of suspiciously wolf-like teeth appeared in a face that elongated and morphed into a Were's head. The Were was fast but Picus' intuition of some terrible danger had bought him just enough time to sidestep and then flit deep into the hedge before the Were could turn and charge again.

By the time it had slowed enough to wheel around, the Were had completed its transformation back to its more usual wolf-like shape. Sniffing the air, it identified Picus' scent and plunged into the hedge after him. Picus knew he had to disable the predator before it raised the alarm. Pulling out a long strand of his own hair he started to make rapid stretching and weaving motions. The magic had to work instantly. If I'm in luck, he hasn't raised the alarm yet because he knows I'm close and thinks he can handle me on his own, Picus thought. He had never done this before, still less under pressure, but the hair in his hands had now changed and stretched into a sticky rope-like web; he blew gently through his fingers, concentrating hard and it billowed out like a silk scarf caught in a strong wind. The light, sticky net fanned out perfectly, Picus noted with satisfaction and stuck to the hawthorn stalks that criss-crossed the path. At that moment Mab's Were came barrelling towards him, straight into the makeshift trap. The web caught it square in the face, not only immobilising its limbs but also acting like a gag on its jaws.

Its huge muscles knotting, eyes flashing yellow, the Were struggled in the trap as Picus prepared for flight. He was crouching, making ready to spring, when a Faie arrow flicked out of the trees and pinned one of his wings to a hawthorn branch. Damn! His first instinct was to pull away but he realised that if he damaged his wing membrane he couldn't fly, and his best option for a quick escape from the trap would be gone. As he turned to pull the arrow out, another caught him on the shoulder, and then another on his thigh. Picus stumbled to the ground, swearing and pulling the last arrow from his leg. He heard the unseen Faie cry out, a strange yapping noise similar to a fox's bark. It was answered at once by an identical call to the east and another, very close, to the west. When he'd laid the trap for the Were he hadn't reckoned on Mab's small band working in pairs; he had assumed they would have spread out, so as to cover a greater area.[20] The voice in his head had been a warning but he had panicked and walked right into a trap! Even through the pain, Picus was furious with himself.

Before he could recover, the Were had broken its bonds and charged him. The beast hit him across the face with one colossal fist, ripping the arrow from the tree, sending Picus sprawling.

But the Vampire reacted with blinding speed.

---

[20] [Translator's note] Further reading of Faie texts would suggest that unbeknown to him, Mab had rejected this idea. Firstly because she didn't fully trust the Weres (they'd been getting sullen and aggressive of late) and secondly, she'd rightly assumed that Picus could have easily dealt with any one of them, except perhaps her, on his own. Dealing with a fit Were and a fully armed Faie would have evened the odds. She'd also correctly predicted that Picus would head in the opposite direction to the Smithy, away from the natural Faie stronghold of the mound.

Ignoring the pain from the arrows he spun on his heels, keeping perfect balance, and sank his teeth into the Were's neck. It tasted terrible, making him gag, but he held on grimly as the Were yelped first in agony and then fear of its life, thrashing from side to side. Picus waved his hand and thought hard about heat and light. Energy seemed to well up in the ground around him as the hawthorn suddenly sprang into life, green shoots bursting out of the soil, creating a natural barrier of briars between Picus and whoever was firing the arrows.

Initially it seemed to work and the Were, blood pouring from its huge matted neck, began to weaken and sink to the ground. But a voice Picus had come to fear cut through the Were's weakening cries. 'SLEEP!'

The Queen had arrived. I'll be forced to stand and fight, Picus thought with a mixture of dread and keen anticipation as the Were's blood hit his heart. His pulse raced.

Immediately the growth stopped. 'NOW WITHER!' The fresh green shoots immediately blackened and died back. Two arrows shot into the glade from different directions – the first missed Picus but hit the Were in the small of the back, making it roar with primitive anger; the second glanced off a branch and gashed Picus' cheek. He let go of the bleeding, howling Were just in time to see the three remaining Faies charge into the glade followed by Mab, carried by her Weres on a tilted litter.

Picus called to mind all he now knew. He hit the first two Faies with a bolt summoned from the energy stored in the soil from the sun's heat. The Faies stopped in their tracks, screaming and clutching their burning eyes, faces blistering as if hit with a scalding iron bar. The next Faie jinked, deftly avoiding the bolt, and loosed an arrow at Picus who whispered quickly to the evening breeze, asking it respectfully to blow the arrow aside. Then he called on the stones, in the language of the rocks, and talked to the sharp flecks of chalky flint that littered the ground, reminding them of their kinship with the Vampires who had known them since birth. Instantly they sprang to life and peppered the remaining Faie and Weres with sharp fragments.

Mab watched all of this with a strange look of contempt on her puffy face. She clicked two fat fingers dismissively. 'Oh, enough,' she said in a sort of bored whisper and fished inside the folds of her gown, bringing out a handful of crushed charcoal. Instantly the sharp slivers of flint veered away from the Weres and buried themselves in the ground. Mab threw the charred remains of the Faie, John Baggs, into the air with a flourish. A choking black mist appeared, enveloping Picus. He felt his chest contract. His breathing stopped as if a giant fist had gripped his lungs and was squeezing out the air. The pain from the arrows was nothing compared to this suffocating, choking feeling.

Close to panic, he tried to focus as he sank to his knees. Through swirls in the black fog he could make out Mab's leering face watching him stagger about as she looked on with obvious and immense satisfaction. 'Oh my, you've been a naughty boy,' she said.

Spots danced before Picus' eyes and he realised with dismay that he was on the verge of blacking out. He also knew that if he did, that would be it. She would bundle him up and prepare him for torture at her leisure. No more lucky escapes. Three times he had met her and three times he had been so easily beaten!

A new feeling rose up inside Picus. Rage. Thrusting aside his panic, he decided there and then that, at all costs, he wasn't going to die here, he had to get back; he had to find Lark. He had to return Exkylipyr.

The Sword!

NO! Cried a voice in his head – the very same that had warned him of the impending danger. But he ignored it. Using all his remaining energy, he brought his uninjured arm over his back and drew the weapon, which was strapped securely between his wings. Almost as if it recognised him from the night in Wink's chamber, the blade sang as it carved through the night air, cutting aside the choking mist like a widow's veil being sliced in two.

It had been years since he had wielded a blade in anger, not since that night in the Gathering Room; but decades of practice with the best tutors, the thousands of hours of sparring and the natural gift for swordplay that resided in the fantastically complex helix of genes all Vampires were born with, sprang to life in a heartbeat. And Exkylipyr instantly worked its own magic for its new master. The arrows that pierced him were pushed from his flesh, the bleeding stopped and his chest sucked the fresh night air into his lungs.

Picus had never felt so good. He had never felt so much righteous anger either.

The remaining Faies had drawn their own swords and now ran towards him. Picus waited until they were a microsecond from gutting him; allowing each razor-sharp blade to come less than a hair's breadth from his exposed body.

Only then did he move.

Exkylipyr seemed feather light in his hands as he rolled his wrist, setting the blade in a tumbling motion like a majorette's baton. It tore through his assailants' defences, slicing through the steel, heavy armour and flesh with almost no resistance. Picus pirouetted, hacking off one of the Were's arms at the shoulder, decapitating the lead Faie and slicing through the torso of another Were. He moved his head back a fraction, allowing the third Faie's sword to pass under his guard – so close that there would have been scant room to run a silk scarf between the tip of the blade and the pulsing artery in Picus' neck. The Faie blade stopped dead as the Vampire straightened his arm and struck out. All the while, he could see Queen Mab, moving as if in slow motion, fist bringing up another handful of the Faie's charred remains. At the same time Picus' lunge found its mark and penetrated the Faie's platinum breastplate, through flesh, pushing between his ribs and into his heart that stopped beating the instant Exkylipyr's steel tip punctured it. Ignoring the death of one of her most trusted knights, by now Mab's fingers had released the ash. It billowed up, a swirling pillar of noxious gasses that twisted and solidified into the trunk and neck of a blackened and insane beast – a reptile, part primitive dragon, part dinosaur that tilted its cobra neck backwards, preparing to strike at Picus.

The Vampire did not hesitate. Flying in a complicated twisting manoeuvre, Picus ran the tip of his deadly blade from the base of the dragon's thorax to where its grizzled throat joined the lower jaw, spilling the monster's windpipe, fire-making organs and still-beating heart onto the dirt. The dragon's roar was silenced as Picus sliced through its voice box and its thick trunk crashed to the ground.

The Queen watched his progress with growing alarm, realising too late that she had to react. Still in the air, Picus now came down at her like the Final Judgement and drilled Exkylipyr through the top of her skull.

She died in an instant.

The night became still once more, stars shone down coldly, leaves moved in the breeze, and a fox barked.

Picus' first feeling was that of joy: Mab was no more; he'd killed his mortal enemy! Then he turned to look around the clearing. At the Queen's bloated corpse lying with the ragged, bone-splintered hole in her head, blood beginning to ooze from her ears; at the twitching Weres; and at the beheaded Faie's heels, who'd only just stopped kicking a *danse macabre* on the bare earth. Picus felt sickened to the core of his soul.

Death came.

Picus staggered back, sword trailing in his hand, and then turned and ran from the horrors in the glade.

With nearly all magical creatures who can pull it off, flight has more to do with how that creature is feeling than with pure aerodynamics. A depressed Vampire can hardly muster the energy to scramble along the ground from one blade of grass to another, let alone fly.

Chapter 17

Wandering

Over a thousand leagues away, Lark tested the strength of her bonds – grimacing as the silver cables cut into her thin wrists, and blood began to trickle down her arm, falling onto the stone tiles with a faint *pat*.

From a hidden gallery, Corbeau watched her closely. His features, illuminated by the single spiderwax candle that spat and guttered in the corner, were almost impossible to read. In recent weeks his skin had seemed to pale and his cheeks hollowed, so that he looked a lot older. However, a new light burned deep in his eyes and those who knew him well now saw shades of his mother's sickness swirling in each dark iris. Even his father, Raben, could no longer look at his son directly without feeling a deep sense of disquiet.

Lark was as close to despair as she had ever been. As the Sanguine, Drontie, had helped Raben tie her to a wooden crossbeam he had whispered the news that Picus had been asked to carry out a mission for the Eltern. The Ducesa had not lied. A friend of his, a guard at the Keep, had escorted him to the edge of the forest but had seen Picus turn back, effectively desert his mission. This meant that he was at liberty, somewhere near. But, if that was the case, why he hadn't warned her of the danger of coming back to the Keep? Nor had he come for her here. She tried to quell rising panic and the feeling that she had been abandoned by her only friend. She was lost.

Picus, too, was lost. He drifted aimlessly for days, still in shock, not eating and barely sleeping. He hardly even thought: each time he tried to arrange his thoughts, an image of the blooded corpses and the carnage he had wrought with his own hand returned to him and blocked everything else out. If he closed his eyes at night, he dreamt of rivers of gore.

His feet carried him south and east, making a vague line towards the coast, although his mind still wandered haphazardly.

On the fourth day after the battle he encountered a dead rabbit, its half rotted body lying across a deer track. Picus listlessly heaved away the maggots, using his bare hands, and fed on the dead blood, not caring if it tasted putrid. Later, he approached a group of Stone Wights who were digging for semi-precious metal in a chalk pit. They became agitated by this wandering scarecrow who muttered to himself in a language they only half understood and they threw rocks at him. Though the rocks struck Picus on his head and shoulders he continued to stumble towards them, so they picked up their picks and shovels. In response, Picus bared his fangs, making the foreman Wight step back in fear. Then they noticed Exkylipyr, still covered in blood, hanging from his back. Still in a daze, he wandered on, then stopped. The Wights, standing about a head shorter than Picus, cringed in fear now as he walked back towards them. Their terror, though, turned to amazement when Picus handed the foreman a diamond the size of a fist and a deep blue sapphire. As soon as he had got rid of the last of Mab's treasure he felt somehow lighter. Picus smiled grimly to himself. Somewhere between the blood-filled glade and this deserted landscape he'd lost his taste in trinkets and perhaps thieving. For good.

Still, he could scarcely summon the energy or the enthusiasm to fly, so he walked along a Human road that ran over the top of some wind-blasted downs, and seemed to take him in roughly the right direction.

When he thought about the murders back in the glade he felt panicky, sick and terrified. Picus was still just a Strigoi and right now, most of all, he just wanted the comfort of his mother. No sooner had he thought this than he felt like crying and laughing hysterically at the same time. To crave the comfort of the one person he knew to be incapable of giving it seemed at once both funny and unbearably tragic.

The landscape, in keeping with his mood, was resolutely barren. Day after day he saw not another soul apart from the Wights. He was surprised, then, to be woken one night by the tramp of several dozen feet. Picus carefully lifted the corner of the dock leaf he was sheltering under and looked along the weather-beaten road. Coming up the hill was a company of Roman soldiers, marching in a closely formed block. Their faces, cloaks and armour shone eerily silver and white and Picus realised that they were spectres of soldiers who died many years before. As they marched past, short swords slapping against their thighs, the young Vampire was surprised to see their huge shadow-bodies veer around the spot where he lay – like ants avoiding an obstacle – to reform after they had passed. The countryside behind them was unpleasantly visible through their translucent bodies.

Before he drifted back off to sleep, Picus wondered idly what their fate had been to all end up as ghosts, silently marching across the chalk downs each night. Two days later his question was answered when he came across the scene of a small battle. The area was strewn with rusting armour, broken swords and spears – and the gigantic remains of Human skeletons, half covered in couch grass, grinning at him as if their violent deaths were all one great joke. The horror of the glade still very fresh with him, Picus took to the air in terror at the sight of this ancient carnage, simply to get away and as far from it as fast as possible. He flew until nightfall, eventually collapsing, exhausted and emotionally drained, into a boggy ditch where he slept soundly for the first time in days, until dawn.

The sound of crashing waves woke him.

Shaking the freezing dew off his wings, Picus stretched and looked out over the cliff at the great expanse of blue and at the start of the end of his journey home: a childish smudge of land on the horizon. He sucked the juice from some sloe berries growing nearby, grimacing at their bitterness, and then flitted slowly down the sloping rock face towards the deserted beach.

About halfway down, something made him pause. Here and there the face of the cliff had fallen away in huge slices of brittle grey rock, which had shattered on impact with the ground to form the shale upon which he walked. What was left, scattered across the perfectly flat cliff face, appeared to be imprints – similar to etchings – on the newly exposed surface. It was almost as if dozens of living things had been squeezed between the shifting stones, like giant pressed flowers. These were mainly the ancient remains of simplified sea creatures, trapped in the mud for eternity; or flora from pre-history, single-stemmed blooms with pouting lips for buds; and curious cockroach-like bugs in possession of long curving antennae and complex mandibles. Picus has seen this type of thing before but never in such profusion of species or in such numbers.

However, towards the top of one of the largest slabs was the particular pressed outline that had originally caught his eye. Picus flew up to take a closer look. At first glance it resembled a leaf, or perhaps the skeletal depiction of one. But Picus knew better. It was the exact replica of something he saw every day.

A Vampire wing – impossibly old, preserved there in fossil form. We've been here on Earth a long time, he thought.

Up until now, he had had every intention of taking Exkylipyr to the nearest ocean and hurling it in, to be swept away by the complex currents, deep down where it would burrow into some forgotten seabed and rot. Now that he was there, staring at his forbears from pre-history, he suddenly found he couldn't do it. The act would have been too like giving in, conceding that the Sword was responsible for what he had done and not Picus himself. The truth was that he had wrought the massacre in a blind rage of self-righteous, self-serving fury. The Sword had simply been the tool to make it possible. Nothing more. If anything should be cast away, to sink without trace under the waves, then it deserved to be him. But he still had a job to do. More than ever, he felt that Lark was in trouble and that he had to get back as fast as possible. The Eltern would know what to do with the Sword.

At that precise moment he looked up and saw a small wooden boat on the horizon. It was moving through the thick morning mist that floated just above the surface of the water. There was no sail, nor was there any sign of oars and yet it cut through the water steadily, in a perfect line, making its way directly toward Picus. At the prow of the boat he could make out a dark figure, sitting hunched over what looked like a small stove. Whoever it was, they seemed to be alone and wholly unconcerned by the fast approaching shoreline; in fact the figure appeared to be lost in thought, facing away, wrapped tightly in a woollen cloak with the hood up, so Picus had no idea who or what was making a beeline for him on that deserted shore.

To deepen the tension Picus was beginning to feel, a low moan suddenly issued from the figure, clearly audible over the noise of the waves that lapped against the sand. The lament was followed by an unworldly chattering sound. Picus took an involuntary step backwards and readied himself. The moaning became louder and the chattering noise more rapid. By now the boat that moved under its own power was almost at the shoreline, yet still the figure remained seated, facing away from Picus, patently ignoring his presence. Picus was in two minds as to whether he should wade out to board the boat or run. In the end he simply stayed where he was.

The terrible wailing reached a peak just as the prow of the boat touched the shore. The speed of the small boat was sufficient for the keel to cut a neat groove in the sand so that it remained upright. Picus saw smoke-blackened talons draw away from the heat of the stove and pull back the cowl. He readied himself for flight or a fight.

Ever so slowly the figure turned around to reveal its ragged face. 'Bloody 'ell, it's freezing out there. Wot nitwit ever sed sailing wos fun? I fort me 'ands were gonna fall off ...'

Picus would have known that voice anywhere. 'ART!'

The cowl fell back and fully exposed the Wight's kindly features, mapped with wrinkles and ink, like a system of deep coloured canyons on his leathery cheeks and forehead. Picus felt the horror of the last few days fall away from him as he launched himself at his old friend.

'Who'aar, *blimey*! You nearly 'ad me in ... hey, HEY? ... OK, it's alright, there you go son ... you 'av a good cry, there's no shame in that. Art's 'ere now ... you'll be alright ... I promise.'

Chapter 18

Eltern

It was mid-morning, and they sat at either end of the boat enjoying a brunch of smoked mussel, crusty white bread, and hot milk laced with calf's blood, which Art warmed to near boiling on his stove. The sun shone and the sea was calm.

'So,' said Picus, wiping his mouth and burping so loudly that Art winced, 'remind me how this boat works again?'

Art regarded him slyly. 'I nevvir sed,' he said. 'Us Wights have more common magic in us than you toffs ever suspect, with or without your so-called Old Lore an' whatnot.' He sniffed just before a clear drop of snot fell into his drink. 'Your Eltern appreciate that, leastways.'

'Ah yes, *the Eltern*,' said Picus with what he hoped sounded like menace. 'It's all coming back to me now ... how long have you been working for them?'

'*Wif*, young man, *working wif them*, there is an important distinchion you know.' Picus shrugged noncommittally and Art carried on. 'Troof is, they got me same way as they got you. *Iver work for us* OR *get locked up somewhere damp an' 'orrible for a few centuries.* That woz more or less the deal on the table – or the rack, in my case ...' Clearly uncomfortable with this line of questioning, Art changed the subject. 'Anyway, look, I got you a pressy, son!'

Picus looked at the boots in Art's grubby hand and then at his own feet, that had been bare for weeks, since he'd lost his last pair in the fight at Wayland's Smithy. He wondered at the events of the past couple of months and how much he had changed in such a short space of time. Despite his fatigue he smiled ruefully as he pulled the beautifully made Unicorn hide boots over his lacerated feet. If you looked at it one way, this whole adventure had started over boots in the first place. 'Thanks Art,' he said sincerely. 'But you didn't come all this way to give me footwear.'

'Nah – I came to find you 'specially. The Eltern were, well, concerned, shall we say. You've bin gone a long time ...' Art paused and looked serious.

Sensing a change in his friend, Picus looked up. 'What?'

'Something else has happened.'

'Lark?'

The Wight now looked surprised. 'How did you know?'

Picus shrugged. 'I guessed, I guess.' He shook his head. 'But how I know's not important. What's happened to her?'

'I won't sugar-coat it, Son, she's been taken. We fink Raben's got her but that's not all.' He leant forward and grabbed Picus' hand. 'The Eltern fink your ma's got somefing to do wiv the 'ol business. If I were you, painful though it might be, you'd best pay the Ducesa a visit.'

'Oh, I will,' Picus said darkly, 'you can be sure of that.'

It was Art's turn to look sharply at Picus. He had expected him to make a joke as he usually did or at least look worried at the prospect of coming against Raben. He hadn't yet heard about Queen Mab but this was a new, harder Picus he had in the boat with him. And Art, for one, was glad: he would need an edge if he was going to go up against a Vampire like Raben or the Ducesa but the old Wight couldn't help feeling a sense of loss, too. A kinder, more innocent Picus, had been lost somewhere along the way.

He glanced at what the young Vampire had strapped to his back. He had ignored the Sword up until now and Picus, following Art's gaze realised that Art had been more concerned with his friend and with Lark than Exkylipyr. He immediately felt absurdly grateful that life had seen fit to give him a friend as caring and true as the old Wight. Even if he did occasionally stitch him up with the authorities.

Realising Picus had seen him looking, Art gestured. 'I see you managed to get your paws on the Sword,' he commented.

'Yes. But the next time I lay a finger on it, will be to hand the thing over to someone who knows how to use it.'

Art looked thoughtful. 'Was that what all that on the beach was about?'

'Yes,' Picus nodded, studying a point on the far off horizon. 'Mostly.'

'I also have another message for you,' Art said as gently as he could.

'What is it?' Picus turned his head as if to shake off the raw memories in the glade and the terrible, gnawing worry that sprang from his imagination of what Raben and his mother might be doing to Lark.

'It's from the Eltern.'

'WHAT IN HELL'S TEETH!'

The gold cup sailed through the air, spraying blood across a tapestry and narrowly missing the Karl. It bounced off the portrait of an especially grim-looking Vampire and fell into the fire.

'How can she have disappeared? This House, Vanquish, has been inviolate for centuries, no-one has crossed the threshold without the express permission of the Karl.' The Ducesa snapped her fingers and the glowing cup flew out of the embers and into her hand.

Raben did his level best not to wrinkle his nose at the revolting smell of burning flesh. If the old hag felt any pain, it didn't seem to stop her tirade.

'She was in your care, you thick troll!'

Raben lowered his head and thought, *you'll pay for that last comment one day*; but for now he said nothing.

'Chained in silver, under a full span of solid granite, guarded by you? Where was your son, whom my Sanguine tells me has kept vigil on her night and day?'

Raben, as was usual when he was in the Ducesa's presence, hadn't got the faintest idea what to do with his hands. 'Corbeau was sent away by me, I feared he was getting too close to the girl.'

The ancient Vampire gave Raben an appraising look. 'See that he is not informed that she has escaped. It is best if this intelligence is kept to just you and me. But this still does not explain how she vanished.'

'Believe me, Your Ladyship, when I say that I am as angry and incredulous as you.'

The Ducesa took a deep breath and looked at him, her features returned to their usual blank mask. 'Oh, I doubt you can even imagine the depths of my rage,' she said levelly.

I'll be very lucky to get out of this room alive, Raben realised with an abrupt jolt of clarity. Even by his own estimation, Raben was not the world's cleverest Vampire but he had a mind uncluttered by intellect and it had served him well. He shook his head and did his best to think clearly. 'This changes nothing.'

'What did you say?' The atmosphere in the room felt as if someone had just opened a door a crack to a cold, icy hell.

Here goes, thought Raben. 'You still have your bargaining chip. No-one apart from us knows that Lark has escaped. My spies tell me that Picus and the old Wight are nearly here. We will watch them closely – if Lark tries to approach them, we will apprehend her before she does. But Picus will still come here first to use the Sword to free his cousin, because this is where he still thinks she is and you remain confident of trapping him when he does, I am sure.'

The Ducesa gave Raben another appraising look, which bore with it centuries of power and arrogance. 'I hope you do not doubt my ability to stamp my authority on my own son?'

'Not in any way.' And Raben found he had very little difficulty sounding sincere.

Art and Picus journeyed together for half a Moon cycle, crossing the dark, confusing Frankish woods with their untamed Weres who roamed at night in search of food. Sleeping by day and travelling by night on foot, they used the stars as their guide when necessary; although the old Wight's sense of direction turned out to be unnaturally good, so much so that most of the time he seemed to navigate by instinct alone. As the summer sun sank to the sky road it travelled in winter, the nights got longer and the mornings far colder. The first frosts came as they crossed the border into central Carpathia. Art complained bitterly about the weather, food and lack of a decent bed, but each day in his company Picus' spirits revived and he got stronger.

A few days after they started the ascent into the Carpathian Mountains, they came across their first poppy field and, shortly after that, the familiar battlements of the Keep, a murky outline in the distance.

Art sat on a rock to warm himself in the mid-afternoon sun. He stared up at the Keep. 'That's wot I never understood about you Vampires. All that power and yet you lock yerselves away in these big old places and all but ignore everyone else. Anyone might fink you were anti-sociable or sumfing.'

Picus smiled. 'I guess you're right. I've never really thought about it.'

'Well I 'av,' said Art, 'and the more I fink about it, the more I fink it's fear that keeps you in your castles, your strongholds and those creepy crypts of yours.'

'Fear?!' Picus was incredulous, and not a little indignant despite being aware that Art's judgements on most matters were rarely serious. 'I think you must be going senile Art.'

'Now don't be cheeky, little biter. I'm still hale and hearty enough to give you a run for yer money, if I had a mind to.'

'OK, OK!' Picus said, grinning. 'But I wasn't being cheeky, I'm just concerned for your mental health. So what do you think we're supposed to be scared of?'

'Yerselves.'

'Oh really?'

'Yes. Truth is, you're the most talented species on the planet. Fact is you could rule the lot of us wiv one wing tied behind yer well-tailored backs but you don't. Now, why is that, I'm finking? I can't see the 'Oomans giving the rest of us the same freedom, given 'alf a chance and as for Faies – well, every time they get uppity, you lot 'av got an habit of putting them back in their place sharpish.' Art shook his ugly head. ' 'Av you got any idea why I stay loyal to them in there?' he jerked a thumb up at the Keep. 'I thought you said they were going to put you in prison unless you helped them?'

'That woz centuries ago. My debt 'as been paid off long since. Nah, the reason I'm still tooling about, 'alf killin' meself chaperoning wet-behind-the-ears-all-fangs-an-hair types like you is *loyalty*. Pure and simple. Loyalty to a cause.'

'What cause?'

'Decency, my son, good ol' fashioned decency.'

'Sorry Art, I don't get it.' Picus shook his head. 'You've always claimed loyalty doesn't exist, so why the boring speech?'

'It's easy, you nitwit but I'll 'av to spell it out for you as usual. The Eltern believe in "live an' let live". They only get really nasty when people frettin something close to them, like the treasures or the Keep itself. Apart from that they're quite chilled out an' generally willing to take a step back so's to give everyone else a chance to live life on their own terms an' keep themselves 'appy wivout some interferin' Vampires sticking their teeth in everywhere. I love that about you lot.'

'OK, I guess you might have a point, somewhere in all that garbage.'

'Too right I do,' said Art. 'So it's like this. The Eltern 'av an 'elfi fear of their power, BUT,' he raised his finger in mid-air, 'they know that not all Vampires are as scrupulous and fair as them, so they create this 'aven for their kind – that's the Keep to you – an' then, 'an this is the really good bit, they put all the bigwigs – the Clans, that is, in it where they can keep a beady watchful eye on wot they are up to. Nips any troubil in the bud.'

Picus shook his head and laughed. 'Very flattering and how do you know all this?'

'Oh gosh, you're right, a little bird must've told me or sumfing... don't be daft! I fort it frew myself. It's pure genius – take it from me.'

Picus had to admit, it sounded plausible. Who knew what the Eltern were thinking anyway? His mind drifted back to the secret message Art had given him on the boat, which had been rolling over in his mind every waking moment since. As usual with the Eltern, Orielle, it raised as many questions as it answered.

Art got up, cleared his throat and stuck out his hand. Picus knew what was coming. 'Well, I'll have to leave you 'ere now, son, can't be seen to be loi'ering too close to the Keep, might start tongues wagging. Anyway, you know where you've got to go and what you've got to do. Good luck and take care of yourself. First sign of trouble get out of there, like you promised!'

Picus shook the leathery old hand, looked at his friend and smiled. Despite the risks, he felt no fear now but he did know he was going to the most dangerous place in the world. A Vampire's home, if you were unwelcome, would make Mab's burrow seem like the safest place on Earth in comparison. 'Cheers Art,' he said. 'For *everything*. And don't worry about me, thanks to you I'll be fine. I'll see you before the next full Moon!'

And with that he flew down the hill towards his home, to find Lark and to face the wrath of his bloodlines.

Chapter 19

ducesa

They stood in the dimly lit audience chamber, two floors below ground level: Picus, Raben, Corbeau, his father, the Karl. And the Ducesa.

The Ducesa, seated at the far end on an onyx dais, looked at her son and fought the almost uncontrollable urge to fly forward and gouge her nails across his cheek – just to hurt him, or perhaps simply to feel something herself. His youthful face stared calmly back at hers, dark blue eyes inherited from his equally ineffectual father. I carried him, she thought, he is mine but I feel nothing more for the Strigoi than this chair I am sitting on. Less! The chair serves its purpose. What is the purpose of offspring, unless it is to obey their parents, to further their needs and enhance their standing? A small voice in the back of the Ducesa's mind – one that, thankfully, had steadily been getting quieter for years – pointed out that there must be something wrong with her to feel this way about her own son; the loathing she felt was probably self-disgust.

'How I love you.' She spoke the words. There! It was easy to say. Does saying it make it so, she wondered? The Ducesa's white-powdered brow wrinkled; despite all her learning, her age and perfect breeding, she found she never knew the answers to that sort of question.

Picus did not reply, just regarded her with a strangely flat look on his face. But an invisible hand seemed to squeeze his heart – his mother's lie triggered regret for something that might have been but never was.

She tried again. 'You carry our name, the headship of the Clan will be yours one day. You are the flesh of my flesh and, paramount, the blood of my blood. Everything I do is for your own good, I have no care for my own needs or feelings.' Now she felt self-righteous anger begin to simmer to the surface. She was the injured party. Her own son had disobeyed and deserted her!

Picus still did not move, except his eyes, which flicked briefly to his father who stood at the far end of the room, half behind his Sanguine. 'Yes, Mother,' he said very quietly.

This might work! The Ducesa tried not to stare at the Sword, which was strapped to her son's back. *It cannot be seized* – the manuscripts on the Lore were all clear on that matter. Exkylipyr, the Sword of swords, wrought in the belly of the Cup of cups was not for the taking, only for the giving. How exquisite! She had thought triumphantly upon reading this in the ancient text. *Giving* could be coerced. Persuasion. So Exkylipyr *could* be acquired by force after all. Not physical perhaps, but a far more satisfying and long-lasting process, the same power she had used to break the Karl and rule the Clan herself all those years ago.

Force of mind.

She just had to get to Picus before the Eltern took the Sword – and now there he was! Her spies confirmed that he had come straight here, no doubt worried about his cousin, defying orders as usual. As Raben had said, she was sure he intended to use the Sword to get Lark back. Perhaps even to use it on his own mother! Well, knowing that would make the next bit easy. Picus was a long way from being won over, she was clever enough to see that; but the Sword was here and so was he. She had supreme confidence in her abilities.

'We are a dying breed,' she said, now controlling her anger, making her tone conversational. 'All species must eventually wane and, when one does the others may wax.' She paused to glare at her son, whose face had inexplicably broken into a smile. Imbecile! She took a deep breath and continued. 'There is no dishonour in this, or so we are told. We have lasted longer than most and should be grateful that the gods have allowed us such a long run – existing, fully formed, when the Earth was young, the continents liquid. And here we are. How many species have we seen come and go? Until just a few years ago, I too believed that we should die out naturally – I accepted it as our lot, as

Nature's plan. But then I took to studying the slow beasts that were replacing us. Where had they come from, these Humans? Do you know, Picus?'

Her son, by way of an answer, moved his head a fraction she took to mean no.

'Then I shall tell you.' She raised herself up, leaning forward, claw-like hands gripping the arms of the chair, so that her scrawny muscles bunched and forced blue veins to appear in her forearms. 'APES! BABOONS! Chattering, swinging, flea-infested, tree-infesting simpletons. With nothing but a couple of decent thumbs to differentiate themselves from a sewer rat – they should have died out after a few thousand millennia. But instead they survived. In fact, they THRIVED!' The Ducesa paused to take a sip of something from a cut diamond cup at her side. Picus noticed that her teeth were stained dark red, almost black. Faie blood: really not a good idea, the species were too close. She took a deep breath, calming herself. 'So how to they do this, I thought? The question haunted me night and day. What had we Vampires missed, with all our hard-won talents? To be vulgarly blunt, what had they got that we hadn't? For years the question revolved in my head until I gave up ever finding the answer. Then one day, whilst studying a picture of a fish that had actually sprouted wings, the better to evade attack, the answer came to me. It was so simple.'

'What?' Despite himself, Picus was half-interested.

His mother smiled at him, almost warmly. 'They adapted.'

There was a long silence. Picus shuffled his feet, he hoped convincingly, and looked up. 'Adapted?'

'Why yes!' the Ducesa exclaimed triumphantly, as if Picus was a bright child who had just come up with the answer for himself. 'They change according to their needs. They make clothes, so they no longer have need for fur, their brains get bigger, and so they climb out of the trees and build hovels to squat in. Then they make weapons, so they no longer need what little magic they may have once possessed.' She pointed dramatically at the Sword on Picus' back. 'Weapons like that!'

Picus took two steps back, feeling giddy. He'd almost forgotten this repugnance since he'd left Vanquish, the family seat. The rage and hate from the Ducesa was stifling him. The room suddenly felt very hot. Warmed by the fires of hell. 'So where do I fit in? You banished me, remember?'

The Ducesa smiled with as much love as she could force upon her rigid features. Then she got up and walked towards him. From the corner of his eye, Picus saw her make a complicated gesture with the tips of her fingers. Instantly the room seemed to brighten and the atmosphere became lighter. It was like someone had stepped off his chest. 'My boy, my dear sweet Picus, my only son, *my* blood. You simply need to give me Exkylipyr and all will be forgiven. We can go back to how it was.' Fleetingly, Picus had a powerful vision of his mother in another age, her face close to his, youthful and fresh, holding him, rocking him gently on her knee. *She's using magic now, but in far subtler ways than I imagined possible,* he thought.

The Ducesa spoke again, ever so softly now. 'Oh! Picus, it will be better than it was. Our Clan will rise above all other Clans. Just as Exkylipyr has worked for the Humans, so it will work for us. It will be a rallying point, its power will bind others to us and we will sweep away the old order, the *hocus pocus* of Faie magic. The old tricksters up the hill might impress the common folk with their pranks and hoaxes, their fairy dust, their sleight of hand – but who ever saw magic mend a wheel, train an army, conquer and lay waste to another nation?'

Picus forced himself to stare at his mother, allowing a tiny glow of hope to form in his eyes. He took a step forward, towards her. Behind him, Raben moved a step closer too; but, apart from his mother, the person who Picus was most aware of in the room was – strangely – Corbeau. His brooding presence filled the shadows and his eyes had not stopped boring into the back of Picus' neck from the moment he had stepped into the room.

'Join us, Picus, you have shown strength of character in fighting your own path. Prove your worth now by fighting for a cause that you can actually believe in. One that you may profit by!'

The Ducesa felt blood well in her chest; her ancient experience told her that Picus was so very nearly there but still he remained undecided. From where she stood she was almost – but not quite – close enough to read his mind. Although did she really need to? Was she not too powerful to resort to those tricks now? He was her son, by now she had convinced herself she could actually feel his yearning to be back in the fold, part of the Clan again; but she also sensed his indecision, it was as if his mind balanced on the edge of the keenest razor – poised on its impossibly slim blade, and so his decision could still fall either way. But she had one more card to play. It was now or never.

'I know you came to free your cousin Lark. I applaud your courage. Join us. You have my word that if you do, she shall be freed. More than that! She will be reinstated with her family, with full honours!'

And that decided it. The Ducesa could see a decision in his soul before he had even taken it. She'd won!

As for Picus, he simply stepped forward and gave his mother the Sword.

Instantly the light seemed to leave the room, as if sucked away by an invisible vortex. The atmosphere reverted to how it had been a few minutes before, worse if possible, and the sense of stifling heat made Picus gasp out loud.

The statues and carvings that studded the arches and friezes across the ceiling now came to life, each turning to leer obscenely at him. 'F O O L!' They cried and the words boomed around the room, filling his head.

'NO!' cried his father unexpectedly as the Ducesa took the Sword with greedy, claw-like hands.

She spun around with incredible speed and bought the flat of the blade across his face. 'Silence!' she screamed and turned immediately to look at Picus, barely heeding her husband who had crumpled without a murmur. 'Ssso,' she hissed, almost more serpent now than Vampire, the mask of kindness gone in an instant. 'The great pleasure in dealing with credulous fools is that sooner or later they believe what you say, however great the lie. Why? Because they are cowards! They want to believe nice things because thinking nasty things,' she pretended to pout, 'is just so horrid!'

Picus didn't say anything, he couldn't move. He just stared at the Sword in horror. Nothing had happened to her. The Eltern were wrong! The message they gave to Art had been wrong! Why had he listened to his old friend on the boat?

He was so shocked he hardly flinched when his mother bought the Sword down and severed one of his wings from the shoulder. She rapped her knuckles on the wooden table and green shoots shot out, binding his arms. Now taking a pair of silver pliers from a fold in her cloak, she flew across the room.

After the first three teeth were removed, Picus blacked out.

When he came too, blood pouring down his chin and neck, Raben stood before him, flanked by his son Corbeau; his face, the very opposite of his father's sweating jowls, showed no emotion, just refined interest. Picus turned slightly and saw that his mother now sat by the fire in a Troll hide chair. Her left hand, covered in Picus' dried blood, held his teeth, palm upwards as if she was about to toss some dice. In her right hand, Exkylipyr trailed. The pain in his wing joint and mouth was unimaginable.

Yes, the Eltern, for all their wisdom, had been wrong. The plan they had got Art to pass onto him had not worked. Everything he had fought for was lost.

He coughed thickly, turning his head to spit a thick stream of blood onto the flagstones. He opened his toothless mouth to speak. 'Where's Lark?'

'She's dead.' It was Raben ready with the lie he had rehearsed with the Ducesa alone.

Behind him, Picus noticed Corbeau's shoulders sag. No-one

knew it then, but at that moment the last truly sane part of Corbeau's soul broke away and fell into the Chaos.

Picus closed his eyes briefly. When he opened them again, he gazed into Raben's eyes, searching out the truth and saw nothing but the usual swagger and the gloating. Was it true? He also perceived something else: fear. Raben was out of his depth.

Lark dead. The whole thing had been a failure, he had lost the Sword, lost Lark, lost his family, his honour! Perhaps his mother was right. The only causes worth following were those that you got something out of personally. Helping others was just a useless waste of time. Look at him now: toothless, half wingless. And Lark. His father mewed weakly where he lay, barely conscious. At least she couldn't kill him, Picus thought with some satisfaction. She might want to get rid of his gentle, cowardly father but killing a Clan head would bring every other Vampire into play against her, whether she had Exkylipyr or not, and although he had only seen part of its devastating power, he doubted she would survive long. The Eltern had other weapons. They had the Chalice. As for Picus, he'd probably bleed to death if he didn't get help soon but she couldn't kill him either, not without producing the same uprising of other Vampires against her. Vampires only had one or two children over hundreds of years. Killing one of your own was considered perhaps the greatest of all crimes. His mother might be partly mad but that also meant she was partly sane. But Lark was dead.

The Ducesa's eyes rotated towards Raben. She lifted her left arm, proffering him Exkylipyr. 'Take the Sword, Raben,' she rasped, 'with my permission. As you have all just seen, it has worked for me and now I gift it to you ...' she raised a finger as Raben halted in front of her. 'For one task only, mind!'

'What is that?' he said, staring greedily at the blade. Raben had always loved swords.

'Kill my son!'

He's *no idea* of the risks, thought Picus struggling to concentrate through the pain, his vision blurring as he lost yet more blood. But what do I know, the Ducesa had used the Exkylipyr to half-kill him and she seemed healthy enough. All this stuff about the Sword being loyal to one wasn't true.

'Give her the Sword!' Art had said to him back on the boat. That was the message he carried from the Keep, all the way to Picus. 'Don't ask me why,' he had said gruffly, 'but Orielle charged me with finding you to tell you this. Sounds risky, I know but the longer I live the more I realise the Eltern know what they're about. Anyway it's their sword, so I guess you've got no choice, Son.'

Well, they were wrong! Picus thought dully as Raben walked over to the Ducesa, took the Sword and turned, drawing the blade across Picus chest in one movement. The cut was not deep but the instant his blood wetted the blade something unexpected happened.

At first it was not much. Picus noticed a subtle change in the room temperature again. From the corner of his eye he also saw his father stop murmuring to himself and look up expectantly. Exkylipyr gave off a faint hum as Raben brought up the blade again, meaning to cut downwards into Picus' torso, probably killing him.

The Ducesa was too excited to notice the Karl stagger to his feet behind her.

'Do it!' she cried. 'The books are clear. The sacrifice of a pure blood Vampire will enhance the Sword's power. We will be unstoppable, the Brasov Clan will brush the Eltern aside. All other clans will rally around us. And you will be my General!' She pointed at Raben, whose right arm was moving downwards in a cleaving motion.

Then, as it came down, the Sword actually spoke: 'Lubire este un fel auÁi da.'

Picus instinctively knew that no-one else could hear it. 'Lubire este un fel auÁi da,' he echoed aloud, without knowing why. The Sword's voice had been light and full of love. The tones of a mother he had never heard.

Instantly his head was filled with a burst of bronze light, its searing heat radiating out of his body, sealing his wounds, filling the chamber with an expanding orb of pure energy that met the falling blade at the precise moment it came down towards his head. The instant the metal made contact with the outer fringes of the power erupting from Picus' body, the blade turned, shattering into several pieces. The bronze light continued to expand, knocking Raben off his feet and throwing Corbeau, who stood behind, against the wall. For a few heartbeats it looked as if it would envelope the whole room; but just before it reached the Ducesa it contracted back in on itself, to the centre of Picus body. His soul awoke.

Picus had never felt so alive.

All the pain in his shoulder and mouth was gone. His head felt clear again as he turned to look at the broken form of Raben lying by his feet, and then at that of his son who lay slumped against a far wall, blood oozing from a deep gash in his temple.

In a daze, Picus gathered up Exkylipyr and was surprised to discover that it felt dead now. Just any old sword – broken and inert. Shocked, he realised that the power he felt within him was the magic that had been contained in the Sword.

He scanned the room, noticing that he could see though the massive walls, out beyond the Keep, beyond the woods surrounding it and across the hills. He heard the chatter of a million voices in a thousand tongues, cocked his head and zoned in on the delicate footfall of a Sprite a thousand leagues away, listened to Wight child singing to her doll, conversed pleasantly with a stream that tumbled through an unknown forest that grew across a dead sea. Then he looked further and saw Wink laughing at a table with his mother and father, Ambrosias burning herself on a candle. Close by, Art argued the price of an uncut ruby with a Dragon Clan trader, the Eltern played canasta in a shaded courtyard hung with vines…

And Lark was close by. She was alive!

All this took place in a microsecond, even before the Ducesa had time to draw a small blade from a concealed pocket and throw it at him.

Picus looked heavenwards and saw the movement of the stars speeded up in his mind. He read his future; and was awestruck.

Turning back he glanced languidly at the tumbling knife, now halfway across the room, flashing silver with each turn. He had all the time in the world, he thought ... just as his father flew into his field of vision.

As ever it seemed that no-one, not even Picus, had paid the Karl any attention until it was too late.

The blade was no bigger than that of a fruit knife, barely long enough to reach any major arteries, even if it did strike home cleanly. But one small nick was enough, one tiny scratch allowed the poison on the blade to enter the Karl's bloodstream like molten larva running through his system, convulsing his aged muscles, burning everything in its way until it reached his heart which – after decades of regret – simply burst.

Picus fell to his knees as the new horror sank in, and felt the core of his being weep with the terrible pity of it all. His father, after a lifetime of keeping out of the way, of avoiding conflict, had used his last and only true act of defiance against the Ducesa to save his son. He thought he was being heroic. He *had* been heroic! But in truth the knife aimed at Picus had presented no threat: Picus could have evaded it twenty different ways. In his present state, with the strength of Exkylipyr transferred to him when the Sword broke, nothing the Ducesa could do to him would amount to anything. But his father had not known that and had flown into the path of the blade, sacrificing himself to save his son.

Giving the Karl's body no more than a fleeting glance as she stepped over it, the Ducesa approached Picus. He swayed where he was, on his knees, immobile with shock. She approached him with something like a swagger, lips smiling, eyes baleful. Picking up a shard of Exkylipyr that lay close to her son, she went to bring it up.

Picus' left hand moved a fraction.

The angle of her hand suggested she was aiming to cut his throat, but before she got midway there her wrist caught on something. She looked down and tugged her hand, frowning. It didn't move. She twisted her arm, yanking it one way and then the other, this time in clear frustration. Picus' right hand now flicked outwards and away. The Ducesa tried to bring her other hand around, only to find it too was tied fast to the heavy table – tied with the bonds the Ducesa had previously created for her only son.

If Picus hadn't been numbed with grief he may even have permitted himself a thin smile at this point. It had taken no magic to use the remains of the ligatures that had held him to tie his mother's own wrists, just good old speed of hand. Any thief worth his salt could have done it.

As he stood up, the broken hilt and shaft of Exkylipyr still in his hand, the Ducesa flinched away, suddenly fearful of her own life. He would kill her, surely, in revenge for Lark and for his father.

But instead Picus looked silently at his mother for the last time, turned, and gently lifted his father into his arms before leaving the room.

Vampire Se'ers had been foretelling it for centuries but the Age of Aquarius, when it came, took most by surprise.

Chapter 20
Interesting times

Picus sat in bed, half listening to Orielle as he gazed out of the window at some trees, now decked in their autumn garb, leaning away from the Keep. They looked like they were sulking.

'We owe you an apology.' Orielle was saying. 'We misjudged, thinking the Sword would work only for you, but your mother is half your flesh and Exkylipyr probably didn't notice the new owner at first – it's only when she gave it to Raben that it reacted to save you – at its own expense, something which we find um, *surprising*. Truthfully there is much we do not understand about Exkylipyr.' He stopped and took a deep breath. 'So we have taken a decision not to re-unite the treasures properly in a binding lore until we do. Picus, you can help. I understand that the sorceress Ambrosias took a shine to you. She is a good friend of ours and has many answers. I would ask you to go back to her, to live with the Humans, to study under her care and come back when the time is right.'

Picus had hoped to stay at the Keep a while. 'How long must I stay?'

'Oh, centuries I daresay!' Orielle said carelessly, and offered him a buttermint. There was a knock at the door.

Picus looked up, and when he saw who had just walked in he was filled with a sense of joy he'd not felt for months, not since Wink had been cured.

Lark grinned at him from the end of the bed. 'It's Picus, by gum!'

'Oh, very funny.' Picus tried to dislodge a lump of sweet from the back of his mouth. 'Anyway, thanks to whatever the Sword did to me, they're growing back.' He opened his mouth to show his cousin the neat row of milk fangs poking through. Even his missing wing was growing back, something that Orielle found endlessly fascinating. Picus wished he could have got up and hugged Lark but was under strict instructions not to move from his bed for another week at least. He had been allowed up briefly to view his father's cortege as it took him to the Crypt; apart from that he had seen no one but his Sanguine nurse and, until this morning, Orielle. He looked at Lark and smiled for the first time since his father had gone. There was hope. 'How did you get away from Vanquish?' he asked.

Lark patted Orielle's wrist, making the old Vampire look immensely pleased. 'Thanks to Orielle, they got me out under his nose. The Eltern have tunnels *everywhere*. Actually, the hard part was getting past Corbeau, but when Raben sent him away, the Eltern took their chance in case they didn't get another. There was no way of letting you know but we all thought you might go to the Eltern first. I'm sorry Picus, we all misjudged you in that respect.' Lark's eyes shone. 'You went to save me first and nearly got yourself killed.'

Picus shook his head, as if it were nothing and changed the subject. 'What happened to Raben and Corbeau?'

Orielle cleared his throat. 'Well, it's somewhat delicate … obviously we can't broadcast the events of the last few days. It would be embarrassing to say the least to have people know how close we came to civil war. We've let it be known that Raben has been arrested for treason, which is true in all but the finer details. His son Corbeau caused a good deal of discussion amongst the Eltern. He has great potential, as much or possibly more even than you, Picus, but there is no doubt that there is something dark in his soul. A stain, if you will. With time it may fade or perhaps disappear, but only years of patience may help. He is staying at the Keep now, with relatives, and we shall watch him carefully. He professes great shame for what he has done.' Orielle saw the look on Picus' face. 'He *is* still young,' he added gently.

Picus shrugged. He wasn't so sure. He noticed that Lark was unusually quiet, too. 'I suppose you'll be going back to the Café du Clairvoyant in time for the evening shift?' he said, mainly to lighten the mood.

Lark seemed to shake herself out of her thoughts and smiled. 'It's very tempting, obviously, but actually I've been offered a job here with the Eltern.'

Picus looked at Orielle. 'Bit risky putting her on the books isn't it?' he remarked, and dodged a pillow.

'You're very lucky you're still ill,' Lark continued, 'anyway, in my new very important role I'm off shortly, too. I'm going to be visiting some of the other Clans, far away from the Keep, sort of like an Ambassador. First stop though is a Human – the girl who seems to have followed me all the way to the Keep. Her name is Aliya and we'd like to talk to her.'

Picus felt another surge of disappointment tinged, although he hated to admit it, with a good dose of self-pity. A small part of him had hoped things would go back to normal now.

Lark saw the expression on his face. 'Don't worry,' she said, and squeezed his leg. 'I'll be coming to Angleland at least once a year. Our kind has been gone from those shores too long. Anyway you'll be too busy, from what I understand, to notice that I'm not around anymore to keep you from getting yourself captured, eaten, chopped up into little pieces or any of the other things you seem to go in for these days.'

'That's a bit rich coming from you,' Picus said. 'I'll be fine.'

Lark looked serious. 'Hmm. Well, I'll be popping in to check on you anyway, but you have to be more careful these days. You're the Clan Head you know. The new Karl.'

'I was sort of hoping that it might pass to your father for a bit.'

Lark gave a short laugh. 'I think he'd like that! But it's not how the system works. Picus –'

'Hmm?'

'There's something that needs saying.'

'What's that then?'

'You father was a timid Vampire but he didn't die in vain. If it wasn't for him the Eltern would never have been able to get into Vanquish and save me. He told them Corbeau was out of the way and he opened the last gate. And he finally got to show that he loved you more than anything, even living.'

Orielle had already briefed Picus on what had happened after he left the house. 'And they still haven't found *her*?' He asked.

'No,' said Orielle. 'But I don't think we'll be looking too hard. When she used one of her own tunnels to escape, she left a magical trace by flying in the direction of the Black Sea. Wherever she is, it will be far away … in our experience, exiles of her tremendous age rarely return.'

'Anyway,' Lark said, 'you've got more important things to worry about for now.'

Orielle nodded. 'She's right. You carry an immense power now within you. Possibly greater than any other living Vampire can imagine. We don't know how it happened, or why the Sword transferred its magical potency to you, we only know that it has happened and you must come to terms with it. I have spoken to the others, persuaded some of the more old-fashioned Eltern that its power is in safe hands for now.' He stared at Picus as he said this, the ancient eyes of a fully-fledged Nosferatu boring into the young Vampire's soul, making him squirm. 'You have made mistakes but you have learnt from them. And both of you have shown courage, which is also good in a Vampire but, most importantly, you have displayed a loyalty to one another that comes through honour and a good heart. I have said this to you before – young Vampire – there is a great conflict coming that will involve all species, even the Humans! But I am convinced that how it plays out – for good or bad – is down to our kind.'

In truth, Picus had spent most of the time in bed these past few days simply sleeping and drinking huge quantities of blood. Whatever power the Sword had given him, it was also exhausting. He had a feeling that it would take some time to get used to the energies that now ran through his system, and a still greater period before he gained some mastery over them. Even now he had to concentrate quite hard to drown out the chatter of voices he could eavesdrop on, and blank out the potent visions his new power gave him. He thought about what he had read in the stars. The Age of Aquarius. Quite frankly it was all a bit scary. 'What about the remains of the Sword?' He asked.

'Well, I have a feeling that someday the time will be right for it to be repaired and perhaps re-united with its power. But for now the pieces are in ... well, safe hands, shall we say.'

'Art!' guessed Picus and Lark together.

Orielle looked a little embarrassed. 'Ah, ha, yes, quite so ... good guess, but I'd be grateful if you kept it under your hats.'

Picus watched as the Eltern got up and left for his morning nap. He had a feeling he'd be keeping quite a lot under his hat from now on. He settled back on his soft pillows and looked at Lark, who propped herself up at the foot of the bed and smiled.

She raised a neat, quizzical eyebrow in his direction. 'Interesting times,' she said.

Picus nodded. 'And I've a feeling that they've only just begun.'

One cannot help wondering just what Humans could achieve if only they lived past one hundred years.

Chapter 21
aliya revisited

It was raining outside and Peter was bored to tears. As was often the case when he could go outside to practise his hunting, he eventually drifted into his sister's chamber to see what she was up to.

Aliya sat cross-legged in the corner by her bed surrounded by blocks of wood.

'How's the carving going?' he asked, squatting down beside her.

Aliya looked up and smiled briefly at her big brother. Over the last few months he'd got even taller and his legs and arms had begun to fill out. They had a long way to go before they were as lean and muscled as their fathers' but he could already pull a bowstring back as far as anyone in the village and just last week he had easily beaten a boy three years older than him in sword practice. Peter picked up a wooden block at random and studied it.

'I think I know what this is,' he said with more humour than he actually felt. Instinctively his hand went up to the two tiny pinprick marks on his neck. It was odd for such a small thing to leave a scar. He studied the intricately carved dragonfly wings and the small but powerful-looking body for a few moments. His sister really did have talent; the carving's stare seemed to drill into the back of his skull. He almost felt relieved handing it back.

'Do you like it?' asked Aliya a little shyly. Her brother was still the one she wanted to impress most of all.

'I think it's incredible Aliya. Did you ever find out what it was?'

'No,' she said. She had kept quiet about leaving her babysitting duties that day and following the golden thread. She had also not breathed a word about what she had seen at the pool and how she had then followed a single thread all the way to the hills until a sudden disturbance in the air had caused her to hold back as she was assailed on all sides by some nameless fear that felt like magic. By the time she had come to her senses she had lost the trail and she had returned home, through fields of poppies, before anyone noticed her absence.

Aliya looked out of the window at the driving rain and thought about the thousands of species out there, hidden away in the quiet places. Things that kept away by stealth, things that watched quietly – creatures the Human imagination could only grasp at with clumsy fingers. Aliya shook her head, '… but I have a funny feeling it's not the last time we'll meet,' she murmured, before going back to her carving.

Epilogue

by Robin Bennett

And so here ends the first Volume of my translation.

This story takes place eighteen hundred years ago – in 266 AD – at a time when Vampires and Faies still possessed almost all of their magic and yet Humans were beginning to dominate large parts of the world. It was shortly after this that Small Vampires and Faies began to retreat to the hushed places: Vampires to the snow-tipped forests and lonely crags, Faies to the shaded thickets, the hollows and the lost woodlands.

As my dear wife advised, we haven't taken ourselves into hiding (not that I imagine now it would have ever done much good). Instead we continue in our daily lives, although I am more vigilant now and I feel sure the house is being watched. By Vampires, by Faies, perhaps, or one of their agents – who knows?

Before I end this first volume, I'll leave you with two things:

What follows is firstly a thumbnail guide to magical creatures that I have taken the liberty of adding to this text for the sake of the Human reader who knows nothing of the Hidden Kingdom and suspects less!

Secondly, the author if these volumes – **Moüsch** – has also added a few extracts from the library of the eminent Faie, John Thistle. You may remember that this was the very same library that Picus used to improve his own version of natural magic whilst staying at Camelan Castle. Just how this library passed from Ambrosias' possession into Moüsch's grubby paws is explained in a later volume. I include it here to give you a flavour of the kind of magic that Picus was learning at this time. It is by no means the only kind of magic that Picus was to go on to master in his long, eventful life but Faie enchantments have a style all of their own and make good reading. Feel free to try some, you may find you have a gift for it!

THUMBNAIL GUIDE TO MAGICAL CREATURES

VAMPIRES The story of *Small Vampires* is a long one, for the species is very ancient and near immortal unless burnt or poisoned. In a nutshell, any tale about *Small Vampires* nearly always involves swordfights and something to do with blood. *Small Vampires* are surprisingly *Human* to look at, on the very rare occasions they have stood still long enough to be studied. *Small Vampires* possess qualities of good looks, humour and magic that make them compelling as a species.

Between the ages of 0 and 50 they hold the rank of *Milk Imp*; 51-100, *Strigoi*, and thereafter they become *Vampire*. If one is lucky enough to attain the age of millennia (1000 years old), the rank of *Nosferatu* is bestowed.

Fields of poppies are a sure sign that *Small Vampires* live close by.

These days their numbers are few but next time you are walking in the woods and are bitten by something that leaves two holes and not one, then it is very probable indeed that one of these beautiful, yet dangerous creatures is close by...

FAIES (AKA ELVES, FAIRIES) *Faies* are the closest thing that a *Vampire* has to a cousin, genetically speaking.

The main difference is that they have lost the power of flight and, over the last few hundred years, they have adopted many *Human* ways such as travelling by boat (*Vampires* really can't stand water) and going to bed early. Many have also taken on English names – the British Isles being the place they feel most comfortable. *Faies*, like *Vampires*, love all finery and precious gems and gold and both species are as vain as the other. This does not make them petty or stupid: *Faies* are almost as old as *Vampires* and possess bucket loads of magic and ancient wisdom.

They are pretty untrustworthy though, ranging from playful to downright malicious.

※

SANGUINE (AKA BLUTSCHPEND) Originally wild, flightless creatures, rather like chubby *Vampires* without wings, but the terrible truth is that over hundreds of generations *Vampires* had bred them as a living food source. *Sanguines* have carried blood for *Vampires* when the Earth was mainly inhabited by fish. Think about it, cold blood tastes about as bad as it sounds, and insects' blood frankly doesn't bear thinking about. As the mammals took over and blood became plentiful, however, the *Sanguines*' use changed from provider – much like *Humans* use cows for milk – to servant and now faithful companion, each attached to a particular *Vampire* family, sometimes for hundreds of years.

A sort of Butler-cum-buffet.

Sanguines have their own language and even their own god: a horned deer they called *Vlad the Impala*.

※

WERE (AKA WEREWOLF) A true *Werewolf* might not be nearly as large and imposing as a normal wolf but they are almost as strong and as intelligent as a *Small Vampire*. In truth, they have nothing to do with wolves or *Humans* but represent an entirely distinct species in scale with all other magical creatures. They have a thick greasy pelt (usually black), which stops just below the neck and rough, pinkish skin that covers the face. Their features are pointed and cunning in aspect, with a pronounced jaw and horrifically sharp teeth. They are roughly the same size as a *Small Vampire* and share the same craving for blood. All the stuff about them hunting on a full Moon is perfectly true, but only because it is easier to hunt with more light. They can walk upright, hence the rumours about them being related to Man, but prefer all fours, as it is faster. They have a limited power of speech. This doesn't mean they're stupid; they just have too many large teeth for the job.

Their deep dislike of *Small Vampires* (and most other magical creatures – they'd pretty much like to rip to shreds anyone they meet) is partly understandable in that it stems from *Vampires'* and *Faies'* early treatment of them as mere animals and therefore as good sport for hunting. *Faies* and *Vampires* have had some success in 'taming' *Weres* to the extent that they can be used in battle or as guards.

Depending on the Moon cycle, *Weres* can morph between most species (not just *Humans* as people have suggested in the past). *Vampire* historians have therefore been known to speculate that this is how they get the name '*Were*': as in, 'Where's that bloody great wolf just gone? ... Oh look, a baby rabbit ... what the? ... aaarrghh!'

WIGHTS A general term for those supernatural creatures who do not necessarily have a proper species designation. This includes *Imps* (workers) and *Fiends* (entrepreneurs). A Wight can be a half-breed *Were* or *Vampire*, or indeed the offspring of a *Sanguine* who has married a *Faie*. Large *Wights* are often called *Trolls*.

THE THIN MAN One of the (many) *Vampire* names for The Devil.

THE CHALICE Well now ...

Long before the Wandering Kings had journeyed the wilds of the Hidden Kingdom and settled the Wild Woods, long before the Craggy Peaks had become the tottering foundations for their strongholds, and really not that long after the Great Father Of All pricked his finger and made the whole round world with a drop of his own blood, Somebody made Something rather important.

Some say it was forged in the fires of volcanoes from precious metals mined from another star; some say it was carved from the glaciers of the gods who inhabited the Snow Mountains, and made of an ice so ancient that nothing - not even the core of the Sun - could melt it. Others, of a less enquiring nature, pick their nose thoughtfully when this mysterious object is mentioned and ask you to pass the salt, if it's not too much trouble.

The strangest thing of all is that nobody knows exactly why it is so important. But, for want of a better name, it is called the Chalice, and it is the most powerful and important of the *Seven Treasures*.

The *Small Vampires*, noble and proud descendants of the Wandering Kings, believe it belongs to them and that, in discovering how to wield it, they will defeat their sworn enemy, *The Thin Man* and that the wisdom contained in *The Chalice* will finally show them the way home.

Wherever that is.

EXTRACTS FROM THE LIBRARY OF THE LATE JOHN THISTLE, ESTEEMED ANGLELAND FAIE

ON ... THE RULES OF MAGIK

Everything on Earth that exists is in a state of Being and is therefore aware of Itself and, most importantly, it is Biddable.

It follows, then, that all magik is essentially a conversation. Anything that is in a state of Being has to listen, that is the Lore. For example, if you wish'd to have the sky go black, you cannot simply make the sun disappear from the Heavens but you *can* cover it up with storm clouds, provided you know the correct form of address to ask a passing storm cloud for a favour.

So magik is all in the *asking*. However, beware, sometimes the price of a favour is high.

The tale of Bek, a Scottish Wight who lived some 6,000 years ago, shows us why.

Bek, like many Wights (and Scottish Wights in particular), lived on his own in a dank little cave on one of those chaliceforsaken, rain-swept isles off the Western coast of what we now call Scotland. In those days it was even colder and more miserable up there, especially so in winter, and Bek took to eating cheese to cheer himself up.

He started with wild goat's cheese, which he liked at first, then began to find a bit crumbly for his taste. Then he had a go at cow's cheese, which was also delicious and put him in a good mood after supper – but it gave him strange, frightening dreams at night, which is not good if you spend the majority of your life in a cave with plenty of unexpected corners and shadows. After that, he tried sheep, osprey, rabbit, fox and even cheese made from rat's milk. All were fine in their own way but eventually, one by one, he grew tired of them and so he went back to staring miserably out of his hovel at the driving rain and screeching, mad-eyed gulls – the island's only other regular inhabitants.

Then one day an Irish peddler Wight visited him unexpectedly. After a few minutes' seemingly idle conversation he learned of Bek's love for cheese and insisted that you hadn't lived unless you tried the cheese that came from the Moon.

Bek was intrigued.

'All you need to know,' the peddler asserted as his coal-black eyes, flecked red, flicked around Bek's cave, 'is that the Moon was once, a very long time ago, part of the Earth. However, being made of cheese, it crumbled and broke away from the Earth eventually. Very rarely a small lump will come down to Earth but mostly it just hangs about up there, remote and utterly delicious!'

'So what do I need to do?'

'Well, first of all you need to remind the Moon where it came from and all the lovely things it might be missing down here. Then you need to point out how lonely it is all the way out there in space and what good company it is depriving itself of, not being down here with you,' the peddler had the decency to look doubtful at this stage, 'ahem ... sharing some of its delectable flesh with such a hearty good friend as yourself.'

At this Bek leaned forward until his long, crooked nose was practically touching the other Wight's long, crooked nose. 'And just how do I do that?'

'I have a spell written down,' the peddler replied, not blinking once. 'Just the right words that will charm the Moon out of the sky.'

'How much, peddler?'

A long, thin finger shot out from inside the Irish Wight's robe and pointed at something that glowed faintly in the corner, hidden by a rag. 'That will do nicely.'

The bundles of rags he pointed at contained a ruby that had belonged to Bek's mother and it was his most radiant possession. But Bek did not hesitate. 'It's yours,' he said handing over the precious rock and snatching the spell from the peddler's extended hand. From the bundle an awful wailing noise immediately echoed around the cave.

'Oh, yes, I see ... bartered like a cheap trinket, a bagatelle of no value ... your poor mother would be spinning in her stony grave, thankless Wight!' The ruby was not only large, it was magik and had this really appalling attitude towards life in general.

'Handed over to a complete stranger ... dishonest by the looks of him ... who knows what will become of me ... plucked from the bosom of my family ... torn from all I love!'

For an instant the peddler's eyes wavered, as if he had begun to suspect he hadn't got such a good deal after all. It was a long crossing back to the mainland.

But before he had a chance to change his mind, Bek wished the peddler good day – meaning *good riddance* – and shot off to find the woolly cap he always wore when doing really difficult magik.

Now, on first reading the words on the scrap of paper meant nothing to him but this didn't bother Bek in the least: he knew enough of magik to have one or two ideas where to start. First of all he assumed that the spell, since it was written to please the Moon, must be written in Her language. The *Her* bit was important because Bek also knew that being female, the Moon would have close affinity with the Tides. The Sea had its own language, too. Bek was all too aware of this because he listened to it, uncomprehendingly, each night; soothed to sleep by the gentle tones, even if he understood not a word. But how could he learn the Language of the Tides? The Wight sat in his cave and thought hard for a whole week, not stirring once, even to eat or drink. Eventually the answer came to him.

Bek went fishing.

Once he had caught enough sprats, he went to see the King of the Gulls on the Island. Being a Wight, he knew the Language of Birds, and he guessed (rightly) that they would be able to teach him the Sea's soft tongue. So he bribed the old gull with leather buckets filled to the brim with smelly fish and learned what he needed to know.

It took him nearly three whole years, and a lot of cold, dreary fishing, but eventually he was able to read the spell in a way the Moon would understand.

Amazingly (especially for those of you who suspected the Irish Wight had tricked Bek), the spell worked. In actual fact the peddler, whose name was Tam, by the way, was just as surprised as anyone when slowly, over a period of a few days, the now thoroughly homesick Moon sunk towards Earth, back to where it came from.

However, as you can imagine, the result was catastrophic: volcanoes boiled over, hurricanes scoured huge valleys in the crust of the Earth and eventually a terrible flood came to pass. Many non-magical and magical creatures perished – including the Unicorn – and those that survived only did so by sheer luck. A Human named Noah somehow got wind of the impending tragedy and built a vast boat which he filled up with all sorts of creatures, quite a few of whom took to eating one another to pass the time on board.

As for Bek, it is supposed that he died in the flood; but perhaps not. There are those that say he had charmed the Moon so effectively that She rescued him from the floods and the storms. It is certainly very true that if you look at the Moon when full, Bek's face seems to stare out at you.

ON ... THE SIMPLE STUFF

Clearly, then, a lot of the ambitious magik is not such a fabulous idea. Far better, perhaps, to concentrate on enchantments closer to home. In fact, magik carried out in one's own home or on land that belongs to the practitioner is always the most effective. Indeed, it is the mark of a truly gifted Faie, Vampire or Wight that can conjure even a spark of fire far away from his home on a dark night in a howling gale.

John Trott of Kente was one such Faie. Many years ago he was travelling through the kingdom of Mercia late in autumn on his way to visit a sick, yet very rich aunt. Whether it was *her* sickness or *his* poorness that prompted his concern for his aged relative is lost to us in the mists of time (see Chapter 12, *On ... unravelling the past*) but what we do know is that John Trott found himself struggling hatless (and coatless) through a sudden squall that forced him to take shelter in some nearby caves. Luck was not on his side, for no sooner had he entered the cave, shaken the rain out of his locks and caught his breath, than the ceiling fell in and he found himself trapped and alone in the dark.

Undeterred at first, he struck out deep into the cave in search of another way out, but soon found himself completely and utterly lost. Cold, wet, and by now most probably regretting that he even had an aunt – rich *or* poor – he sat down where he was and tried to conjure a small fire to cheer himself up. However, he was altogether out of sorts by now and every spell he tried fizzled to nothing. His usual method of taking some suitably enchanted powder (namely a pinch of salt that had been struck by the lightening of a summer storm) and adding water from a clear pool in the cave just gave him a sludgy mess.

However, like all Faies he also knew that fire retains the memory of itself and that rubbing the ash of a burnt oak on stone would cause flames to gut from chalk, lime or granite. Unfortunately he had no such potash. Faie eyes are not as good in the dark as Vampires but he saw enough in the pitch dark around him to know that he was very far underground and quite alone.

John felt like crying. And he probably would have burst into tears there and then were it not for him noticing some crystals that ran along the rim of a hollow near to where he crouched – a hollow made by the ancient volcano that had spat flame and formed the cave, its terrible heat leaving the white crystals behind. *Fire retains a memory of itself*, he thought again, and I *do* also have red granite. In fact the cave was made up of practically nothing else. He had the ingredients – the spell itself was easy – but more than this he had hope.

Magik thrives on self-confidence and before long John had his fire and felt much better.

This story has a further happy ending too. His aunt, Mistress Trott, knowing very well her nephew's propensity for mishap, sent two of her clever Wight servants out to look for him. By now the storm had passed but the servants noticed smoke drifting up through a pothole in some local caves. They investigated by another entrance further up the hill and soon found John sleeping soundly by his fire.

Escorting him back to his aunt's bedside, Trott – who may have exaggerated the story of being lost and alone in a cave somewhat – delighted his aunt with the tale of his adventure, as well as delighting many of her elderly friends with similar stories. In fact he made himself so agreeable to several old ladies that he not only inherited his aunt's estates but several more besides, and became a very rich and respected Faie indeed who could chuse to leave home with a dozen different hats if he so desired.

On ... old magik

This comes from the Lore, passed down by the wandering Kings and rarely practised by Faies though it is still used by our cousins, the Vampires.

Lore is the old ways – and it makes up the blueprints for understanding this world we live in. To understand Lore is to talk the slow language of the Earth as it navigates us, its children, through cold space over millions of years. This is a very different language to that of the other Beings on Earth. It is more like music – a slow steady beat, with many long pauses.

The Vampire mastery of Lore marks them as the most sophisticated practitioners of old magik in the Hidden Kingdom – although some might well remark that that's just showing-off.

Seeing the future is one of the skills mastered by Lore. In fact the Vampire Clan of Sgi gave up the sword over a dozen millennia ago, the better to concentrate on this particular skill. The last in their line, which is lost now, was a Vampire known to his friends as Perroquet and he was perhaps the greatest Se'er of the Clan. So honed were his skills, he could read the future accurately in almost any object – the trajectory of a snowflake, the path taken by a spider as it stalked through a meadow at dawn, the flight of swallows …

Late in life, when he was well past a thousand years old, he liked to explain that the trick to peering into the future was to appreciate that all events in life are linked. Once you had satisfied yourself that this was so, the only thing you needed to do was open your heart (and mind) to the thousands connections all around you. It literally meant letting the speech and the rhythms of the Earth into your mind; letting the movement of its creatures, the flow of the rivers, the ebb of tides and all the continuous dialogues wash over you. At first this is a confusing and disagreeable sensation but, bit by bit, with a couple of hundred years of practice, the Vampire mind, in particular, is strong enough to withstand the millions of strands of information.

Unfortunately, reading the future can be depressing, so Perroquet spent another couple of hundred years unlearning his art and died (quite unexpectedly) a happy Vampire.